PENGUIN BOOKS

WISE VIRGIN

A. N. Wilson was born in Staffordshire and grew up in Wales. His first novel, *The Sweets of Pimlico*, was awarded the John Llewelyn Rhys Memorial Prize for 1978. His other novels are *Unguarded Hours*, *Kindly Light*, *The Healing Art* (Penguin, 1982) which won the Somerset Maugham Award for 1980, the Southern Arts Literature Prize for 1980 and the Arts Council National Book Award for 1981, *Who Was Oswald Fish?* (Penguin, 1983) and *Scandal*. He has also written a study of Sir Walter Scott, *The Laird of Abbotsford*, which won the John Llewelyn Rhys Memorial Prize for 1981, and a biography of Milton. He has edited Sir Walter Scott's *Ivanhoe* for the Penguin English Library. A. N. Wilson is a Fellow of the Royal Society of Literature. He received the W. H. Smith Annual Literary Award for 1983 for *Wise Virgin*.

A. N. WILSON

WISE VIRGIN

Penguin Books

Penguin Books Ltd, Harmondsworth, Middlesex, England
Penguin Books, 40 West 23rd Street, New York, New York 10010, U.S.A.
Penguin Books Australia Ltd, Ringwood, Victoria, Australia
Penguin Books Canada Ltd, 2801 John Street, Markham, Ontario, Canada L3R 1B4
Penguin Books (N.Z.) Ltd, 182–190 Wairau Road, Auckland 10, New Zealand

First published in Great Britain by Martin Secker & Warburg 1982
First published in the United States of America by The Viking Press 1983
Published in Penguin Books 1984

Made and printed in Great Britain by
Cox & Wyman Ltd, Reading
Filmset in 9/11½ pt Monophoto Photina by
Northumberland Press Ltd, Gateshead

*For
Caroline*

I

'Marry me,' said Louise Agar.

She stood behind Giles Fox's chair, quivering with the novelty of the gesture, and cast her arms around his throat, so that, as he sat there, stonily upright, he could feel the thick folds of her hair hanging about his carefully shaven cheeks like a false beard.

Silence followed her exclamation and they listened to her heart beats as she nuzzled against his long pale face. At length, quietly, he spoke.

'I don't know if that is a request or a command.'

The words were cold, but they could scarcely disguise the excitement he felt. As silence descended again, the atmosphere of happiness quickened between them. Giles felt it spreading through his body in a warm glow. It was the first proposal of marriage he had ever received. He could not recall ever having proposed in any formal sense to his first wife, Mary. To Carol, his second wife, he had proposed, and known all the anguish, throughout his brief marriage to her, of being uncertain of her affection. Absurd, when Carol was so *uncomplicated*, but he had always somehow feared her. Now was the first time in an unhappy life of nearly fifty years that anyone had verbally declared a passion for him. He chose to savour the experience, unexpected as it was, by a prolonged interrogation.

'It is a request, Giles.'

'It seems very precipitate.' He stroked her fingers as he spoke. One of her hands rested at the top of his punctiliously arranged silk necktie. Another strayed in and out of his waistcoat, playing with buttons, and running its fingers through the neatly tailored crevices until they found a shirt and more buttons.

'And it is also a command.'

'What makes you feel able to command me?'

'Because I love you.'

He sighed and said nothing, the deep waves of joy sinking deeper into his breast at the words. He wanted her to say them again and again.

'Please,' he began.

'Oh, but, Giles, I do. I can't keep it to myself any longer. I know that I should . . . and yet I must . . .'

'Louise.'

'You'll say I don't really know you. It's true. But I still love you. Oh I love you.'

He felt her crying now. He wanted to convey that these words, *I love you*, were making him more painfully happy than he had ever been in his life. They were words which he felt he had been waiting forty-eight years for someone to say. And now he had heard them. And he had heard them from a young girl, half his age, with soft hands and thick, abundantly long hair.

He said merely, 'It is true, you don't know me.'

'I have been coming here every week for a year. More than once a week lately. Have you not noticed? Oh Giles, the first time I came here I loved you. I thought at first it was just a childish crush . . .'

'It is, perhaps, no more than that.'

'Giles, this has eaten into my life. I dream about you. I long for you all the time. Oh God! There is no point in trying to explain it all, and probably now I've told you, you'll tell me that I mustn't come again. But I had to tell you, I had to.'

'Oh, Louise.'

'But Giles, it is true.'

'No, Louise, I am not contradicting you. I want merely to hold you in my arms, and not to talk to you as a voice which is coming from the back of my head.'

She moved silently, stealthily, not allowing herself to let go of him as she sidled awkwardly round the arm of the upright Windsor chair and knelt before him. It seemed – to them both

– a natural obeisance, as he ran his thin bony fingers through her hair, now spread upon his knees like a rug. He fondled her cheeks too and felt them wet with tears.

'Come on,' he said, raising her and plonking her a trifle heavily on the fiercely pressed pleat of his trouser knees. He merely added her name again, 'Oh, Louise,' before their lips met fumblingly in their first kiss. 'Oh, Louise.'

It was what Tibba, Giles's daughter, in earlier days of her childhood, would have called a 'film kiss'. It went on some time, and there they sat, Giles's knees becoming numb, as they clutched at each other and at the new excitement of recognizing their love.

It was a striking sequel to an interview which had begun, as usual, with the arrival of Miss Agar at Hermit Street to help with the transcription of a medieval tract on virginity.

'Finally, my dear sisters, commend yourselves to His pitiful care; that, when that cry goes up, *Behold the Bridegroom cometh*, you may be found watchful, with the lamps which are your immortal souls shining brightly, and your brows moist with the oil of that unspeakable gladness which is His most Holy Unction, and His faithful vouchsafing of your Heavenly reward. Then, you will think not of the hardships which for His sake you have undergone, here in this cloister which is the muddy frame of your carnal selves, but only of the joys of Union with Him. For He cometh forth as the Bridegroom out of His chamber, and will receive each of you, pure and unspotted, as His holy brides to live with Him unto the end of ages.'*

Robert of St Victor's voice was still. The last of his orations was complete. Tomorrow, he would leave the little convent of Willerton Magna for the last time and return to his abbey in Paris.

The eight women who attended his homily did not look up as he left their tiny chapel. But two of them, who were his sisters indeed according to the flesh, being the Mother Prioress and the

* Quotations from the *Tretis of Loue Heuenliche* are taken, with few exceptions, from the translation *A Treatise of Heavenly Love* (St Mawr Press 1982).

9

Sister Almoner, bade him farewell next morning in the pretty little convent yard before he went his way. It was the last time they saw him, or any other member of their family. He died in Paris, twenty years later, aged forty-five. Their elder sister was married to a powerful baron in Shropshire. They had not seen her since her wedding. Their elder brother looked after the family estates just outside Hereford where they had all been born. The youngest sibling, Brian, was fighting for Our Lord Christ in the Holy Lands, and was never to return. So it was that this by the Priory gates was their last family gathering before they committed themselves to another twenty years of pious solitude on the edge of the Welsh marches.

It was an aristocratic family, but the holy wars had limited the supply of eligible husbands, and urged on by their pious brother Robert, the two women – they were at this date sixteen and eighteen years old – had given themselves to holy religion. At first, they had lived as anchoresses on the edge of the village church. But then other women, of similar breeding and inclination, had joined them. And when Robert had returned from the Abbey of St Victor in Paris, where he had studied for four years, he had helped to form them into a community of Augustinian canonesses. They had built a Priory on the edge of their father's lands and devoted themselves to prayer.

Robert had visited them regularly, and given them his counsels. They had asked him to draw up for them a Rule of Holy Religion. But this he had not consented to do, for they were not a new religious order and they lived under obedience to no one. Their servitude to Christ was voluntary, and it was seemly that Robert should offer them no more than counsel. At first, he had tried to instruct them in Latin, but this had been of only limited help, since, apart from being able to follow the Mass and a few other prayers, the women understood little of that tongue. They had asked him to distil for them, rather, his acquired knowledge of the Holy Scriptures, of the Fathers of Holy Mother Church, and of Her mystical doctors and teachers. It was this which determined his course of sermons to them, delivered sometimes in

French, and sometimes in English. But when they had been joined by women who, though landed and aristocratic, were of less exalted birth, he had spoken only in English, a homely vigorous English, full of images and examples drawn from natural life: as when, telling them how the Devil would tempt them even in little things, he spoke of the sin of wrath, which could distract the mind from prayer, even if it were directed to the buzzing of a housefly.

After he had been visiting them and instructing them for a year or more, his sister Katherine, the Mother Prioress as she now was, of the small community, had implored him to write his homilies in a book, so that she and her sisters could meditate on his words even when he was gone. And he had done so, reordering some and expanding others so that it formed a continuous treatise. And he made the book an extended meditation on the gospel parable of the Wise and Foolish Virgins. The Foolish Virgins were those who believed that there was yet time before the Bridegroom came. They tasted the fruits of forbidden concupiscence and earthly lust. They married and feasted and knew the pains of childbirth and the squalors of the infant and the cruelty and fickleness of man. But the Wise Virgins gave themselves to Holy Religion; in place of feasting, they sated themselves with the nourishment of holy meditation; and in place of carnal concupiscence, they were satisfied to know that they were the paramours of Christ Our Lord, who came to their souls and took possession of them, as a Knight Errant might rescue a damsel from a besieged tower; which tower is the Flesh, being besieged by the Seven Deadly Sins who make war on the Five Wits.

His little book was called *A Tretis of Loue Heuenliche*, and he wrote it out in a small calf-bound codex in the perfect hand which he had mastered in the cloisters of St Victor. So ardently did the sisters study it, and so much was it admired by visitors to their cloister, that copies were made either of the whole, or of part. The nuns of Burnham had one, and the Franciscans of Hereford, and the Dominicans at Oxford. And the great central passage, a hymn in praise of virginity, was copied out into dozens of preaching-books and commonplace books, so that by the time its language was obsolete, there existed over a hundred copies of the *Tretis* in over twenty shires.

But time passed, and our language changed, and the dialect of Robert of St Victor and his sisters, the speech of the West Midlands, became forgotten, until in time it was as incomprehensible to English readers as Latin had been to Dame Katherine in 1216. The little volume was still kept at Willerton Magna in the cell of the Mother Prioress; but it was never opened.

Eighteen years had passed since Giles first began work on *A Tretis of Loue Heuenliche*. He had now found six manuscripts of which no one hitherto had known the existence.

The work was a prose effusion of the early thirteenth century, bidding young girls leave their father's house (by which was signified life in the body) and to pursue all spiritual good in the cloister; exhorting them to preserve the oil in their lamps (that is to say to keep alive the mortification of the flesh) and to be not like unto the foolish virgins who numbed their dread of the last judgement with dissipation and worldly lusts. There was (in the Pottle version, though not in the manuscripts in the Bodleian or in Trinity College, Cambridge) an eloquent hymn in praise of virginity; a slightly different version of this hymn, an excerpt, as Giles now realized, from the larger *Tretis*, existed in the British Museum (Cotton Nero Ms. xxvii). It was only the familiarity of this hymn which had alerted Giles, all those years ago, to what the Pottle manuscript *was*, and how it related to all the others. By patient collation of all his discoveries, Giles had managed to establish almost beyond doubt the date, the provenance and the dialect of the lost 'original' text, and he was beginning to believe that the Pottle version, if not the original itself, was something very close to it, of which all other manuscripts were copies.

Hardly a day of Giles's life in the past eighteen years had passed without the devotion of an hour or two to thinking of this medieval treatise and its obscure origins in the reign of King John. He had stoutly proprietorial feelings about it, regarded it as his own, and enjoyed the thought that, even when other scholars took an interest in it, they could not know as much about it as he did. Indeed, in order to establish the closeness he felt towards the little codex, he had evolved a theory of its linguistic origins which all his colleagues in the field, on the rare occasions they had been consulted, regarded as heterodox. He had decided that it was Kentish, while all other scholars whom he had consulted, showing them specimens of the book's language, were convinced of a Western origin, possibly in the Welsh marches.

Far from being disturbed by his difference with the other experts, Giles gloried in it. When they read his final edition they would, he knew, be proved wrong; for they had none of them understood the full extent of his argument, which depended on a complete linguistic analysis of every word in the treatise. The language of the thing would have been incomprehensible to all but a handful of present-day English speakers: and yet it was more familiar to him than the debased modernity of speech (which he much deplored) of television and wireless functionaries. Almost every sentence in the work could be, for him, a subject of a prolonged discourse: not a discourse on virginity, but on sources, philology, intellectual or linguistic *origins*. Here the author had been thinking of a passage in St Bernard of Clairvaux: there, one hears an allusion to St Augustine on the seven sacraments; here, incongruously, an echo of Ovid and of Anselm, in the same sentence. It was written for an aristocratic audience. The girls – how old had they been? Fourteen? Sixteen? No older, certainly, than his own daughter Tibba was now – had been called away from sexual entanglement by every rhetorical trick the author could devise. Sometimes, echoing St Bernard on *The Canticle of Canticles*, he would implore them to pursue the ecstatic delights of mystical union with the Deity. At other times, more sternly, he would point to the near impossibility of salvation in this world. There were narrative passages recalling how women were to blame for most of the calamities in history. Eve, Dalila and Bathsheba were invoked as terrible examples of how not to behave. And there followed expositions, hierarchical in tone, of the superiority of the male sex to the female: and, within this second and unfortunate category of human beings, the superiority of virgins to widows and of widows to wives.

There was perhaps nothing very striking in *A Tretis of Loue Heuenliche* which could not be found in other medieval books. But Giles had laboured at it, the only person in the world to know the whole of its contents, since none of it had ever been published. The world awaited his edition.

When the year 1536 had passed, none of the Augustinian canonesses were left at Willerton Magna. By then the community had grown to twenty-five. After the dissolution, some of the younger nuns married, the older ones dispersed, and led bewildered lives in the houses of their relations. The Priory was occupied by a successful but illiterate wool merchant who had been honoured with a knighthood by Henry VIII. The chapel was converted into a stable for his horses, and he rebuilt the refectory, lowering the ceiling and installing mullioned windows. He had no time for the popish library of his predecessors. By the end of two years, he had wiped his arse on half their Origens and Austins and Tertullians; while with the other half, his wife had lined pudding-basins. The painted mass-books, with their idolatrous and decorated pages, stiff with whorish colour, served no useful function in the kitchen or the privy and were assigned to the flames. Thus perished one of the finest small libraries in the West of England.

But the last Prioress of Willerton Magna, Dame Agnes D'Arcy, lived on in her brother's house, thirty miles away in Worcester. When she had received her peremptory dismissal from the King's men, she had not resisted, but had made a hasty escape, with her bags and her mules, taking with her as many jewels and treasures as she could inconspicuously carry. The little book, *A Tretis of Loue Heuenliche*, which had been lying in her cell unread for more than two centuries, caught her eye just as she left the cell with a final imprecation, and she had slipped it into her jewel-case, for what reason she could not tell, beyond that it was small and that it was old.

The brother of Dame Agnes, Sir Henry D'Arcy, was a lawyer, who clung to the old religion and ruined himself with fines, so that his son, John Daker, stayed in London, after passing through Clifford's Inn, in the hope of resurrecting the family fortunes. When the Prioress eventually died in Worcester, her possessions passed to John Daker, and since he was still a young man with a way to make in the world, he felt no inclination to hold on to any of it. The jewels of an earlier time would scarce have suited his wife, Doll, who held after the new fashions, so the boxes – of brooches and necklaces and silver rosaries – were sold to a Genoese merchant in Cheapside to pay for a mortgage the Dakers had taken out on a property in Southwark. The Genoese merchant made a profit on the jewels of some three hundred per cent. But at the bottom of one of the cases, he found the little book, written in the Dutch language as he guessed, and gave it as a curio to a bookselling friend in Aldersgate Street. The bookselling friend left it on a shelf, unread, for forty years, where it was found by his son, who published the books of William Camden, the headmaster of Westminster School and a famous antiquary. Having no use for the volume himself, he gave it to Camden, who perused it for a week or two and then gave it to his pupil Ben Jonson. For, though neither of them could understand its language, Jonson had admired the hand.

Ben Jonson pawned it some years later, together with an early printed text of Geoffrey of Monmouth's Histories, and an edition of Ovid, printed in Leghorn. He never redeemed his debt, and there the thread was broken.

Somehow, however, the little book, this *Tretis of Loue Heuenliche*, survived the Civil War, the Fire of London, the Glorious Revolution of 1688–9, and the turmoils and controversies of the early eighteenth century. For, during the reign of George II, it found itself wedged between two volumes of Josephus in a bookshop called Alingham's at the bottom of the Strand.

In 1751, a young clergyman of the name of Pottle, a Fellow

of All Soul's College, Oxford and the Master of the Temple, was busy collecting a substantial library, and thinking Alingham's Josephus cheap, he decided (although he possessed three copies of the great work) to buy it. He also purchased on the same day the complete works of Bishop Ken and a first edition of Dryden's *Fables*. It was only when he returned to his chambers that he realized that, along with his superfluous Josephus, whose chronicles of Jewry he could read with such endless fascination, he had inadvertently brought home a little manuscript book which must have dated from medieval times.

At thirty-two, Septimus Pottle was too old a man, and too sensible, to be seized with the picturesque delight in the Middle Ages which so excited the imagination of some of his contemporaries. He had no taste for grottoes or ruins, no ambition to be, or to patronize, a hermit, no awe in the presence of unbridled nature. Skimming, without comprehension, the dirty pages of his discovery, he concluded that it was Gothick, vulgar and superstitious. But since it was old, and a book, it could have a place in his enormous collection and need never be looked at again. Not long afterwards, Pottle was rewarded with preferment, and he moved his extensive library to the Deanery at Selchester. The house was altogether inadequate, being no more than a converted priory house dating from the sixteenth century. What had been satisfactory for the ignorant monks of a barbarous and superstitious age would scarcely be a fitting residence for a clergyman and a gentleman of the reign of George II. He therefore pulled down the whole house and built a handsome, well-proportioned Deanery, with an ingenious hexagonal library which provided wall space for his magnificent collection of quartos and folios. A talkative wife, an early addiction to port, and a passion for cards, ensured that Dean Pottle never perused more than a handful of his precious volumes in the course of a year. In the twenty-five years he spent in that house, he grew fatter and redder and, thanks to the acquisition of a number of country livings in addition to his decanal stipend, quite considerably richer. But his early reputation for learning was not fulfilled. He died of apoplexy upon hearing of the American Declaration of Independence.

The more portable, or attractive, volumes in his library were housed by his descendants, who tended to be parsons unremarkable for anything except their idleness and their longevity. The bulk of the library, however, remained in the Deanery, and the volumes were untouched as one Dean succeeded to the next, a gaitered procession of well-meaning nonentities who occupied the house until the nineteen-sixties. It was then taken over by a dean of the modern school, denim-clad and mindless beyond the claret-induced dreams of his predecessors. The house into which he moved had, in the previous two centuries, accumulated a mellow, antiquated atmosphere which was inimical to his aggressive modernity. Victorian corridors were duly ripped out, sleek radiators were put in, and every available wall was injected with damp-proofing. In the course of this operation, the library was housed in the Chapter House and, in order to offset the prodigious cost of these renovations, the Dean resolved to sell the volumes (irrelevant to his own quest for something designated 'the nitty-gritty') to an antiquarian bookseller in Hastings. Among the tea-chests which were unloaded in that bookseller's warehouse was the little *Tretis of Loue Heuenliche*. It was a momentous event. The bookseller, perceiving its age and its rarity, sold it to a college friend called Giles Fox who had an interest in medieval languages. Robert of St Victor was to have his first reader for more than six hundred years. Few authors have ever waited so long for publication.

For Giles himself, the actual contents of the treatise, once its sources and analogues had been traced with reasonable thoroughness, held no interest. Familiarity had blurred any sense of oddness in reading a book furiously devoted to the notion that sex was evil. And he had long ago abandoned the rueful, sometimes bitter, contemplation of its inapplicability to his own life.

His first marriage, to Tibba's mother, had been hideously

painful for almost all of its ten years. He had married Mary because she was pregnant and this fact alone (not her pregnancy, but the ignominy of marrying for this reason) had poisoned his early affection for her. He had scarcely been able to look at the baby during the first miserable year of Tibba's life. The little bundle of squalling pink flesh, wrapped at the groin in stinking white plastic, seemed such an irrelevant reason for being obliged to live with Mary Hargreaves for the rest of his life. *What of the night foulnesses and the constant giving of suck?* fulminated the medieval author. Giles could have lived happily without them. His passion for Mary had been almost wholly sexual. In the months before she tricked him (so he saw it) there had been long blissful days and nights in which they had made love over and over again. He was drunk with her beauty. The howling arrival of Tibba (it was he who chose the name*) put a stop to these amorous excesses. With sex gone, everything went. As his sister often complained, he made no *effort* at all to 'get on' with Mary. After a while, they no longer even quarrelled. An iciness descended upon them from which it seemed they would never emerge. More and more of her time was spent with her boring horsey family in Hampshire and when, in the fullness of time, she chose to have sordid little love affairs, he affected an indifference which grew to be real. *What more are they than liars and harlots, this sex of yours, my sisters, who from the first deception of our father Adam have brought into this world death and lamentation and provoked the ire of our heavenly Father?*

It was in this period that his obsessive interest in *A Tretis of Loue Heuenliche* had begun. A bookselling friend, required to value the contents of a deanery library in the south of England, had discovered the cache of manuscripts in an old orange box twenty years previously. Most of them were of little interest: deeds for eighteenth-century houses, a seventeenth-century commonplace book, a will or two. But then, incredibly, at the side of the box, wedged down as one might a paperback novel

* After an East Saxon princess of devout life who flourished in the sixth century.

at the bottom of a suitcase, was the small calf-bound codex, no more than five inches by four, on yellowing paper, and in a hand which was unmistakably of the thirteenth century. When Giles read it, and realized that he had found an unknown medieval prose work of considerable linguistic interest, his excitement had been unbounded. It was an excitement pure in itself, a delight in learning, and in the discovery of a lost treasure. But it was a delight soon alloyed by the worldly satisfaction that the discovery would 'make' his career. He knew that it would guarantee him advancement, freedom from the tedious thraldom of a rather junior librarianship.

This had in course of time been the case; by the age of thirty-five he had secured an important job as Keeper of Manuscripts in a prestigious London musuem. It was a job which brought him a salary that seemed at the time princely, and which gave him more time for his researches.

He took some cynical pleasure in the fact that this unworldly tract on the virtues of virgins and the deceitfulness of married women should have brought such material advantage to Mary, then at the height of some deceitfully operated attachment to a much younger man. In the year he got his job, they had bought the house in Hermit Street: it was a time rather before Islington became fashionable.

They both loved its Regency simplicities. While the rest of the world rediscovered William Morris, they took their pleasure in spindly staircases, white panelling, and a few well-chosen pieces of Chippendale. The house provided their first shared interest, and, by then, Giles had come to love their child. Tibba had been eight. The smelly, noisy infancy was over. A serious, beautiful (she was an image of Mary), intelligent little creature had emerged and it had gradually dawned on them both that their years of iciness had been wasted years: home and children and shared experience were as much parts of love as what our medieval sage called the vile and damnable sin of concupiscence. Their love-making, once resumed after the years of abstinence, had nothing of the early abandonment, no romping about the house with no clothes on for hours upon end. But there was a quiet gentleness about it, a deep peacefulness, a longing at last that they should be together and that they should have more children.

How short it had been, this period of reconciliation, when measured beside the years of estrangement, the silent breakfasts, the cross little meetings on the landing, the slamming of separate bedroom doors. When she became pregnant again, he had feared that all his old feelings of anger and revulsion would return, but this had been so different. There had been so much happy hugging of one another in those last months.

And then she had died. Only in other people's lives, in newspaper stories and in Victorian novels can people die in childbed. But Mary had done so. To the loathsome agony of her death was added all the bitterness of self-reproach. The gap between the first child and the second was thought to have been too long. Mary was a little old. Dear God, at thirty-nine she was a little old. The labour had been premature by two months. Her blood pressure was uncertain. Completely to Giles's surprise, and to everyone else's, she had died (and her baby with her) with cruel and unannounced suddenness.

In the shocked months which followed, he had consoled himself with rather a promiscuous sex-life: but marriage was out of the question. For one thing, there was the little girl. The more time he spent with Tibba, and tried to penetrate her increasingly taciturn mysteries, the more puzzling his marriage to her mother appeared. It had been a mistake, he told himself, because he was not a marrying man. There was something in his temperament which was too romantic to endure the disillusioning recognition that the beloved belonged to the race of humans, sharing with that race the ability to forget appointments, to lose her temper or to burn saucepans. The brief entanglements which he allowed himself at this phase of existence were all firmly a matter of suppers at Italian restaurants and the removal of underclothes in bedrooms other than his own. They were not allowed home, these entanglements. *For knowe this in thin herte that al prickynges of the fleshe and al lustes thereof are but the nette in whiche Satan doth fisshe for the soules of menne. And al the warme heate of that fleshlie prickynge is but the first taste of fires whiche burne hot forever in the pittes of helle.*

His days were thus devoted to the library, his afternoons to little Tibba, all available time to the wise thirteenth-century virgins to whom his *Tretis* was written: it was only 'spare' time left over to the foolish maidens (never virgin for long) of the *tagltatelle verde* and bedsitting-rooms in Belsize Park.

And then calamity had come again, within a year of Mary's death. Long before, there had been trouble with the nerve in his right eye; and for some months before his operation Giles had suffered from violent pains in the head. But no one had warned him what 'the operation' would mean. The weeks of trekking to and from Moorfields Eye Hospital in taxis brought little hope. He lost his right eye, and soon he learnt that the nerve was suspect in the left eye also.

Anyone confronted with this horrific experience would feel anguish, despair, horror. But for Giles there seemed a particular cruelty in it. The edition of *A Tretis of Loue Heuenliche* was still far from complete. True, he knew the six separate manuscripts almost by heart. He had transcribed them all and had made all the major decisions about variant readings, collations, etc. But there remained the actual knocking of the whole into shape, the presentation of a typescript, not to mention the reading of proofs, which would be the necessary stages before his final ambition was realized – a neat, brown volume published by the Early English Text Society: '*A Tretis of Loue Heuenliche* edited by Giles Fox'. To shirk the completion of this task would involve a diminution of self which would have made life intolerable. Obsessively, painfully, stumblingly, he had worked on, sometimes with the help of research assistants, sometimes even getting members of his family – his sister Margaret, or his daughter Tibba – to read the unfamiliar Middle English words aloud to him, letter by letter on some occasions to be sure of exact spelling.

Margaret, being a sensible woman, was torn between objecting to the tyranny thus imposed and a recognition that her brother's life would become quite meaningless unless he were able to finish his edition. Giles's unreasonableness was a shared joke between Meg and her husband. They liked to picture him (a not wholly false picture) as pernickety, selfish, imposing. This dictation seemed the last straw.

'I couldn't make head or tail of it so what poor little Tibs made of it, God knows. And, my dear, it's such morbid stuff – going on and on and *on* about all that side of life . . .'

'Just like old Giles, though.'

But though they both laughed, Meg and her husband admired Giles's doggedness. Another man would have been worried about the future of his job in the library, or by the blank domestic horrors which blindness would be bound to impose. Giles spoke only of his *Tretis.*

What a rum life for little Tibba, Margaret had thought (what a rum name, she never ceased to exclaim). Thirteen years old, and condemned to live the life of a domestic recluse with only a blind father for companionship! It wasn't *right* (Monty had said). It wasn't natural. So, for a brief period while poor Giles had been taken off to Moorfields yet again, Tibba had gone down to Pangham to stay with her aunt and uncle Monty. And it was then that Giles had surprised them all.

Margaret said it was impossible to know with Giles (he kept things so bottled up, and Tibba was just as bad) how long he had had Carol up his sleeve. She was a nurse at Moorfields and probably Giles had known her for years – ever since his first trouble. So Margaret chattered to every distant relation who asked.

But the truth was (Giles had not chosen to admit it all at the time) that he had only known the girl a few weeks when they decided to get married.

Giles had worshipped and loved Carol in a way that he had revered no other woman. Her touch, her voice, her cool hands on his brow, had from the first something angelic about them. How pained and shaken (with one part of himself) he had been when a rather coarse male nurse had conveyed to him that Carol was 'a bit of all right', the phrase suggesting physical contours and facial features of which she had reason to be proud. Giles from that moment (with another part of himself) made up his mind to attain her. He knew, from what the male nurse had said, that Carol was very beautiful, and he was in love with her beauty, even though he had never seen it. The sexual attraction of it was enormous. And Carol's strange combination of sweet kindness and a sort of *distance* made her all the more alluring.

What a mystery! She had accepted him at once, and married him with such speed and such seeming joy. Giles knew that if once they started to discuss it, their love would be engulfed by such arrangements, such clashes of will. Their love! They lived in its selfish and ecstatic privacy with such intensity for those first few weeks that sacrificing it for prudency, expediency, what not, would have been impossible. Giles knew that Margaret would think it was mad to marry a woman he had never seen and whom he had known only a few weeks. He could not face the conversation in which this jaunty common sense would be enunciated. And what of Tibba? Would his little girl (she was thirteen by then) welcome a stepmother, or be repelled by her?

These questions, so necessary to answer from a common-sense point of view, had to be shirked by Giles. They had married, he and Carol, at the Register Office in Finsbury Pavement, and he had written to tell Margaret only after a few days had elapsed.

Those days had been the strangest of Giles's life: the awful heartbreak of his loss of sight was not alleviated by the joy he felt in Carol's love. He felt these two profound extremes of emotion at the same time. *Disappointment*, magnified to an almost intolerable degree, was the name by which he labelled his pain.

On a minor scale, in times past, it could be caused by waking up on the day when a picnic had been planned, and watching the pattering of rain on the windows. It was a feature of early waking, this *disappointment*, it was connected with the cruel oblivions of sleep, the harsh reminders with which the mind jolts itself to life at the beginning of a new day. You have been hoping to get a new job: and you failed to get it. It is in the morning, when the heavy knowledge returns like a dull weight to the stomach, that the pain is worst. Rejected lovers and recently bereaved widows both dread the dawn. So it was with Giles, who woke, forgetting his blindness. He would lie, half asleep, planning his day – a day in the library, in which, around his ordinary routines, he would be able to fit in an hour or two on the *Tretis*. A thought would occur to him about the handwriting on the fifth folio leaf and he would plan, as he lay there, to peer into the microfilm machine and compare it with the hand of another, more famous manuscript. What else would he enjoy about the day? A stroll at lunchtime down the Charing Cross Road to look in the second-hand bookshops would be followed, perhaps, by a glimpse of his favourite pictures in the National Gallery. If it was fine, he might walk further. What was the weather like? And he would open his eyes to see whether the sun shone through the gap in the curtains. He would blink at the darkness and then with sickening suddenness the disappointment would return, the knowledge that he would never see anything again, never have anything to gaze on. The mind would go on supplying him with visual images – of London, of Margaret, of Tibba, of the manuscripts. But cruelly, no optic function would ever satisfy these memories.

Was that, in part, what made the presence of Carol such a cause of joy in his heart? His mind played no tricks with her. He *felt* her to be beautiful and he loved her for it. But there was no image which relentlessly flashed into his mind whenever he thought of her. She was the first major impression of a non-visual kind. He accepted, in an anguished way, the fact that she was invisible, because she had never, in his life, been anything else. She felt, instinctively, the pain of his life. When he woke to these moments of acute horror for which the word disappointment appears cruelly and hideously mild, Carol was lying there beside him, and could supply wordless comfort for the pain she intuitively sensed him to be feeling. Sometimes she would merely hold his hand and stroke his brow, as in the old days when they had first met in the hospital. But more often, she calmed his waking anguish with exquisite and leisurely lovemaking, in which she guided his hands to be aware of her complete nakedness as she stood beside his bed before creeping in to be with him once again. These morning idylls had something in them of Paradise. It could not be said when, precisely, the lovemaking stopped and the business of the day began, because after bed, it would be bath-time, which they shared, and even the way she helped him dress had an erotic playfulness which marked his helplessness.

All this had happened in the space of a long school holiday, and when the term began again, Tibba, who was a day girl, came back to London. In those painful weeks, Giles began to wonder whether these qualities of *distance*, which he found so fascinating in Carol, were not actually mere symptoms of his own blindness. Tibba seemed distant too. He had always found her a slightly impenetrable child, prone to taciturnity. But he had never reckoned before on how much he had interpreted her silences by the expression on her face. Now that he could no longer see whether she was smiling or sullen, pale or flushed, he felt that he had in large part lost the Tibba he knew and loved. Her silences troubled and frightened him. They *felt* like hurt silences, but he hesitated to trust wholly to such fears. Carol, he came to realize, was not particularly sensitive in this respect. She delivered herself of ominous sentences to the effect that all children find it difficult when their parents marry again. Giles suddenly wondered, when she said this, whether class had anything to do with it, since Carol (another reason for marrying in haste and not consulting Margaret and Monty) spoke with an 'accent' and did not profess to share what she jokingly regarded as Giles's pretensions to gentility. So, to the pain of his blindness was added the pain of Tibba, her silent ability to convey hurt which had finally cracked one evening as she sat with him reading aloud from one of the *Waverley* novels: her voice was half choked with anguish and she had sobbed, and put her head on his knee and cried, 'Oh, f-father, f-father, f-father.'

He, without requiring an explanation, had asked, 'Is it Carol?'

'Oh she just hates me – she's a pig – oh f-father, why did you m-marry her – why?'

Giles sometimes thought that the silence which followed these words was more painful than anything that had ever happened to him; worse than the knowledge that he was blind or that his loved ones were dead. The alleged 'hatred' of Carol for Tibba was doubtless exaggerated in the child's mind: perhaps fabricated altogether. When it was possible to investigate what she had meant, it all seemed to come down to a few cross words over a household chore Carol had expected her to perform. But the outburst could not be forgotten and, in the light of subsequent horrors, it paved the way for the future of Tibba's life with her father.

Carol and Giles were married a little less than a year. None of the three living together in Hermit Street – not Carol, nor Giles, nor Tibba – ever alluded to the child's assertion that she was hated by her stepmother. But it left, as the silences of the household grew longer and deeper, no doubt as to the nature of Tibba's position. She had staked out a claim for her father's heart which was in direct opposition to Carol's. She never seemed, didn't Tibba, to be obstructing their marital happiness by design. But she was able, by a quiet self-assertion just on the border of politeness, to establish herself clearly as Carol's rival. There was no reason why a young teenage girl should not have developed the habit of a morning bath. But she did so with such perfect timing that her father's ablutions, in a house of one bathroom, had to be deferred to the evening when Carol was busy with the preparation of a meal. And it was doubtless a genuine kindness and generosity, to save Carol the troublous ten minutes each morning with foam and razor blades, to provide her father with the simple electric means to shave himself. Nor was Tibba to blame if Carol had never mastered French, and if she practised reading aloud in that language to Giles from the plays of Racine.

Little by little, and with nothing so crude as a spoken rivalry, Giles had *felt* Tibba and Carol disliking one another. He had sensed their glances and their coldnesses. But nothing, after the outburst, had ever been spoken.

Tibba had been so calm when she told her father that Carol was dead. Though there was affection and kindness in her voice, she did not pretend to be grief-stricken, nor even remotely sorry. Indeed the child was so matter-of-fact that he could almost have believed that it was some cruel prank to tell him that Carol had been hit by a taxi in the City Road – killed outright, stone dead, less than a year after the wedding.

'Father, listen to me, Carol is d-d-dead,' the child had said. Child! He hardly recognized the womanly form, so tall and with fully developed breasts, who held him in her arms while he shook and sobbed. Tibba in the most matter-of-fact and yet kindly way had, simply, taken control from that afternoon onwards. It was Tibba who had made all the initial telephone calls, to Carol's people, to Margaret and Monty, to the doctor and the undertakers. When the grotesquenesses of the funeral were done it was Tibba who was patiently there, by his side. It was as though some natural order was reasserting itself.

For the widower, the shock of Carol's death had full impact only some weeks after it all happened. Insomnia set in, punctuated only by appalling nightmares. In his exhausted, weakened anguish, he would be uncertain of time, person, place. Dozing off for a few horrid minutes, he would awake to imagine himself a boy again – or still married to Mary. Then blindness, Carol, the present, would flood back in all its dark cruelty into his consciousness.

From this phase, which lasted six months or so (he had, he supposed, been mad) Giles emerged. But he emerged changed and chastened. At the library they were still kind enough to pretend that there were things he could do; he still went in a couple of days a week. Apart from that he was at home, and home meant the domain of Tibba. It was the phase of Tibba triumphant, and it was a phase which was still going on.

Tibba, as a patient, self-willed seventeen-year-old, now ran the household and she was the very centre of Giles's life. After

Carol's demise there was no recurrence of the sexual promiscuity which had followed the death of his first wife. He no longer sought female companionship. His evenings were spent with Tibba. Sometimes he played, or she played, the piano. Sometimes the wireless set or the gramophone were resorted to. They came to know and love intimately the operas of Handel, the chamber music of Vivaldi, but more often than not Tibba read aloud to her father. Her voice was not unmodulated but the variations of tone were quiet and subtle. The stammer interrupted fluency, but she made no real attempt to imitate the voices of Nichol Jarvie or Meg Dodds any more than of Mr Crawley or Lady Lufton – for Scott and Trollope were the favoured novelists. The literature they fed her with at school and which she seemed to like was, in Giles's view, shallow piffle: Pinter and Tom Stoppard and *To the Lighthouse* and the poetry of Wilfred Owen. But Tibba, while keeping her literary tastes distinct from her father's, had no objection to reading from the giants in the evening. And sometimes, as when she read *Northanger Abbey*, their tastes would gloriously overlap.

In this way, for some years, Giles's life had passed. Tibba still had school, A-levels, and hours on her own about which he did not inquire. A woman 'did' the house, and the shopping. There was no reason why he should not have braved the rough tides and married again but it was simply, until Louise Agar's dramatic proposal, that he had never thought of doing so.

Even Louise had been produced as a result of Tibba's organizing powers. The girl had no time – nor inclination – to immerse herself in *A Tretis of Loue Heuenliche*. Moreover she lacked the necessary expertise, for it was all but done: a typescript was made and almost ready for the presses. A more regular research assistant must be found than the stray graduate students supplied by Giles's friends at London University. He should advertise. Tibba had framed the words of the advertisement. *Scholar*, she had read aloud, but she had put *Blind scholar: requires research assistant to complete edition of Middle English Text. Must be trained in palaeography and linguistically competent.*

Few responded to this attractive proposal, even though it lingered for a week on the back pages of *The Times*. The young clergyman would have had to come in from Croydon and his Latin was lamentably poor. Tibba had thought the swabsy girl working on Sagas had had a sly look. It was a relief when Giles declared her palaeographical skills inadequate. The sweaty young man with very short hair did not appear to know what Middle English was: his appearance at Hermit Street had been an irrelevance, an intrusion. And then modest, self-effacing and certain that the post would already be filled, Miss Agar had appeared.

She had called when Tibba was out. Giles had vetted her on his own and, since beggars cannot be choosers, he had offered her the post. Eight pounds a week for a weekly afternoon regularly spent on the *Tretis*; three pounds an hour for any extra endeavours on his behalf. The young woman had been at Girton College, Cambridge. She had written a doctoral dissertation, which had been failed, on a subject of staggeringly peripheral importance, but she had made herself the mistress of Anglo-Norman, Latin, Old High German, and the early manifestations of English. She could read old handwriting and she lived with her mother in Northwood Hills. She was the best that they could muster.

When Tibba had first set eyes on Miss Agar, this figure her father had hired without consultation, her heart had felt childish stabs of pity. She was so very plain, so boringly dressed, so heavy of chin and cheeks, so dull (behind the unattractive spectacles) of eye. She was five foot ten, and lumpish. Her legs were unshapely, columnar. Her complexion was poor. Her only redeeming feature, in Tibba's searching gaze, was her hair, which, if it was not washed with sufficient frequency, was at least abundant and long.

Tibba could allow herself reflections so devoid of mercy partly because she was young and partly because she was such a beautiful person. It was not a beauty one would ever have thought flashy or obvious, but in its English restraints it could be perfectly, tastefully self-confident. Thick, long hair was nowadays 'up', and swept back from a smooth pale brow. Her eyebrows were perfect little arches over good, searching green eyes. Her pallor was slightly freckled above the cheek-bones. Her nose was small and straight. Her lips (though she hardly knew it herself) were her glory, a little cupid's bow, always unadorned and open, slightly parted, to reveal teeth which were large and (in the most attractive way) uneven. A good chin, and a long swan-like throat, where her simplicities of dress began: Shetland jumpers, kilts, dark red tights, all a schoolgirl innocence of style.

Miss Agar could not compete! Had any such cruel conception flashed upon Tibba's subconscious, forgetful of the vanity of appearance in competition for the affections of a blind man? *For knowe the wel, as seint Austin witneseth, that al erthly fairness and the likerous painting of outwarde shewes is a snare and deceit unto oure hertes.*

With no little condescension, Tibba had deemed Miss Agar admirable. Her father admired her philological grasp, the speed with which she had mastered the manuscript tradition of the *Tretis*, the precision with which the task seemed to go forward now that she was Giles's collaborator. At last it made sense to dream of submitting a typescript to the Early English Text Society before the year's end.

Week by week, and more than once a week, poor, plain Miss Agar had come, and spoken to Giles about matters so minute in their orthographical and typographical exactitude that he had sometimes felt his gift of sight had been a superfluity. With Miss Agar at his side to spot variants, marks, spellings, what man needed eyes? Their talk had been all practical, formal. Stiffly they avoided Christian names. They clung to their Foxes and Agars. She had never been Louise until that very afternoon when she clambered heavily on to his knees. But Louise had, in the stiffest manner imaginable, become a 'family friend' to the extent that she had occasionally partaken of a meal at Hermit Street; that she had 'remembered' Tibba's birthday with a postcard from the Tate Gallery (Waterhouse's 'Lady of Shallot'); that she had even, during Giles's and Tibba's absence of a fortnight one precious summer, slept in the place and put on and switched off lights to the confusion of potential burglars.

Such was the extent of her intimacy with Giles Fox before she wildly exclaimed, 'Marry me!' that afternoon. And when he comfortingly took her in his arms, murmuring, 'Louise, Louise,' she knew next to nothing of his emotional history. She saw only a slightly small, punctiliously neat man in a suit, a man whose neatness might hoodwink the casual observer into supposing him a homosexual or an ambassador. In fact he was Giles Fox: not a name known widely to the world but familiar to Louise from the beginnings of her career as a medievalist. Had he not written the definitive article, in the *Journal of English and Germanic Philology*, on the language of the *Ayenbite of Inwit*? And for anyone wishing to familiarize themselves with that area of knowledge, was there a better way than reading Fox on *The Early Developments of London English and the East Midland Dialect*? Was it not his note in *Neophilologus* on 'Some early Middle English diphthongs – au, ai, oi', which had first inspired Louise Agar to quit the comparative frivolities of medieval literature and history to cleave only unto language, language, language? To encounter this legend, this Fox, had been no small experience for Louise: it was as if an average man had answered a newspaper advertisement and found himself face to face with M. Larousse or Mr Chambers, or some such monumental authority. Of the hundred or so people in the world who knew what Giles was 'up to' in the scholarly field, Miss Agar was the closest he had to a 'fan'.

Her own work with the diphthongs had failed to result in a doctorate and, such is the world's poverty and cynicism, she could find no institution willing to employ her on the basis of her researches. With a sense of failure, she had exchanged her uncomfortable lodgings in the brickish outskirts of Cambridge for her old bedroom, with its cosy carpet, its teddy-bear, its poster of Winnie the Pooh, in her mother's half-timbered house in

Northwood Hills, and its jangling, ill-rendered noises of Handel's Largo. An ability to type brought financial relief, but it had been depressing to be designated a 'temp'. Miss Agar felt herself to be one of nature's permanencies. Then the blind scholar had advertised and to her amazement, at the cost of less than a pound, she had been conveyed from that dingy 'front room', with its potted plants and its somewhat melancholy photographs of Mum and Dad on their wedding day, to the spotlessly neat elegance of Giles Fox's study. She had not moved so little in academic circles as never to have met anyone whose name had appeared in print. Her old tutors at Girton had both written books, the Mistress wrote books. But these had not the magic of Fox on 'Some diphthongs'. From the first, when she found herself in Giles's presence, she was transported. It was a journey far deeper than the outer eye could have perceived, if it only saw her clambering (or, unkindly thought, her galumphing) aboard the red electric train at Northwood Hills in that brown coat of hers. Metropolitan Line down to King's Cross; change to the Northern Line, and it was only one stop to the Angel. On subsequent visits, what *double entendre* she had injected into her words as she had said to the ticket-vendor at Northwood Hills, 'I am going to the Angel!'

Angels, of one sort or another, lurked all over London: this was the city's magic. The bus or the underground railway could whoosh you away from your dull room and your dingy street until, in no time at all, you stood outside the door of the Queen or the Foreign Secretary or the Poet Laureate. They put up blue plaques on these houses when the angels flapped their wings and sped towards the greater light. How much more exciting their houses seemed before the blue plaques went up. The twitch of a curtain, a light being turned on in an upstairs room: evidence of the Presence! All over London, these Presences, less than a pound's journey from our own front door.

Giles, it need hardly be said, had almost no sense of himself as angelic in this regard; he would have been too distracted, even though not too modest, to think of himself as Fox on some early

32

Middle English diphthongs. Life over the last ten and twenty years had bombarded him with so many experiences that he did not devote much thought to his early monographs. Nor, it must be confessed, had he ever, before today, devoted much thought to Miss Agar. He had admired her punctilious accuracy of method, the speed with which she had managed to collate and assemble his material, the painstaking patience with which, sometimes letter by letter, she had read aloud the pages of typescript and verified spellings over and over again. Her diligence had impressed him, her industry, intelligence. It was a pity that the Cambridge examiners should have condemned her to residence, until the death of her mother, in Northwood Hills. She was as good a medievalist as many he had met in more exalted academic spheres. That was all he had felt.

Or did he, he now wondered, as she sobbed on his collar and clawed at his neck and kissed his mouth, did he not always sense her reverence for him and (with a part of himself insufficiently disciplined to feel shame) did not a little sycophancy always please him? Now, he felt himself luxuriating in the worship. No, there had been nothing like it in his life. Mother had never been much a cuddler (perhaps this was why he had turned out by turns so cold and so promiscuous, and why his sister Margaret was so *brisk*). Mary had never *doted* on him, never taken him seriously enough to adore in the way that he could sense in every kiss and stroke and wordless gasp, Miss Agar adored. The maidens who belonged to the phase of the Italian restaurants of Frascati and fornication had never doted. There had rarely even been tears. And *he* had been the worshipper in his marriage to Carol. The relationship of patient and nurse had never been abandoned wholly. He was always in her power: she always, therefore, could retain some of her mystery, hold some of herself back from his possession.

This adoration was more than comforting. Even a few minutes were habit-forming. He felt her gently, stroking, squeezing, a sort of amorous Hoodman Blind. He felt good round shoulders and a fleshy back, covered with an acrylic cardigan and quivering

33

with emotion. He felt her wonderfully large, protuberant breasts beneath the acrylic. He lingered over them, wishing he could remove them from their bondage to appear naked to his touch, but no obvious way out – or in – suggested itself to his fingers. He felt her waist on his groin. He stroked her legs and tried to feel up into the skirt, which seemed to be of a slithery rayon fibre; but there again entrance, if not barred, seemed awkward in her present posture.

How much of his history did she know? How much should she now be told? What wrong guesses had she made?

'Don't love me too much,' he advised.

'It's too late to tell me that, Giles.' Her hands now held his cheeks between their palms. 'I love you too much already.'

Silence intervened; a long silence, before he asked, 'Do you often fall in love in this way?'

She was slightly flattered, apparently. There was a giggle. How good it would be to have her undressed; to feel these great balloons soft, not acrylic, to the touch, to know that natural, quivering, drooping shapeliness, detached from the absurdities of dress!

'Giles, I have never been in love before in my life.'

He sighed at the painfully obvious sincerity of the confession. Its truthfulness shot through him sharply. 'Never?'

'Never, oh never, my dearest, like this. I have never ... held ... a man in my *arms* like this before.'

He stroked her head as, once more, she cried a little. They were tears of release, not painfulness. But he was at last troubled to find himself at the centre of so important an epiphany.

II

If there was a touch of mist in the air, as there was today, Tibba eschewed the bus and walked towards Hermit Street in a dream. It was not a noisy walk, nor ugly once she had quitted Clerkenwell Road. A little clutch of streets unpested by the bombs, or by the bulldozers or the conservers and lovers of English architecture, still survived in a convincingly grubby and habitable state. The roar of main thoroughfares was held in check by good, old brickwork in the pretty terraces and high Victorian tenements.

Anyone who saw her drift along, this modern girl, could have been forgiven for thinking that she carried about in her person some of the sad dignities of long ago. Her beauty was not completely of the present age, nor even of this world. Today, her abundantly thick brown hair fell over the shoulders of her white jersey and was almost damp with the yellowing swirling mist. She wore a dark blue skirt, and a rather thick white wool covered her sturdy legs. She wore plain, black, sensible shoes, and carried a little music case, which contained *Phèdre*, *King Lear*, *To the Lighthouse* and her diary.

She had never read *King Lear* before; they were reading it aloud in class, and she kept wishing to read the whole thing at home. But she was so pained by it that she couldn't. Its noise and cruelty appalled her. This afternoon, Miss Russenberger had corrected Melanie (a girl in her set) for reading with insufficient vigour.

'Bind fast his *corky* arms!' she had gleefully, lugubriously exclaimed. Melanie had repeated it in the same flat tones which she had used the first time. Miss Russenberger was reading Gloucester's part, so she had to be quiet while Melanie said, 'Bind him I say' in the dullest, quietest voice; then Chantal (who hated Miss Russenberger) had injected real venom into 'Hard, hard. O filthy traitor,' and lots of the set had sniggered. Tibba had sniggered with the rest, but only because she was hating the play so much. It did not seem to be a dignified *tragedy*, like *Phèdre*, nor written in beautiful language, like *To the Lighthouse*: the language Tibba herself tried to imitate in her school essays and in her diary. The language of Shakespeare was grotesque, not beautiful in the way Mrs Woolf was beautiful. It was like eating too-strong curry when Chantal asked, 'Wherefore to Dover?' and Miss Russenberger answered:

> Because I would not see thy cruel nails
> Pluck out his poor old eyes; nor thy fierce sister
> In his anointed flesh stick boarish fangs.

You wanted to gasp at its terribleness.

The whole experience of doing it with Miss Russenberger was upsetting anyway. Tibba longed to do well for Miss Russenberger. She had done well for her in *Comus* and in *The Knight's Tale*, but could not see herself rising to the occasion when it came to writing essays on *King Lear*. She was shocked by it all being so like – and yet in many ways so unlike – her own life. Giles, after all, wanted to give up responsibility in the library after he lost his sight and like King Lear, 'unburthen'd crawl towards' an early retirement. Yet he was always complaining at the inadequacy of his successors and about the fact that when he *did* go into the library, they did not give him enough to do. In this, he was Lear-like. There were no other children beside herself: she did not know whether, if there had been, her relations with him would err in the direction of being a Goneril or a Cordelia. The rejection of Cordelia at the beginning of the play seemed to her almost intolerably cruel, a cruelty of which her own father would have been incapable. But there was surely much of Giles in Lear:

> I lov'd her best and thought to set my rest
> On her kind nursery ...

It was only now, at the age of seventeen, that Tibba was beginning to discover that other girls of her age had what they called 'a life of their own'. Tibba was not sure, entirely, that she would want this. It was not that she was not in love: she was. With the most romantic despair and pain, she loved a man. But there could be no fostering of this affection by visits to the cinema or discothèque. She loved Captain de Courcy, and there was no likelihood of his ever asking her out in the evening, nor of her having the courage to accept such a suggestion if it were made. Hers was a true love, of the kind which breaks hearts. But even if it were possible to imagine Captain de Courcy in a discothèque, it is unlikely that Tibba would have been in a position to join him. Chantal went to a disco several nights a week. So did Melanie. Sue had been sleeping with boys, with her parents' full knowledge and connivance, since the age of fourteen. This very weekend, Rosemary and her boyfriend were going on a motor-bike to Dorset. The time of these girls was their own.

Tibba's life and time were not her own. They belonged to Giles. This was something taken so much for granted that she had barely recognized it as a fact. How *could* she arrange her life differently? Supposing ... but such a thing was impossible: it made the blood leap in the face and the heart pound and the loins ache and melt as in D. H. Lawrence, but it *was* as impossible to imagine Captain de Courcy on a motor-bicycle as it was to picture him cavorting at a discothèque. Suppose then she had a boy-friend in the *ordinary* way, of the sort who conveyed you by motor-bike to Dorset; of the sort who revealed, when the luggage was unfurled, that he possessed a *double* sleeping bag (Oh the excitement of Rosemary's life!), well, *suppose*. What could Tibba do? Who would look after father?

It was no good forever reckoning that he could 'go to Pang-ham'. Aunt Margaret did not, probably, always want to have him. He hated going. He did not get on with Uncle Monty, and Pangham was, in itself (how often she had heard him say it) detestable to him. Without Tibba, besides, where would he be? Could one imagine Aunt Margaret reading Racine, or Uncle

Monty? Trollope they managed – he was a favourite author of Monty's. But father said that no one read like Tibba. And there were the meals. He did not eat much, but he always complained of indigestion if he were exposed to a regulation much different from that Tibba provided. Cold meat, noodles, and olives were his staple food. Supper was always a variant of this, followed by fresh fruit. She left soup and cheese for his lunch, boiled eggs were sometimes eaten at breakfast. Tibba wearied of this routine and pined for variety: chilli con carne, Wiener schnitzel, fish and chips, biryani, *boeuf en daube.* Father merely said that life was too short to spend more of it than one had to sitting on the lavatory. This brisk view settled the matter. Tibba compensated by tucking in more heartily than most girls of her age to the school food.

She knew about her legs. There was nothing she could do to make them lithe and thin, like Chantal's. Sometimes she would stare at them for hours and hours before the glass in her bedroom: and the longer she stared, the more they seemed to become solid and swollen. On happy days she could tell herself that no one could quite call her legs fat: not fat in the way that Debbie's were, sort of quivering with surplus flesh. But, if only those sturdy calves swooped *in* a little more towards the ankle! Perhaps they did: but no one had ever *told* her she had nice legs. They told her she had nice hair, and she believed them. How gaily she brushed it, how frequently she toyed with it, stuck bits in her mouth, wove little plaits with it while she dreamed of Captain de Courcy or Virginia Woolf. But her legs no one had ever mentioned. And she had only, as today, to glimpse Chantal's slight, shapely little twigs in their dark blue tights, to be filled with the most profound despair. She knows not what the curse may be, and so she guzzles steadily. Day by day, when the others nibbled cottage cheese from plastic boxes, Tibba still pined and slavered for the school lunches. And little other care hath she. Irish stew, with lots of potatoes; roly-poly pud; cottage pie; jam tart; toad in the hole and Eve's pudding. Always lots and lots of lovely gravy at the meal's beginning, and at its end plenty of delicious custard: the things you would never bother to make for yourself at home.

So, her appetite at school lunch was a little sign, not comprehended by her fellows, that Tibba was set apart. They knew, vaguely, that she had rather a sad home life. They gathered that her mother was dead and that her father had some kind of disability. Some of them knew that he was blind. She was on the whole a popular girl, but her aloofness was unmistakable. She was cast off from them all partly because she was much cleverer, but largely because of the huge difference of life-style between herself and them. She was, though she did not know it, living the life of the grown-up married woman while having to perform the tasks and rigours of the schoolgirl. It was she who had to see to the running of the household, and who had to get her father to sign all the cheques; it was she who did the catering, the shopping and the cooking, paid Mrs Tucker and chatted to her on Saturday mornings. Without Mrs Tucker, of course, the whole enterprise would have been unendurable. But it was enough as it was to give Tibba the air of belonging to an older generation than her coevals.

If that did not ensure it, her life and conversation with her father would have done so.

'You and I are born out of time,' he had said to her so often. It might have been true of him: Tibba had not been given the option. When she heard people at school discussing Kojak, Space Invaders, or Pink Floyd, she had almost no idea what they were talking about. In 'current affairs' lessons, she tried to keep quiet, but if they made her speak it was to reveal her ignorance. Miss Russenberger had been told, and frequently repeated it with enthusiasm, of Tibba's comment that the Prime Minister was a 'Whig'. It struck some of the class as quaint at the time, but Miss Jackson-Downes had said, with Miss Russenberger's agreement, that it was a remark of 'scholarship potential'. What did they mean? Tibba had seized the name 'Whig' out of the air, as one which she knew attached itself to politicians. She had no idea whether the Prime Minister was in fact a Whig or a Fascist, or a Sinn Feiner, or a Republican. 'Most schemes of political improvement are very laughable things,' she had parroted, again earning the delighted praise of Miss Jackson-Downes. It was something her father said every day. Tibba barely knew that it was a quotation.

The modern world, its tastes and fashions, were for the most part unpalatable to her father, with the result that Tibba had only tasted it in patches. He never took a newspaper. The wireless was turned off whenever news or 'current affairs' were mentioned; it was solely, for him, a musical box. He did not read modern literature – he claimed (but she knew it was untrue) not to have read a work of literature written after 1914. His idea of an evening's entertainment was for Tibba to read aloud from authors whose work was wholly unknown to the majority of her immediate contemporaries. The whole inner furniture of Tibba's mind was different from theirs. She was bashful because of it, but in an inner way serene, because she knew herself to be more knowledgeable as well as more clever. She did not know who was the Prime Minister of Iran or what a quango was or whether the dollar should be devalued, or even, with much accuracy, how her own country was governed. But such knowledge is peripheral and, on the whole, transitory. She knew Racine and Scott; she was a deft embroiderer and a good household manager, she loved Captain de Courcy, and she was – that was it – she was *invaluable* to her father.

Goodness knew how he had lived through the torments and trials of the previous few years. No one could write a line like *'Out, vile jelly'*, still less could they snigger about it, if they had actually lived with someone who was going blind. Miss Russenberger had said that she would not rebuke Chantal for sniggering. *King Lear* had produced laughter in more than one audience when performed. It was what Wilson Knight called the comedy of the grotesque. It was like, Miss Russenberger had said, laughing at funerals. It was a relief of tension, a form of mild hysteria. It was a tribute to the play's extraordinary power. All this was gibberish. Chantal was laughing at Miss Russenberger, not at

King Lear. But Shakespeare had written '*Out, vile jelly*', and it was too painful and disgusting to think about.

Life, it seemed to Tibba, was divided absolutely into its own equivalent of BC and AD. Before her mother's death (when she was twelve), there had not strictly speaking been any unhappiness at all. She had *thought* she was unhappy. She had felt chilled with horror when her parents made it so obvious that they disliked one another. She had hated it when her mother spoke to Trevor on the telephone (Trevor had been the 'man' in her mother's life) and then crossly fidgeted about for her car keys and went out for hours on end. And she had known acute pain – or thought she had known it – over all the usual childish sorrows – the breaking of favourite dolls and toys; the getting to the zoo and finding it closed; the opening of the large parcel (what else could it be *but* a doll's house?) on Christmas morning and finding it a toy fort. A fort! With medieval soldiers; and then they had wondered why she cried over her fowl and stuffing and brussels sprouts before the Queen spoke to the Commonwealth.

That had been what she thought was meant by the word *unhappiness* in the days of BC. And it had gradually, with such cruel, deceptive gentleness, receded. Mother and Father were no longer foul to each other. She left the school where the girls were foul to her and fell under the spell of Miss Russenberger – 'Imagine a child of eleven writing an essay on poetic metre!' that female had exclaimed to her parents – and she had made friends with Chantal and Debbie and Sue and all the others. Pubescence had its pains and embarrassments, of course, but life, on the whole, promised to get better. And as life lulled her with this falsehood, Mother began to grow visibly pregnant, and she began to share her parents' excitement about the coming child. Father had been bothered for months with pain in his eye. The phrase 'optic neuritis' of which there seemed to be fear, meant nothing to Tibba. She won a poetry prize. And her mother grew daily larger and rounder and pinker-cheeked.

Tibba had been in love with her in those weeks, she was so beautiful. It made the girl so happy that there were no more

41

telephone calls, no Trevors, no searches for car keys. Her mother had come *back*. She was so fine-looking, with her large hazel eyes, and firm oval face, and straight white teeth, that she did not need the attentions of a hairdresser. Tibba had always felt that it was nicer when mother's hair was straight, before Vidal Sassoon's got at it with their curling tongs in Sloane Street. But the curls were a frivolity which Mary had enjoyed, and when she returned to Tibba in dreams it was usually as a face framed with curls.

There had not been the smallest indication, not from her father, nor from the doctors, nor – and this was the most reliable guide by far – nor in Tibba's bones, that her mother was in any danger when she entered the maternity hospital. She came out of it a hideously white, slightly greasy stiff *thing*. Tibba had insisted on seeing it before it was put in the undertaker's van. Where was she, where had she gone? This grimacing, seemingly thin-lipped object was not her mother. It seemed like the most hideous trick of supplantation or substitution. There was almost (in this point of view she saw what Miss Russenberger meant) something hilarious about it: the whole substitution was so fantastic. One day there she had been, sitting up in bed, munching grapes, clutching the Penguin English Classic of *The Moonstone* and telling Tibba the plot with her mouth still full of fruit. The next day, the telephone had rung at Hermit Street. Margaret had gone to answer it and come back looking shocked and troubled. It had been Giles, ringing from the hospital. They had gone round at once, and there it was, this horrible thing which hardly looked like Mary at all, and mocked at them and at her with the stiffness of the Vidal Sassoon curls.

No words could describe Tibba's grief. She was still mourning her mother even now, four years later. Yet the absolute savagery and injustice of it all was just the first act of an appalling drama in which, as Miss Russenberger said so often, 'one woe doth tread upon another's heel'. Whenever something appalling had been about to happen in the past, in BC, the Golden Age, Mary had usually managed to avert it. The queue was so long that they could not get into the film; but Mary's ingenuity would quickly think of some other treat, equally alluring. The cake fell flat; but there would follow a happy half-hour whipping up cream in a blender and squeezing it into brandy-snaps.

That is to say, life might be hard, but there was always a happy ending. But since the disappearance of Mary, it seemed as if it might all be cruelty and relentlessly unhappy.

> I've got a wonderful feeling
> Everythin's goin' ma way . . .

Carol had mindlessly trilled. But Tibba had the opposite feeling.

First there had been the era which in Giles's life had been taken up with promiscuous and compensating evenings out with a whole series of inappropriate (usually) young women. Tibba knew nothing of the Italian restaurants, still less of the removal of underclothing. All she felt was a combined anger and shock with her father. Her loneliness was appalling: he did nothing to lighten it. There were some weeks when he was out almost every night, and she would have fallen asleep, after several hours of sobbing, long before his return. He appeared able to accept her mother's death. This was what was so painful. Death, surely, was unacceptable. You couldn't accept it, it was so disloyal to *her*: it contradicted one's very being to accept that she could be the victim of this vile game: that all her loveliness could be transformed into this terrible gaping doll-like thing. But all grown-ups were the same. Margaret and Monty were positively breezy.

She knew that Margaret tried to be kind. It was something that she kept repeating to herself. But the company of Margaret had never been congenial, and when Monty was there too it was intolerable. They seemed to be having some private joke all the time. They kept smiling and laughing. Tibba feared they might be laughing at her, only they were always like that. And the laughter seemed so loathsome, so cruelly inappropriate, now that her mother was dead.

Of course, as her father always dutifully said, Margaret and

Monty were *very good*. And they meant so very well. Tibba dreaded their visits to Hermit Street and she herself hated going to stay at Pangham. But this had been her lot, for a portion of the holidays, for the last three years. In the terrible months when her father was going to and fro to the eye hospital, there almost seemed the possibility that Margaret would take them off to live at Pangham permanently. There was something overwhelming about Margaret's bossiness. And yet, as Tibba knew (and this made her hate herself for having unkind thoughts about her aunt) there was no one else, and without Margaret's help in the weeks that Giles lost his sight, what *would* they have done?

Blind! How could life deal out such blows? All her father's work and nearly all his happiness depended on his being able to see. With excruciating pain, and quite terrifying surgical experiences, he had lost the fight: that was how the doctors saw it. He had lost a battle for his sight. But why did there have to be a fight? Who or what was it in the cruelly indifferent world of nature that forced these fights upon us, making of her mother a lifeless pale dummy, and of her father a blind man? When they had taken all the bandages off, he looked less sinisterly like the invisible man. But she had been unable to stop sobbing at the sight of him, perched there in his chair. His tie was crooked, an unthinkable thing in 'real life', in 'normal circumstances'. And his face was sadder than anything Tibba had ever seen in her life.

Margaret had told her that being sad wasn't going to help Giles and that they must try to be bright as well as practical about it. Well, of course, she was right and tears *help*, strictly speaking, no one. It had been necessary to do lots of practical things about the house and Tibba had enjoyed helping with that. And yet she couldn't stop crying. It was heartbreaking. There were boxes and boxes in the study labelled *TLH*, which was what he often called *A Tretis of Loue Heuenliche*, this medieval tract or whatever it was which was the most important thing in his life. And now he could not even read a cereal packet. This again, like her pretty mother turning into a corpse, had for Tibba some of the ghastliness of a joke. It made her retreat into a greater seriousness.

Tibba had spent that holiday at Pangham. She had never much cared for the place before, but now she would always blame it for the disaster of her father's second marriage. Even so few years later (three only was it, but she had changed and the difference between thirteen and seventeen, as Miss Russenberger had said, is not four but Eternity), even so few years later she forgot the details. Her father had to go *back* to the hospital after his unsuccessful treatment. Monty and Margaret had simply whisked her off to Pangham for a purgatorial four weeks of rain-swept walks and the banter of cousins. When she had returned to Hermit Street – to her *mother's house* – That Woman had been in residence. Married!

This had felt the worst, this had caused the most pain; more than her mother's death or her father's blindness. The ordinary terms of dislike or disapprobation are too mild to convey the immediate and atavistic disgust Tibba felt when she first saw Carol and apprised herself of the situation. In the subsequent painful months, she had sometimes tried to explain the thing: had That Woman shared some of her father's interests; had That Woman had a pleasanter voice . . . But reason did not enter into it. Her father had perpetrated the Ultimate Betrayal. Tibba was not merely shocked by it. She was shaken, upended, disrupted. Before, the earlier disasters had been an upsetting of her old self. The arrival of Carol meant not an upsetting, but a new Tibba: harder, colder. She no longer expected Life to be anything but miserably harsh and painful. She had gone through the most searing experience possible: she had lost her faith. Giles, in short, had been what she put her trust in. Even as she had tried to comfort him – or had merely shared in his unhappy silences – she had believed in him. But the arrival of Carol destroyed this belief.

It sickened the child to see Carol writhed around Giles's neck like a cheap woman in a film. It was all so entirely inappropriate. Few people in the world could have been expected to have much to say about medieval treatises: it was not to be expected that anyone would wholly share Giles's intellectual interest. But a certain level of bookishness, while her mother lived, had always been taken for granted. Carol might almost have been the sort of person who read true-life Romances and comic-strip stories about Doctors and Nurses. In fact, apart from the occasional desultory turning of pages of the more vulgar women's magazines, Tibba had never seen her stepmother reading during the whole sorry year.

She had tried not to let her feelings show. Her father had suffered enough, she knew. And yet her anger with him and her disillusionment became entangled with her hatred of Carol and her general sense of the pathos of it all. The evenings were intolerable. Tibba sat and read to her father when the radio yielded no interest. He couldn't see the looks of boredom, or envy or resentment, on his spouse's face as Tibba read about the loveliness of Diana Vernon or tried to get her mouth round the witticisms of Nichol Jarvie. At any point where it was possible to do so, Carol would interrupt Sir Walter Scott's relentless narratives with suggestions about a drink for either of them, or by asking if they minded her having the radio on very quietly while Tibba read, or by ostentatious bangings and rattlings of coal buckets.

Her father took it all so quietly, with such passivity, that it was as if he did not notice Tibba's miseries. That was why she had her outburst and declared of Carol, 'She hates me – she's a pig – Oh f-father, why did you marry her?' The scene, even in three-year retrospect, embarrassed the Tibba aged seventeen who remembered the gawky child who had made the tearful ejaculation. She now felt that it was cruel to have upset and embarrassed her father. Her objections to poor Carol now appeared very arch and snobbish. Anyone in the place of her mother would have been – would still be – unthinkable. The shock of Mary's death had still been vivid. But did not a lot of the horror of Carol consist in her somehow vulgar very freckly arms, and her plebeian Liverpudlian accent? The seventeen-year-old Tibba

46

was able to view the last disability with more detachment than her former fourteen-year-old self. The seventeen-year-old knew that Wordsworth and Mr Gladstone and Tennyson had spoken with 'regional' accents, and that no disgrace attached to the fact. She knew, too, that Giles himself came from quite modest stock, and that nothing entitled her to suppose, merely on the evidence of her parents' educated voices, that she was superior to those who spoke differently. But in those days Carol had merely been a pleb – the word used by Tibba's horrid little friends to denote anyone of a class poorer than themselves. It had filled her with shame: such shame that one never wanted to have anyone from school to the house. Better to live without friends than be compelled to explain what cruel folly her father had committed, what degradation had come upon the house.

The blatant childish snobbery was not a thing she had ever dared spell out to her father. It remained a shameful secret. Nor, of course, had she ever told Giles about the Curse.

The Curse still troubled Tibba, even though she was now an unbeliever, like Virginia Woolf, in any of what she took to be the superstitious claptrap of Christianity. She was as brittle and as despairing as it was possible to be in her apprehensions of the unseen world. But the effectiveness of the Curse still troubled her even though she tried to dismiss it with the keen satirical vein she was cultivating in place of a sense of humour. The ghastliness of Carol had been so painful and so upsetting that Tibba had been driven to it. The worst occasion of all had been when they were all going over to Pangham to stay with Margaret and Monty.

Giles's sartorial eccentricities had been marked even before his loss of sight, but they were now fixed. He possessed three grey suits: one lightweight for the summer, one heavy tweed for the coldest winter days, one ordinary. He wore these without variation, and when one or other wore out, they were replaced with identical substitutes. He wore a clean white shirt each day, and a silk tie, usually blue, which was taken from the top right-hand drawer from the chest in his bedroom. The simplicity of this

47

design ensured that Giles always knew what he was wearing and did not require the assistance of a 'dresser'. Carol often commented on its dullness, but he always rebuffed her.

It was a cold Saturday in January when they were due to drive off to Pangham. Tibba waited with Carol in the hall. The bags were in the boot of the car and her father was coming downstairs. It was appalling to see the look of glee on Carol's vulgar, scheming, freckly, beaky face. Giles, normally so tastefully punctilious in costume, was wearing a bright orange shirt and a tie of the most florid and vulgar design. Tibba was on the point of remonstrating when Carol had held her nasty painted fingernail to her heavy red lipstick and grinned playfully. It seemed such a cruel jape. When they got to Pangham, Monty of course made no comment, but Margaret exclaimed at once, 'Aren't we gay!'

'What do you mean?'

'Your tie. Rather fun – looks like a Jamaican bus conductor on his night off.'

Giles, in former days, would have been furious. As it was, he was simply crumpled and unhappy. He self-consciously fingered his tie and obviously longed to remove it. No one dared tell him he was in an orange shirt. At the rather stiff little dinner party, attended by other schoolmasters and their wives, he looked woefully ridiculous: and as Tibba knew, Giles could not be happy unless he looked seemly. The next day he appeared in a bright red shirt. He had implored Carol to find him a tie less offensive than the Jamaican bus conductor's, but she had merely come up with a horrible stripy thing that clashed badly with the scarlet shirt.

For Carol, it was all part of an attempt to cheer Giles up, to make his life brighter. She shared with Margaret and Monty a sense that Giles indulged in gloom deliberately. But in contrast to Monty, Carol also seemed to think that anything remotely formal or old-fashioned or seemly was also in danger of being depressingly 'stuffy'.

'Gile looks so stuffy in a white shirt all the while.'

Tibba tried to persuade herself she had misheard, but this

extraordinary and inelegant shortening *was* being applied to her father. Gile. And there he sat, dressed like a cheer-leader on a holiday camp, nervously fingering his tie. It was on that Sunday that Tibba had pronounced the Curse. It was during the morning service in Pangham Chapel which Monty liked them to attend. Tibba tried not to compromise herself by allowing any sound to pass her lips while she was in this edifice. If Margaret looked her way during the hymns she would sometimes, out of politeness, open and shut her mouth like a goldfish. She tried to sit in a rather hunched position, rather than kneel, during the prayers, and she tried to get on the end of the pew so that she did not have to turn left at the Creed. The hour was usually an embarrassing one, not less so because she felt the eyes of all the boys were upon her. These were pre-de Courcy days, of course, so she was, in a sense, free to be stared at. Nevertheless it was an ordeal quiet as excruciating as flattering. But as she stood there in the pew – Monty in an MA gown and hood bellowing some canticle, Margaret trilling in harmony, Carol illiterately losing her place in the book and Giles standing in quiet dignity by her side – Tibba had made the Curse. She knew it was irrational. The whole point of her demeanour, during these embarrassing sessions of Morning Prayer, was to establish her unbelief. But she had made the Curse in the form of a prayer. Whom had she addressed? *Make her die.* Those had been her words. She had said them quietly at first inside her head, but then she had daringly sung them to the tune of the Te Deum. And then later in the service, while the collection plates were being taken round by the boys, she had fitted the words into a hymn tune. Monty had been roaring: rather to Tibba's amazement, Giles had joined in, too, the painful irony of the lines:

> *Immortal, invisible, God only wise,*
> *In light inaccessible hid from our eyes.*

But Tibba had sung merely and persistently

> *O make her, O make her, O make her die soon.*
> *The sooner the better, O make her die soon.*

There was nothing to indicate that the imprecation had 'registered' in any celestial quarter. She did not glow or feel different from any other Pangham Sunday. The routines were gone through afterwards: the roast meat and the pudding, the bracing walk, the usual drive to London. At no point had Tibba's rage against her stepmother diminished for dressing her father in so outrageous a manner, but she had gone to school next day without giving any further thought to the Curse.

It had been one of her father's library days. What could they find for a blind man to do in a library? Only charity could be their motive in allowing him his two mornings a week. He was quick in his mastery of braille, it was true. But the card indexes were not in braille in the library: nor were the books. Anyhow, to the library he had gone, and had been puzzled to return to an empty house after luncheon. Tibba had come back as usual about four, and it was she who met the policeman on the doorstep and received the extraordinary news. Her heart danced when she heard it, but with a jolt of fear as well as of joy. It was the only time she had ever allowed her mouth to open in prayer in the house of God: and the prayer had been answered within twenty-four hours. The odious and unfortunate Carol had been crossing the City Road at lunchtime. There were nevertheless no witnesses. She was found, a few minutes after being hit, lifeless in the middle of the road. But no one had seen the accident. The doctors said she could have felt no pain, she must have been killed outright by the impact of the car. The police were still looking for the car, thought, on no evidence at all, to have been a taxi. The poor young constable on the doorstep had expressed himself of the view that it was a tragedy.

The freedom, the release, the cleansing, the wonder of this tragedy! She had found him in his study. 'What is it? What is it?' he had anxiously asked. The white shirts had been returned to him at his insistence, and Carol had allowed him his dark blue tie for the library. As Tibba had put both her hands on his shoulders – at fourteen she was already a little taller than he – she realized that she had never, in the entire Carol era, felt quite free to kiss him. She *had* done so, of course. But it was as if she did so with the permission of that bitch.

'F-father, listen to me. Carol is d-dead!'

His grief had been awful – and a great surprise. Because she herself had found nothing to like in Carol, it had not occurred to her that there would be anything to grieve for. Her father's helpless sobbing seemed totally unaccountable. But she had held him, and comforted him, and cosseted him: and even on that first afternoon the cuddling had brought a wonderful sense of well-being. Now that she was so fully and uncompromisingly a woman, though not quite fifteen, there could be no more innocent cuddling outside the family circle. The way that Monty, even, held her in his arms was quite embarrassing. So this being able to clutch and hold her father was a great resource. She longed to smother him with hugs.

God knew life had been full of enough unhappiness, she realized, as she walked home now through the mist, the seventeen-year-old Tibba, and thought about it: death, and blindness, and the pangs of her unhappy devotion to Captain de Courcy. Since the death of Mary it was All Desolation, AD, and she could not hope for it to be otherwise. But things were unspeakably better since the Curse had been effectual. No Carol-substitute had ever been suggested. And life had resumed an almost normal routine. Now that he could operate the braille typewriter, which secretaries could transcribe, it was really possible for him to get on with writing his introduction to the *Tretis*. And the edition itself, thanks to Miss Agar, looked like nearing completion.

Tibba was so pleased with herself for having placed the advertisement which landed 'Miss Agar', as Louise still remained in her mind. She was nun-like and a little ridiculous. It was easy to imagine what the Bloomsbury set would have made of her mousy existence in Northwood Hills, her widowed mother and her (probable) subscription to the Christian orthodoxies. Tibba belonged to no 'set'. Captain de Courcy would scarcely have been interested in Miss Agar. Nor really would it be worth risking any displays of shrill malice with him. Nothing, besides, that she managed to say about Miss Agar would be as arch or as funny as the things that Lytton and Virginia would have found to snigger about. Her satirical views were therefore kept to herself. She had no wish to communicate them to her father. It was difficult to find assistants who met with his approval, and he seemed to admire Miss Agar's diligence and accuracy. There was no point in troubling him with thoughts about Miss Agar's legs, or her cardigans, or the incongruity of her long thick school-girlish hair (not unlike Tibba's own) that didn't really go with the chubby middle-aged face. But Tibba smiled about them as she turned into Hermit Street, picturing her father and his assistant busily, and with an absurd appropriateness, puzzling out advice to thirteenth-century anchorites.

III

'On her own?'

'Apparently.'

'But how will Giles manage?'

'Tibba doesn't say.'

Monty Gore laughed at this information. Giles never had been one for 'saying', and his daughter had caught this habitual reticence. The brothers-in-law were as remote from each other as separate orders of creation, as butterflies and bacon.

Monty was not really a soldier, but he sat over his breakfast in the battle-dress uniform of a major and drummed a leather-covered stick on the breakfast table as he contemplated Giles's eccentricity. It was Corps Day, and Monty (Ruddy G. as the boys called him) was responsible for the army branch of the CCF. His short hair and his bland amused mouth, creased beneath a Roman nose which had been designed by a caricaturist, could have been those of an officer in the regular army. Even his spectacles, if one imagined him as an intelligence officer, were not wholly unmilitary. But there was something about his face that gave the lie to his uniform: something about the bright eyes and the turning up of the corners of his mouth that suggested that life, though entered upon in a sporting spirit, was a bit of a joke.

In fact, as Meg sat there at the other end of the table and read aloud Tibba's letter, Monty was made uneasy, a sensation which made him grin even more than usual. There was something about the girl which he did not like to admit, even to himself. It was rum. But he desired her with a passion. It was simply a physical trick, of course. He would never dream of saying to himself that he was in *love* with the girl. What could be more ridiculous? But, nevertheless, he loved her in a way which was excessive in an aunt's husband. Since he also liked her, and felt sorry for her, and since he was very fond of his own wife and family, he had no desire to mess things up by letting his predilections 'show' in any way. But it was one of those little things (more than a little thing) which trouble a man when he hears that phrase in the Communion Service about a God 'from whom no secrets are hid'.

'There will be House Matches on the Saturday, of course,' said Meg, who had as much grasp of the School Calendar as her husband. 'And we mustn't forget that we promised the Bodger that we would do the entertaining of the bish that Sunday morning.'

'The bish?'

'Some OP bish, I forget where of. Peverill reminded me of it yesterday. The Bodger had apparently told *him* about it before telling *us*! And Peverill had invited the bish to sherry in our drawing-room. He really is –' But charity forbade Meg to say what Peverill really was; charity, and the fact that she did not have all morning.

Every housemaster sooner or later finds himself landed with a difficult customer; but Fate had bowled a googly when Monty Gore found himself saddled with four or five years of Peverill.

Monty had felt in his bones, ever since Peverill had been admitted to the school, that there was going to be trouble. First, though his method of entrance had not been 'shady', nor was it entirely above board. Peverill had failed to get into Eton. His Common Entrance papers had mysteriously been 'lost' in transit and so Pangham had been obliged to take him on trust. There had been an interview with the Bodger, and Monty, by one of those unhappy strokes Providence deals out to the virtuous, had found the child had been assigned to Gore's. Nothing could ever prove that the lost Common Entrance papers had been deliberately destroyed; nothing could ever prove that Peverill's father, who held all kinds of directorships, had 'nobbled' three of the School Governors over lunch in the City. They were just feelings you got.

He had been a big, handsome boy from the moment of his advent, arrogantly sun-tanned in the middle of January, clambering out of the back of his mother's Jag. Monty had noticed from the first not a blank refusal (nothing so crude) but a *slowness* about calling him, or any other beak, *Sir*. There was soon enough trouble about fagging. Peverill said that he thought it was 'barbaric', being made to perform the minimal tasks assigned by his fag-master; and, since this was the way the wind seemed to be blowing, Monty had not pressed the point. Before long, fagging had mysteriously 'died' in Gore's, the last House in the School where it had survived.

On the academic side of things Peverill (placed inevitably in the Lower Middles) was not exactly Leonardo da Vinci. His formmaster, Tiger Miller, had thrown up his hands in the CommonRoom and said, 'How that youth of yours passed the Common Entrance I shall never know,' a remark to which, in some sheepish way, Monty had felt ashamed to reply. Peverill had this way of making you feel that you were in the wrong. Nobody could *say*, for instance, that he had actually been blackmailing the Captain of Big Side. The mere passing to and fro of certain types of bounty – illicit cigarettes, free meals at the Stodge – scarcely constituted blackmail. It was merely odd that there should have been this communication at all between a senior member of the School (not in his House and not hitherto known to Peverill) and a new boy who seemed up to no good. Peverill had persistently denied asking Hyslop-Hyslop for the cigarettes. He said that they had been an unsolicited gift, and that the discovery of them in his toye had been profoundly distressing. 'Honestly,' he had said, as he so unconvincingly and frequently did, adding, very much as an afterthought, 'sir'.

Rather to everyone's amazement, Hyslop-Hyslop, Captain of Big Side and a pillar of rectitude, had broken down in the Bodger's study and blubbered like a child when questioned about the incident. The matter blew over, of course, but it had poisoned the lad's last term at Pangham and there had been some difficulty about getting him into the Navy. Peverill, the while, had remained cool as a cucumber, making them all feel somehow to blame: Hyslop-Hyslop for a 'seduction scene' which you could tell Peverill loved making up as he went along; the Bodger for not punishing H-Squared more severely; Monty Gore himself for not protecting the young charges in his House with more solicitude.

It was the kind of problem which would be forgotten about now the school was taking girls. That had been Meg's advice, and Monty had believed it, even though he was opposed to the idea of the old-fashioned Public Schools taking persons of both sexes into the sixth form, on the chivalrous principle that it was draining away the cream of Benenden, Cheltenham and Roedean.

There were no girls in his House, of course. They were all (only about thirty of them) accommodated in the San. But although Peverill was only fifteen, there had been the inevitable rumpus. He had been at the school eighteen months by now and Monty had developed a hearty detestation of the boy. Tall, tanned, idle at work, nonchalant at games, contemptuous of his seniors and beaks, Peverill had developed most disappointingly. Yet, although it was obvious that (for instance) he smoked, and that he went out of bounds, he had never actually been caught redhanded. The gambling ring ('Honestly, it was only a sweepstake ... *sir*') had been something for which any other child would have been expelled: Monty had rung up Sir Anthony Peverill to make the necessary arrangements. But the Bodger had mysteriously moved in to spare the boy. It took the ground from under Monty's feet and made him feel such a fool. The 'sweepstake' had, amazingly, turned out to involve members of staff. A younger physics beak (who left at the end of that term) was actually thought to owe Peverill *several hundred* pounds. Like everything else in Peverill's list of crimes, it was found simpler to let the matter pass.

But the girls were a different matter, and here Monty had felt on surer ground. Even if Peverill had been only fifteen (sixteen by the time Amanda actually had the tests confirmed), the incident was still a disgraceful one; precisely the kind of scandal which communities of mixed sex look to avoid. Peverill admitted guilt, and made a terrific show of contrition, but he had finally shot his bolt. Monty could scarcely conceal his glee as he picked up the receiver of his telephone. He should have known better of course. In a way, that set of what in American political circles would be called 'cover-ups' had shocked him more than the incident of the sweepstake (or, for that matter, than the so-called psychologist's report which had saved Peverill from being expelled for shoplifting the previous half). This incident, of Amanda's misfortune, seemed to demonstrate the blatantly hypocritical nature of Monty's colleagues. Good grief, Monty wasn't a lefty by a long chalk: not even remotely pink. But he did think that principle was principle. Peverill had admitted guilt in the matter, and that, he assumed, was that. In the case of one amorous aberration, it would have been possible to take a more forgiving line, but with Peverill's record, it was *impossible*.

But what did he find? That it would be 'much easier for the girl if too much was not made of the incident'. This from Holy Joe, the School Chaplain! Holy Joe had not thought to mention, however, that his sister was one of Amanda's mother's best friends. That was a fact which had only emerged in a second interview, with much blushing and humming and hawing. Amanda's father, according to a troubled communication from the Bodger, had threatened to sue the school, until the whole matter had been 'settled quite amicably' by the Chairman of the Governors who entertained him at his club in Pall Mall and made it clear that Sir Anthony Peverill was quite prepared to pay for the necessary expenses in Harley Street. Thus, what promised to be the scandal which would finally and for all time entrap Peverill turned out to be an altogether different affair. Amanda was off school no longer than if she had been seized with a fit of influenza. Peverill had emerged, not only flourishing like the green bay tree, but actually stronger. It now appeared that he had not only the Chaplain, but also the Chairman of the School Governors effectively under his or his father's control. Amanda had left that term and gone to live with an aunt in Barnes, where she could attend St Paul's Girls School. Peverill had gone from strength to strength. Having failed all his O-levels twice, he scraped a pass with Biology. An indifferent rugger player in Monty's view, he found himself as a hectoring, bullying captain of Big Side, and, when the Bodger insisted on electing him to the Levée, Monty had been forced, much against his better nature, to make Peverill Captain of House. Hence it was that, when considering the dates of House Matches, or even when entertaining a bish, Peverill's name had to be taken into account. Both Monty and Meg found it so disagreeable that it made a pleasant change to be talking of Giles's troubles.

Meg was a pretty woman who did not look fifty. Her hair was naturally dark, and was only greying around the brow. She had a perfect, rosy complexion and good cheekbones, a perfect set of teeth and bright blue eyes. When you saw her with Giles, you could see that they were brother and sister. But she lacked entirely Giles's meticulous pessimism. Though perfectly neat in her twin-sets and tweed skirts, no one would ever think, as they would have done in his presence, of the word 'prissy'. And though she had known sorrow, it was not, as in Giles's case, written all over her features. Her strong chin and bright eyes suggested a determination jolly well to put up with things.

She and Monty had been married twenty-five years. They loved each other still, in a way that was the envy of the Common-Room. There was already a grandchild (by a daughter who lived nearby); another child was still at the University; the eldest was in Canada. The Gores were a pattern of family happiness and virtue. But they were also devoted to the School in a way which, among the younger members of staff, seemed almost comic.

Monty laughed about Pangham, as he laughed about everything else. There used to be inverted commas around the schoolboy slang when he and Meg spoke to each other about the other beaks or the Bodger (their word for the Headmaster). But the quotation marks had slipped away in the twenty years they had been at the school. He had started as the most callow of apprentices. Then he had got his own form, Lower V G, then a tutorship at School House. Finally, five years ago, a House of his own: Gore's. He would never leave now. He had no desire for Headmasterships in other places. Pangham had taken possession of him. Meg and he now employed a vocabulary which would have been incomprehensible to ninety-five per cent of the inhabitants of the British Isles. It was years since either of them had used the words *lavatory, waste-paper basket, prayers, bath, cane,* or, except in a specifically liturgical surrounding, *master.* Like the arcane private language of love, school slang reflected an attachment to the school which, though they were too bluff to be soppy about it, was almost as deep as any emotion in their lives.

'It's not this week-end anyway,' he said, rising from the table. 'There's plenty of time to sort things out. You could ring her up.' He turned away from his wife as he referred to Tibba, afraid that he might be blushing.

'I hate ringing up,' said Meg. 'Poor Tibba's stammer seems so awful on the phone.'

'That's the bell,' Monty said. Sonorously funereal, the sound rang across the mists of School Field from the Victorian chapel. 'I loathe Tuesdays.'

Meg laughed, knowing that he really loathed nothing and no one, except perhaps Peverill. She decided to write a note to Tibba saying that it would be perfectly all right for her to come but did she really mean *come on her own.* She said, 'Don't forget that pile of prep in the hall.'

Monty picked up the exercise books as he went, calling out 'Bung-ho!' as he stepped out into the Close.

From the breakfast-room window, Meg watched him slouch off into the mists, carrying the worn-out attaché case which was his diurnal burden.

She sighed a little as she contemplated the happiness of their own lives, the wretchedness of Giles's. It was so bleak, him and

Tibba stuck together in that melancholy little house in such a slummy part of London. Meg accepted things as they came. She was not a questioner, as Giles was, nor a rebel. It simply seemed hard, cruelly hard, that her brother had been made to suffer so much in life: his wretched bad luck with wives, his eyesight going, his increasing poverty, the uncertainty of his future. As soon as there was a change of staff in the library they would bring to an end the farce of pretending that he served any useful function there. And then what would he have to live on? Nothing but a little bit of pension. Since he could *write*, his articles and so on, it struck her as mysterious that he did not turn his talent to more lucrative use. She made no distinction between his articles in learned journals and the popular stuff, of which, automatically, she assumed him to be capable. Since he employed a secretary, and was getting used to dictating, and could use a braille machine now (though *what* an effort it had been, getting him to learn), you would have thought he could have turned his hand to something that would really sell, like whodunnits or she did not know what. It was all part of his hopelessness. She regarded her brother as having far more talents than her own; and to her way of seeing the world, they were nearly all talents which were wasted. His obsession with a quite unheard-of medieval treatise was incomprehensible to her. It seemed so wilfully depressing. She had done some of the copying for him a few years back. It was all mumbo-jumbo to her, and then of course he had got cross with her because she hadn't understood about the funny old spelling. And so morbid! She could not understand why Giles, who had no religious belief at all, should be so concerned to publish a book meant for a lot of medieval old nuns, with instructions about fasting and bloodletting and she did not know what nonsense. As Monty said, it made you thankful you belonged to the C of E (though of course there were Anglican nuns, and some of them did very good work, and the left-footers were much less awful than they used to be).

Pangham did not have any left-footers, but she remembered

the awful hullaballoo when one of the boys in Gore's wanted to *go over*: the trouble there had been with his parents, and the embarrassing visits they had had from the little padre at the tallow church. The boy had been talked out of it eventually by Holy Joe, but it had given them a nasty glimpse of the way that church could carry on. Just as bad as the Moonies, Monty thought, the way they get hold of people. Or used to, anyway. The desire to embrace any form of religious obedience other than the one in which she had been born had never entered Meg's head. She was happy in her religion, as was Monty. She wished and prayed that Giles could believe. It would surely have been consoling in all his troubles to have something to turn to. But he couldn't believe, and that was that. She still felt some of the horror which had first come upon her when this stark fact dawned on her. It was while she was training as a physio at Tommies, she remembered. Something that Giles had said over supper: they had met at some super Greek restaurant in Soho, and Giles had said something so awful, so *cynical* about Our Lord that it had become clear. Not only was he an unbeliever; he always had been, it seemed; simply went to church at home to avoid upsetting Daddy. 'That arrogant and over-estimated joiner's son,' he had said, so coldly. She realized it was the way that he must speak among his friends. She hated it. Apart from anything else, the implied snobbery of the remark was quite alien to the whole way in which she had been brought up. She wondered why on earth Giles should have developed this antipathy to the Redeemer; or how one could possibly get through life without the knowledge that God guides and supports us. She had only been eighteen or nineteen when he made the horrid remark. But since then, thirty and more years later, things had never been quite the same between them. She had prayed for him endlessly. And still his heart was hard; and hardened yet further by his cruel experiences of life.

While Meg cleared the breakfast away and contemplated these things, Monty strode across School Field. He tried to banish

thoughts about Tibba by running through his school day. First
school was with the Lower Twenties; they were doing rainfall.
Second school with the Upper Thirds was always rather fun; they
were meant to be doing Africa but he spent most of the lesson
reminiscing about his National Service in Cyprus. Then there
was the Quarter, when he must remember to buttonhole Loony
H. about refereeing the Colts match against Haileybury. Next
school was a Free Period and he would sit in the Common-Room
smoking and marking the Upper Third's prep. Then his own form,
LVG, for Scripture; then back to his House for lunch with the
boys. Signing chits after lunch would be followed by Corps. A
tosh. Tea. An abortive attempt to do the *Times* crossword. Sherry
with Stuffy Smith, the House Tutor who would come in to take
the boys' tea at six and stay on to supervise prep. House dics at
8.45. (Good, they were having *For those in peril on the sea*
tonight); and then, some time after nine, he might hope to see
his wife again. It was a full day, which was what he meant by
hating Tuesdays. But he could not think about any of it. Even
as he dumped his case in the Common-Room, briefly checked in
the *Telegraph* how we were doing against the West Indians, and
upbraided, as he crossed the quad, a little squirt from Loony H.'s
house for having his hands in his pockets, Monty's mind was far
away. And as he entered the vast chapel, and found his place in
the school hymnal (*Come down, O Love divine*), his heart was in
turmoil.

He just hoped that Tibba wouldn't come for the week-end of
the seventeenth. Or that, if she did, she would bring her father
and be occupied with reading aloud in her soft, faltering, stammering voice. But even as he remembered the voice, Monty felt
quite buffoonishly weak, quite mad with engulfing passion. He
had always had a *soft spot* for his niece, from her infancy. Meg
used to tease him that he never bothered to choose presents for
his own children, but that he would spend hours in the toyshop
looking out teddy-bears or rag books that might take the infant
Tibba's fancy. Meg had evidently been pleased by his devotion
to her brother's child. Like Monty, she had felt desperately *sorry*

for the girl. Giles and Mary had neglected her most terribly; both of them either snapping at each other or pursuing more or less independent lives. Mary had been a number one troublemaker and, not to put too fine a point on it, a bitch. She had been perfectly foul to Giles, humiliating him with her boyfriends, snubbing him in front of his own child, and then getting pregnant. Giles had been wonderful about this, and it was true that they had seemed fonder of each other towards the very end. But it was hard, quite honestly, after her record, to believe that poor old Giles had had more than an outside chance of being the father of the new baby. Opinion differed as to the likeliest dad. Someone Monty knew in Hampshire, who knew Mary's people, thought the odds-on favourite was a little nancy called Trevor something, but there had also been a man with a Range-Rover who lived somewhere near Petersfield. Through all this, poor little Tibba had been on the shelf. Then, when Mary finally snuffed it, they had had the girl to stay with them in Pangham, and he had realized how desperately she mattered to him. She couldn't have been much more than twelve then. It was her sad face which got him, and her stammering voice, and her almost-womanliness. But of course, it didn't dawn on him that there was any *danger*.

They had tried endless things for the stammer. Meg said it was because Giles was always correcting her pronunciation, but nowadays they said these things were psychological. Monty had always regarded stammers as a bit of a joke. He sympathized with the boys when they laughed at someone afflicted in this way. He remembered with amusement a rather weedy beak (he had looked younger than some of the elder boys) who had been to the Bodger's dinner one year and drunk sherry all evening because it was the only liquid he felt himself capable of pronouncing. He hadn't lasted ten minutes with the boys, of course. Classics, he had taught. Went into the Civil Service and never heard of again. But Tibba's stammer was not comic. When it became severe, Monty ached on her behalf. He longed to be able to draw the words out of her mouth, and he was always finishing the poor child's sentences for her, which Meg said was just what you shouldn't do. They'd tried speech therapy at the local hospital, and hypnosis; and now she went to some quack in Canonbury. It was much better than it had been, but it still came upon her when she was nervous. Now that it was more slight, it added to her attractiveness.

They hadn't seen all that much of her in the years of Giles's marriage to That Bloody Nurse. They knew it was mean of them, but Monty just couldn't stick the woman. It wasn't that they were snobs, but they didn't like the way she fingered Giles in public.

But the last week-end of Carol's life, when she and Giles and Tibba had all come down to Pangham, was when he had first realized that his feeling for his niece was dangerous. It was when they were coming back from chapel on the Sunday morning. He had helped Tibba off with her coat as they stood in the hall and, just momentarily, his hands had lingered on her bosom as he stood behind her and she fumbled with buttons. And the full erotic excitement of her womanliness had made the moment electrifying embarrassing. The rum thing was that he knew she felt it too. Not that his feelings were reciprocated. But he had sensed, from the way that her shoulders hunched and froze, that his excitement was not a secret from her any more.

She had not been down to Pangham on her own since that day.

'O, let it freely burn,' he bellowed, noticing that silly little Willoughby, a minor irritant in the Upper Middles, was chatting with his neighbour instead of singing the hymn; he would have to punish him.

> Till earthly paa-ssions turn
> To dust and ashes in its heat consuming!

The prayers followed. Holy Joe did not use the old collects any more. He read to them from some Dutch Johnny called Michel Quoist. The organ voluntary struck up, and the beaks rose to their feet.

'I want to talk to you, Willoughby,' Monty said fiercely as he passed the snivelling offender's pew. Half an hour's litter-duty was what he had in mind. In some nebulous way, Monty always felt more authoritarian on Tuesdays: the effect, presumably, of the rough khaki he wore.

The beaks were followed out of the chapel by the Levée. Monty stood on the lawn outside Old Big School waiting for the juniors to come out of the sacred edifice so that he could buttonhole the offender. The Levée stood a little way apart, exercising with some display their privilege of being allowed on the grass. Peverill seemed to dominate them all. It was like watching a general among subalterns to see the way he addressed them. The Sixth Form came out of chapel first; then the Removes. Then Lower School. Little Willoughby, his spectacles pathetically awry, made his way in Monty's direction, but at that moment his name was bellowed out across the quad.

'Willoughby!'

Which was the superior command? The former injunction to see Ruddy G., who waited there impatiently on the lawn, or the more immediate summons from Peverill? Like a frightened rodent caught between two predators, Willoughby paused momentarily and glanced from side to side. Monty tried to look calm as he stared at the dilemma facing the child. Willoughby quivered, and then, his spirit crushed, he wandered over to Peverill, who strutted about in his morning coat and striped trousers.

'I want you to run over to the Gym and get my track suit,' said Peverill in tones which would have been audible on the opposite side of School Field.

'But, Mr Gore said –'

'Go and do what you're bloody told, Willoughby,' said Peverill, turning to laugh with other members of the Levée. It had been a show performance, put on for their benefit. Although fagging had now been abolished, and Peverill when younger had been vociferous in his condemnation of so barbaric a survival from Victorian days, he did not scruple to treat all younger boys like slaves, making them run errands, do small bits of shopping, and even, on occasion, assist him in a secretarial capacity.

'Hope you didn't want to see young Willoughby about anything important,' Peverill said, as he came towards Monty on the lawn, 'only I have gym second school and I have a lot of work to do before sending out the invitations for the OP's match.'

Monty stared at Peverill. He was furious, but this, like most emotions, only made him grin. What an arrogant figure Peverill was, swaggering with one hand in his striped trouser pocket. The blue eyes which met Monty's were wholly self-confident. He knew that Monty minded about OP's being invited back on the day of the match, and that the task of sending out the invitations had traditionally fallen to the Captain of Big Side.

'Just so long as you're not neglecting your other work,' he said. 'Remember, Peverill, that you've got your English re-sit at the end of term.'

The remark should have been humiliating. There Peverill stood, wholly a young man now, taller than Monty himself; in appearance, he could have been a successful stockbroker, or even, in spite of the slightly too long curly hair, a guards officer. It bloody well should have shamed him that he could not even pass English O-level. But he merely said, 'I shouldn't worry too much about that if I were you.' He smiled at Monty sympathetically. *Sir*, it seemed, was no longer a word in his vocabulary.

IV

'This is Miss Agar; she is my eyesight.'

It had been with this pleasantry that Giles had introduced her to the Library Clerk at Trinity; and the extraordinary privilege of being so described had moved her almost to sobbing. It had added a kind of fervour to her usual diligence when it came to checking the manuscript.

Attend, My Dear Sisters, what is that cry of anguish which I hear, that sorrowful wailing, that bitter weeping, that anxious rending of garments? It is the lamentation of the foolish virgins, who kept not burning that holy light of virginity in their lamps, but squandered it in fleshly lusts and carnal appetites. They have been cast out from the marriage feast of the Lamb.

The passage was so familiar to her now, but how differently she had come to regard it since the wonder of her love for Giles had been declared and accepted. The afternoon, some ten days before, when she had lain in his arms on the study floor in Hermit Street, had been the turning-point of Louise's life. She was no longer the same person. She could hardly understand how it was that she masqueraded as her earlier self for so long: for a masquerade was now what it seemed. The *Tretis*, which for Giles was a mere rag-bag of linguistic data, a quarry of footnotes, a philological gold-mine devoid, however, of any rational applicability to everyday life, had been, for Louise, ever since she first went to Hermit Street and discovered it, a richly beautiful document. In the early months, when she had tried to put her devotion to Giles to one side, even, in her own phrase, to 'offer it up', she had taken the words of the *Tretis* deeply to heart, and had even, without telling Giles, written a translation of it into modern English.

The heartbreak she suffered for Giles seemed, in those early weeks, to be part of some cruel testing, a purgatory through which she must pass. It was a love which could never blossom, or proceed. It was impossible that he could ever return her affections. She must bury her feelings utterly, and seek other consolation. And was it not there, in the manuscripts and micro-films, the Answer, abundantly clear and sure?

Frightened by that stage to call the sense she had by any name (such as 'calling' or 'vocation'), she had felt, ever since under-graduate days, that she was meant for a celibate life. Religion did not merely console her in this thought; it was the primary factor in shaping it. Love, for such as she, was something so much deeper than some of the sordid and unhappy things which her undergraduate contemporaries had got up to. Love filled the whole world; and it was the same Love, Who filled her heart, Who had called those sisters long ago through the words of the *Tretis*. '*Loue is that salue to maken the myrier than al this worldes ioies*,' she remembered, from the 'catechism' passage, in which the medieval author had, in a recounted dream, put a series of questions and answers to a heavenly figure called Genius.

But Love, she now saw, had made her miserable, love as the author of the *Tretis* understood it. What was all that wailing and rending of garments? Louise knew perfectly well that it was the sound made not by the foolish, but by the wise virgins, who had had no option in the matter of whether or not to use up the oil in their lamps. She had tried to kid herself that she was giving herself to her heavenly Lord and denying herself the satisfactions of an earthly affection. But *when*, if she told the truth, had the possibilities of carnal indulgence ever presented themselves to her? If anyone had cast eyes upon her to lust after her in her schooldays, the fact had passed unobserved in Northwood Hills. Such a possibility would not have been smiled upon by her mother, in any case. In Cambridge, when Louise went up to Girton as an undergraduate, matters might have mended. But Girton was still a college of one sex in those days, and all the young men in Cambridge were able to resist the temptation to cycle the considerable and chilly distance to Louise's bower to pay their court. Awkwardness, a desire to do well in her studies, acne and, ultimately, piety, dominated her undergraduate days. There was no chance of her becoming anyone's paramour. And now she felt able to admit the brutal truth to herself.

When she stayed on in Cambridge to do research, her circle of friends diminished, so that she was lucky, in the course of a whole week-end, if she saw anyone, apart from the congregation at church, and Rowena, the evangelical biochemist with whom she had shared her lodgings. The fact that Louise's mother 'needed' her in Northwood Hills had been born, she now saw, out of her bitter loneliness during those Cambridge week-ends as a research student. Even the friars at St Benet's sometimes gave the impression of being bored with her; she began eventually to sense their impatience if she went there to tea *every* Sunday. When they had suggested that she made her retreat with some nuns on the other side of England, she had felt decidedly as though she had been given the brush-off. She had gone to the Priory in question for a few days. It turned out to be idyllic. The Society of the Sacred Passion was a tiny little group of women who had begun their corporate history as 'parish workers' in a High Church slum in Birmingham in the 1890s. They were only formally constituted as a religious order in 1898, when their number was less than ten. Gradually, they had developed a wholly contemplative way of life. They had left their slums and they now inhabited the converted barn of what had been a medieval priory on the edges of the Berkshire Downs.

The peaceful atmosphere of the place, the kindness of the sisters, the decency of the liturgical round, had done much for Louise's spirits. She had felt there, perhaps, that she was *not* a failure, in spite of the fact that her thesis *had* just failed, and she had been unable to sustain any friendships in her grown-up life. With the nuns, it had all seemed rather different. Here, she had felt, she *could* surely find a life for herself. It had been quite a shock when even *they* rejected her. They were much too kind to call it a rejection. The guest-mistress had walked her round and round the cloisters trying to console her and explain that they were *not* saying that she had no vocation. It was merely that nowadays the contemplative life was more demanding than it had ever been before. It was essential, before embarking upon it, to have had some experience of the world. There was nothing specific that they were suggesting. It was not that they felt that she should have travelled more, or done a job. Merely they thought that she should be older and 'Well, quite honestly, Louise, just a tiny bit more mature.'

How she had sobbed, but how absolutely right Sister Philippa Mary had been. Louise saw it now. She despised herself for having even proposed the idea of becoming a nun. Thank goodness Mummy had never known of the scheme.

It was then that she had answered Giles's advertisement and everything had begun to be different. For the first time in her life, she had fallen in love. And, as the weeks passed, and the pain of her love got worse and worse, so that she thought she would go mad with it, Louise had still been gripped by the new (as she thought) concept that she must reject this good thing, this adoration of Giles, and keep it as a bitter secret, never to be revealed to anyone. She had told herself that her reasons for doing this were religious. But she now saw that it was mere funk. She had been afraid of declaring herself.

Thank God that she had done so. In that moment, everything had snapped, everything had changed. For the first time in her twenty-six years, Louise had felt a man's arms around her, and a man's lips were pressed to her own. Even though it had worried her at the time that he so quickly had started to be *dirty*, fingering undergarments which were not in the least romantic, even this had its thrill in retrospect. There had been no repetition of the incident. How could there have been? She had hardly thought he would react so quickly to her proposal that they spend the week-end away together in Cambridge. One session only in Hermit Street had followed the afternoon in which they had cuddled and rolled on the carpet. It had been punctuated by a long, beautiful kiss when she stood up to pass him his tea. But

Mrs Tucker was cleaning, and Tibba had been in and out once or twice. There had not been a chance to settle down to a really good *cuddle*.

Now it was with a wholly profane and new sense, unintended by the medieval author, that she read the famous passage: *But what is that cry of joy, that hymn of gladness, that sweetest of music in my ears? It is the cry of the wise virgins who are bidden to the marriage. Their bridegroom has come and He welcomes them into His presence, where there is gladness and the sweetness of spices and heavenly odours for evermore, Oh, the joy of that virgin who diligently has endured to the end and can present herself spotless to her Lord and Lover.* Giles, and not Christ, was the Bridegroom. The near-blasphemy of this thought thrilled her. But the return of her affection was more than she could have prayed for in her wildest imaginings. It was almost so astonishing that she could call it miraculous. She now felt that the love of any man, at this stage in her life, would have revealed to her the futility of her earlier unhappiness, the lumpish solitudes, the misdirected hours on her quivering knees. But to be loved by Giles Fox, so very distinguished a person in her private mythology, was an accident which inevitably threw her into an inebriation of happiness. It was so extraordinarily moving that she was not merely someone to hold his hand and provide him with domestic comforts.

'This is Miss Agar; she is my eyesight.'

He had said it in that weary, resigned, almost sarcastic voice which he sometimes adopted, but it was meant, she felt sure, to be taken as a warm assertion of his regard. It was extraordinary, not that he had unhappiness in his voice when he alluded to his blindness, but that he had made so public a declaration of his *love*, his need for her. This, anyway, was how she saw it, even though it was an exchange lasting only a few seconds with a person that neither of them was ever likely to meet with any frequency again.

After their session with the manuscript (and it had taken up much less time than she anticipated) they had adjourned to a café for a Cypriot meal. They had been forced down into the basement where it had been rather a squash, and it had been a blow to her, when the food came, to find that he disliked *kebabs*. They had waited for them so long that there seemed no point in reordering. He had drummed his fingers rather impatiently while she finished her meal, and his mouth had been screwed up with disgust at the rather muddy coffee. She felt that a walk after this would do him good. She certainly needed to have some exercise after all that rice! His spirits seemed sunken and depressed, and she did not know whether it was the overcrowded restaurant or something she had said, or failed to say, that accounted for the apparently sudden descent of gloom. Being in Cambridge always invigorated her. She loved its winding little streets and did not in the least mind their being crowded. She held tightly to Giles to prevent him from being buffeted or knocked off the pavement. They walked down Trinity Street and into King's.

'Isn't this your old college?' she asked.

'Are we really here?' It was the first time he had spoken for about a quarter of an hour.

For Giles, there was an intolerable poignancy about knowing that he was there of all places. The very cobblestones beneath his black buckled shoes affirmed the fact, and the cold wind blowing in from the Backs. But apart from these two indications, he might have been in Luton or Chicago. The spindly grey of the chapel roof, pale against a paler sky, the geometrical delicacy of the perpendicular windows, the patch of lawn and the statue of Henry VI, had been the backcloth for many of the most intense and important days of his youth. Now, they were no longer there. His inability to see them made him as sad as if they had ceased to exist. A bulldozer might, for all he could appreciate them now, have destroyed them and replaced them with rabbit-hutches.

They had more of the morning than he would have wished in Trinity, Miss Agar poring over the manuscript and answering his questions. The Trinity *Tretis* only amounted to a small fraction of the full work in the Pottle version, but in the pages which existed there were some interesting variants. They had all been duly noted and commented upon by Giles years before, in the days of his sight. But now that the typescript of his edition was almost ready for press, there was a case for last-minute checks, particularly of a very faint, smudgy page which the microfilm did little to make clearer. Nothing of moment was contained in these 'variants', though Giles, about ten years before, had got excited by the fact that one of the semi-legible smudges might have been a Welsh loan-word, a fact which might have indicated that the Trinity manuscript came from a source West of the Pottle *Tretis*, possibly even from Llanthony.

It was all, even by Giles's minute and exacting standards, fairly footling stuff. The visit to Cambridge had not been strictly necessary. When Miss Agar had suggested it, so soon after their last 'session' in which she had declared her affections so unambiguously, he had been quick to hear the unspoken suggestiveness of the scheme. By going away to Cambridge, he understood (and understood her to understand) the possibility of consummating their attachment. He had not had in mind going to Cambridge for the night. A drive, a morning in the library, and then back to Hermit Street, had been what, in his mind, should have happened.

It embarrassed him, and caused him acute moral pain, to have practised a deception on Tibba. But the girl's presence in Hermit Street would have made it impossible for Miss Agar to share his bed. It was as bluntly consequential as that. The news would eventually have to be broken to his daughter. But he felt unable to do so yet. Let there first be some surreptitious months so that he could be sure of his ground. Miss Agar, pathetically anxious not to tread on anyone's toes, had consented to keep the matter a secret. Even her mother in Northwood Hills – especially she – was to be kept in the dark. It was to be their own delicious secret.

Not without malice, he had therefore proposed to Tibba that she accompany them to Cambridge; a suggestion which had been met with the predictable absence of enthusiasm. He still allowed Tibba to speak of Miss Agar as if she were a joke. It was perhaps disloyal to his new love to do so; but to protest against it would have been to disclose the secret, and the disclosure of the secret at this stage would have damned Miss Agar's chances of ever becoming Mrs Fox. Giles knew his daughter well enough to be aware of how vigilant she would be, how positively hostile, in her attempt to prevent his re-marriage. They had come so much together, Tibba had become so much his domestic companion, that the thought of uniting himself to another would have been, in the circumstances, tantamount to a sort of bigamy.

So he had suggested that Tibba came with Miss Agar and him to Cambridge.

'I am afraid that our conversation will be so *entirely* limited to the *Tretis* that you will be very bored,' he had said, 'but Miss Agar is a very pleasant companion, as I believe you find.'

'Poor Miss Agar,' Tibba had sighed. 'It must be so awful to *be* her.'

Tibba's acquaintance with the plump research assistant was almost wholly limited to the moments in the front hall of the Hermit Street house where she admitted her week by week. Sometimes, the unfortunate had come for Sunday tea and there had been the excruciating difficulty of finding enough things to say to fill an hour and twenty minutes before the poor creature began to gather her things and speak of Evensong. Evensong! How Lytton would have split his sides! Tibba regretted that she was incapable of Mrs Woolf's cruelty. Some acid witticism would have put an end to the possibility of another Sunday tea. It would have been so amusing that witnesses would treasure it and put it into their Bloomsbury memoirs. Such conversational darts were impossible in Islington; the more so if one stammered.

'Then I shall stay at home,' had been Tibba's first piece of rearguard action.

Giles was perfectly capable of meeting this expected retort. How often Meg and Monty had wanted Tibba to go down to Pangham! Only that week – when the girl was at school – Meg had rung suggesting it. He had (thoughtlessly, he now saw) more or less assented to it. He saw no objection. He had never seen why she did not like going to Pangham.

'But *you* hate it,' she had said.

'Only because it is an unfamiliar house.'

True enough, his clumsiness there was invariably pathetic. He bumped into doors and upset glasses with just sufficiently frequent aplomb to make the point.

Her silence had been worrying, nonetheless. Was she about to rebel? If so, the whole scheme would crumble. He could not, after all, *insist* on her going to Pangham. She was perfectly old enough to be left on her own for a single night in Hermit Street. Mercifully, she had relented.

'If Meg and M-Monty are expecting me I shall have to go. I shall be most unsocial. I am trying to read *King L-l-l –*'

'Quite so. You had better write to them and announce the time of your train.'

So, the matter had been settled, and Tibba was now in Pangham.

It disconcerted him, however, to discover that Miss Agar's literalism had taken a night in Cambridge to mean simply that. The social programme she had laid on to please him was saved up as something of a surprise. By the time she had announced it all, there was no wriggling out of the plans. Their suitcases, before their sojourn in the library, had been deposited in a mean little house off the Chesterton Road with Brenda something, a former college friend of Miss Agar's, by now an accredited supervisor at Selwyn.

The social programme which now lay before them presented, in its own terms, an *embarras de richesse*. They were to have tea with Miss Agar's old supervisor at Girton. The Accredited Supervisor ('I hope you like beans') had prepared a cassoulet for the evening which was to be shared by a young couple who, at the State's expense, were preparing doctoral dissertations, the husband on Breton lays, the wife on the stage history of Dekker's *Shoemaker's Holiday*.

Giles was to be accommodated in a small bedroom on the ground floor, next to the tiny bathroom. The bed had had a dampish feel to it when he had fingered the Indian cotton counterpane in the morning. It was a narrow thing. He could not see, even if they found themselves with an hour or two alone in the watches of the night, how Miss Agar's ample form was to be snuggled up beside his own under the flimsy duvet. When Sunday dawned, the round would begin again: drinks with the don who had supervised Miss Agar's thesis would be followed by luncheon in the University Centre.

'I love you so much, I want to show you off, you see,' she said as they stood there in the front court of King's. 'I hope it's not too much for you.'

'There is a syntactical ambiguity in what you say,' Giles remarked. 'But I dare say both that you love me too much, and that you have arranged too many encounters.'

She reacted, as though his words were sentimental nothings, by nuzzling against his arm more tightly. He felt her breath upon his ear.

A don, passing them by, paused to stare. They were a conspicuous, almost grotesque couple; but what first arrested his attention was the rapturous happiness of the young woman's pink features. Her round cheeks were almost bursting with joy. She made an odd companion for the short, sombre figure at her side. In his black, rather clerical hat, his neat, well-cut grey overcoat, his silk scarf and his kid gloves, he formed a perfect antithesis to the chaos of pleasure which clutched him, to the exuberant frizz of hair which blew from the hood of her shabby duffle coat. The dark glasses increased the hint that this might be a Famous Personage in the world. Then recognition dawned.

'My dear Giles, this is an all-too-rare privilege,' said the don's mellifluous tones. 'How can we get you to visit us more often?'

Giles stiffened. 'Henry,' he said.

'Are you here to lecture? You must fit in a moment to call,' said the voice.

'Our time is short and almost over-filled.' Giles disentangled himself from his lover's elbow as he spoke the unintentional pentameter. 'May I introduce my research assistant, Miss Agar. Professor Lightfoot.'

'I am very pleased to meet you. What a happy conjunction; I do not normally come in to college on a Saturday afternoon.'

Louise blushed inarticulately. She knew *of* the Professor, of course. But to be saluted as his familiar was a pleasure she would not have expected in her wildest fantasies.

'But how sad.' He was perhaps a trifle quick to seize on the idea that their social programme could not include a visit to his rooms. 'Next time you come to Cambridge you must give us prior warning. Tibba well? Good, good.'

And he was gone.

'Lightfoot,' Giles said when he was gone. It had the venomous sound, on his lips, of an oath. The Professor's unctuous pomposity appeared to have made his spirits sink even lower. To the perpetual anguish of his blindness, and the present embarrassment attaching to Miss Agar's attempts to make him happy, were added the nebulous sensations of gloom which always threatened to engulf him when he returned to his old university. There was no harm in Lightfoot. In another mood Giles would have enjoyed his company. But the tiny encounter revived all the bitter regrets for the Fellowship he had failed to get twenty years before. Lightfoot, whom Giles considered less able than himself, a solitary bachelor who swanned about the courts of King's using the first person plural as though Cambridge and he were indissolubly linked, a kind of hypostatic union ('How can we get you to visit us more often ... ?' 'You must give us prior warning') while he cowered in Hermit Street.

To be blind anywhere was a living hell. But to be a blind don in Cambridge would not have been impossible. He could still have lectured, and given individual supervision to his pupils. There would still have been the possibility of intelligent conversation. As it was, he was shipwrecked by life in a position of total uselessness. His one scholarly activity was the exact perusal of a set of manuscripts which he could not any longer distinguish from a newspaper. And his professional livelihood, soon, inevitably to be taken from him, depended on library work which, without sight, was impossible.

Life, in that second or two, seemed so intolerably bitter that the blank useless globes of jelly filled with tears behind his rigid features. How dare they punish him so callously, those dons of twenty years before, who had elected some nonentity to a Fellowship which could have been his? Had they done so, his comfort, his professional livelihood, his career would have been assured. And he would have been very learned, very conscientious, very punctilious in his duties. Moreover, he would never, in all probability, have met Mary. The chaos of his personal life might never have happened. It would at least have been different. The books he might have written! His ludicrous marriages, as much as his professional isolation, were the direct consequence of this cruel stroke of luck. And Lightfoot, the suave and honey-toned figure who had now drifted out of earshot, had been on the committee which had decided Giles's fate.

'We must get a taxi to Girton,' he said. 'Thank you for showing me King's.'

'Fancy meeting Professor Lightfoot,' she said. 'Were you students together?'

Giles did not like to consider that he had ever been a 'student'; and he thought that it might have occurred to Miss Agar that the Professor was at least four years his senior. 'Lightfoot was the junior Dean when I was up,' he said.

That was the end of that little exchange. They crossed King's Parade at a pace too brisk to be romantic and looked for a taxi near the market.

'This cold gives you an appetite, doesn't it,' she shivered, unable to prevent herself thinking of the scones and cakes which would be burdening the tablecloths in her former supervisor's rooms.

'I find my appetite is very little affected by the climate,' Giles said. 'I hope that they do not expect one to eat very much at tea in Girton.'

He felt a gnawing awkwardness and guilt which he tried to tell himself was based wholly on his having told a lie to Tibba. To enforce this conviction, he squeezed Miss Agar's hand in the back of the taxi.

V

In prosaic fact, in what she felt obliged so unsatisfactorily to call Life, Tibba never had interesting conversations with Captain de Courcy. It was only when she was on her own that she could really let rip and discover how much he resembled one of the more moustachioed figures in the life of Mrs Woolf. Tibba was not under the illusion that she *was* the author of *A Writer's Diary*, *The Waves* and other works of genius; but it somehow happened, in these reveries, that she found itself, as it were, speaking Virginia's lines.

In the second-class compartment, somewhere beyond West Ealing, Tibba stared towards Captain de Courcy's moist brown eyes and said, 'Did you grow your moustache in order to look like Morgan?'

'Goose!' he laughed, a knowing laugh, for underneath, surely all the Bloomsbury men were really homosexual. What this implied, exactly, was hard to fathom. But she said, in as brittle a way as possible, 'I sit here and try to fix my concentration on the whole incandescent moment, this moment here, today, in the railway carriage.' What did incandescent mean, she had often wondered; but Captain de Courcy did not seem to mind. She saw, as she spoke, that the moustache was far more like Harold Nicolson's: not a bit like Morgan Forster's. 'Sounds flit in and out of my ears – the click of a suitcase being unlocked, the click of the train on the railway track – Lord Tennyson thought trains ran in grooves. And the railway carriage is lost once more, for I think only of Lord Tennyson, moaning a sad lay, as he strides along the cliffs at Freshwater.'

'It is sad that Lytton never wrote a life of Lord Tennyson,' said Harold Nicolson/Captain de Courcy.

'Do not let us talk of Lytton – for sometimes when I think of death, the dreadfulness of it, its absolute ending – I feel myself going mad again.'

Tibba had never been in danger of going mad, and the imagined sentence died on her brain as Captain de Courcy/Harold Nicolson who stared in at her through the window of the train was suddenly clicked out of existence by a passing railway-bridge, as though someone had switched off his image on a television set. She sped on without him. An Awayday indeed.

Her last 'real' exchange with Captain de Courcy had been altogether briefer, colder, less pleasant. She knew even as she spoke that he was not believing her story. It seemed, on the face of it, so very improbable that she would have been summoned to spend Saturday and Sunday with an aunt so suddenly, and on so slight a pretext. The fact that she had made her announcement on the telephone made her gabble. The breathless nervousness when she spoke into that instrument was increased by the excitement of knowing that she spoke to the Man she Loved.

'Slowly now,' he had said. How extraordinary that his marvellous voice could come down the wires into her ears! 'Remember that you have all – the – time – in – the – world.' He said each syllable slowly and precisely and almost absurdly.

'I dddidn't know my ffffather had to go to Cccc; had to go to Cccc; had to go to Cccc.' But the word Cambridge refused to come out.

'Hick – or – y – dick – or – y – dock,' Captain de Courcy had said, with the regularity of a metronome.

'The – mouse – ran – up – the – clock,' she had repeated obediently. The exercise made her able to resume. 'I would have told you sooner, but I couldn't.'

As she spoke, she knew that he would be thinking that she was just a cheap, silly little socialite who had, at the last minute, been invited to a party. If only he could guess how her heart bled to be with him, catching a glimpse of her own reflexion in the flat silver buttons of his smart blue blazer as he stood by her arm-chair.

'There is always next week.' He had said it. But she could sense the chilliness in his voice. 'Don't worry, really.'

Before she had had the chance to continue the conversation, the line had gone dead and he was gone; gone, gone for seven more aching, miserable days. It would make a fortnight alto-gether without seeing him. Only once, on a weekday, had she set eyes on him, inadvertently, in the public library. It was when she was taking back the second volume of Mrs Woolf's letters. He had been hovering by the 'Returned Fiction' with a rather surprisingly middle-brow selection of stories already under his arm. It was a Wednesday.

She felt him to be a man of regular habits, so she stored up the day and the hour in her soul. Nowadays, not a Wednesday passed which did not find her furtively rummaging through the dog-eared cellophane-covered volumes on the Returned Fiction trolley. But he had never come back. *Fled is that music: do I wake or sleep?*

Ye gods, how she loved him. As the Paddington train whizzed towards Wiltshire, she stared out at her own reflexion in the glass and longed for his features to reappear there: the brown, brindled hair *en brosse*, the very crinkly brow; the extraordinarily handsome cleft chin; and the moustache. The truth was that this growth was more military than even Harold Nicolson would have gone in for. She loved Captain de Courcy as he *was*, she suddenly told herself. What though the window-box of the Cap-tain's flat in Canonbury hardly compared with the gardens of Sissinghurst?

She summoned back to her memory his cavalry twill trousers, his silk display handkerchiefs, his manly striped ties and the very faint whiff of after-shave lotion he always exuded. How much she would like to know what sort it was. A bottle of it could then be purchased. Even if she never summoned up the temerity to present it at Christmas she could sniff it in the intervening weeks to remind herself of him. She had spent hours in Boots with her nose pressed to the samples there until her sinuses ached and she could not tell the difference between one and another. They all began to seem merely spirituous. It was like smelling turpentine. And she realized then how very sparingly Captain de Courcy used his own mysterious unguent; and that she loved, not merely the smell of the lotion, but the way it mingled with the smell of Wright's Coal Tar soap, and above all, with the smell of *him*.

'Oh my darling Captain,' she murmured aloud.

No one heard, because the train whooshed so that you could (if you had wanted) have sung 'Lillibulero' at the top of your voice and still not disturbed the other passengers.

She settled down to a conscious self-preparation for the week-end that lay ahead.

'Going anywhere nice?' had been Chantie's inquiry when Tibba had shyly (not without a touch of boastfulness) and swaggeringly hinted that she would be 'Away for the weekend'. (Chantal had kindly suggested a cup of coffee on the Saturday morning in the King's Road, Chelsea.)

'To Wiltshire,' she had said. Saying 'to Pangham' would have made her feel ridiculous. There was nothing disreputable about Pangham, of course, but her father had brought her up to regard Monty and Meg as a pair of idiots, and the institution they served as inescapably inane. But, in mentioning her week-end to Chantal, Tibba had suddenly wanted to add a bit of mystery to her life; let it be thought that, perhaps, somewhere in the background, there might be a boyfriend.

She could not possibly tell them about Captain de Courcy. It would seem altogether childish, too much like a 'crush' rather than being, as it was, the sort of sensation which inspired Dante to write the *Divina Commedia* or Carrington to commit suicide. But Chantal would, she knew, be spending rather a lot of time between Friday afternoon and Sunday morning with a Westminster boy called Napier; and that was his first name. The descriptions of what they had got up to would be graphic, rivalled by Rosemary's love affairs in the extent of their erotic extravagance, but having the edge upon them when it came to social *cachet*. The wonder was, Tibba sometimes thought, that these girls wanted her as a friend at all; as they so plainly did. She never competed, conversationally. That, perhaps, was part of her charm for them. But she did not feel that she could merely confess that she was going to stay with an aunt who was married to a schoolmaster. This would scarcely cut much ice when measured beside Rosemary's adventures at the disco, or Chantie's having to hold Napier's neck while he was sick over passers-by beneath the window of his mother's house in Ennismore Gardens.

And yet, oddly, because there had been a very faint hint of deception in her replies to Chantie – not a direct lie, but an element of concealment, designed to make her week-end in Wiltshire sound more interesting than it could possibly be – she felt a stirring of adventure. It would inevitably be the same dreary round of Meg asking her if she had brought stout walking shoes and their having to eat hard-boiled eggs before setting out to take part in the chapel services. Yet, who knew? Something might be about to happen.

When the word PANGHAM appeared on the little station platform she was quite excited. It was the first week-end without her father for over two years; the first two days in which she was not having to be his nurse, his companion, his help-meet. The combinations of feeling in her bosom were delicious as she stepped down from the train: exquisite and despairing love for Captain de Courcy mingled with a satirical sense that she was playing a little trick on Chantal by having half implied that an adventure was in the air; a sense, as she breathed the damp, grey atmosphere, that she was suddenly free.

Meg, rather maddeningly, was not on the platform to meet her, and no one else got out of the train. Having shown her ticket to the little man, she wandered out towards the small station car-park, swinging her little green hold-all.

It was not a huge distance to the school. One could easily walk. It was just that, increasingly, since Giles lost his sight, he was treated as an invalid, as though he had lost the use of his limbs as well; and Tibba had come to be treated likewise.

Should she wait, or should she walk on up to the school? As she hovered in the portico of the little railway station, she was aware that she was standing next to a rather distinguished-looking boy in Pangham School uniform. He had a blue blazer, not unlike Captain de Courcy's, a striped tie and a fancy waistcoat which did not exactly go with either. He had laughing blue eyes and acne, and his boater sat at a jaunty angle on top of springy straw-coloured hair.

'Have you just got off the train?' he asked.

'Yes.'

She did not know where he had sprung from. He had simply materialized.

'I'm a bit late. Meant to be meeting someone, but I nipped behind the awning for a drag.' He made a lordly wave in the direction of a poster which displayed a glass of beer, some ten feet high.

'Oh,' she smiled nervously. Wasn't smoking against the rules? Would he be so free with his confidences if he knew that he was speaking to the niece of a housemaster?

'There wasn't a rather shrivelled-looking garden gnome in an astrakhan coat on the train?' asked the boy.

'I'm afraid I didn't notice.' It was an odd inquiry. She had not seen into the luggage van, where garden ornaments were presumably stowed. Why should this one have been wearing a fur coat? Tibba had the uneasy sense that there was a joke in the air which she could not catch. Then it dawned on her that 'the Garden Gnome' was a nickname, probably for a schoolmaster.

'Who would it have been?' she managed to ask.

'My father,' said Peverill. 'Anyhow, it looks as if the old man's come by car after all. Are you waiting for someone?'

'Nnnnot really. My aunt mmmight have c-c-come but I c-c-can easily walk to her house.'

'Does she live in Pangham?'

Tibba realized that the young man was not going to be shaken off. As she had turned to walk towards the school he remained persistently at her side. He spoke in a baying, loud voice, as though he was shouting orders. In a strange sort of way, he was handsome. You did not notice the spots. You noticed the tallness, and the straw hair, and the charming arrogance of his smile.

'My old man's coming up from London to take me out to lunch,' said Peverill. 'Then I'm in a match. I'm Piers Peverill. What's your name?'

'Fox.' She began to say *Tibba*, but it remained unsaid.

'Just Fox? You still haven't told me if your aunt lives in Pangham.' This was said in the impatient authoritative tones of one who has an absolute right to know.

'She's at the school. She's married to a master.'

'Oh *no!*' His amazement was either contrived or foolish. Apart from the sprawling school buildings, Pangham was just a smudge of a place, planted with evergreens. There was almost nothing there except a vicarage (now occupied by a stockbroker's family) and a small council estate. The overwhelming probability was, if you were going there at all, that you were going to visit someone at the school.

'Which beak's she married to?'

'Mister Gore.'

'I don't *believe* it! I'm Ruddy G.'s Head of House.'

Tibba knew of course that the boys called him Ruddy G. Even Meg did, sometimes. But it seemed a curiously bold crossing of boundaries for a *boy* to refer to a master in this informal way to a member of that dignitary's family. There also seemed an oddity about saying 'I'm Ruddy G.'s Head of House', as though in some mysterious way it was Piers Peverill, and not Monty, who was in charge of Gore's.

'Are you allowed to smoke?' she asked, a little petulantly, for she felt herself at once being 'taken over' by Peverill, and thought perhaps that he needed to be slapped down.

Peverill replied with a rather melodramatic honking cough, loud enough to shake rooftops, a sound which trailed off into a

sneering drawl which might roughly be rendered 'Eeee-yare –
khum – not *exactly*.' The question seemed to amuse him very
much.

'I mean, would you get into trouble if you were caught?'

'I haven't been caught, have I?'

'You have by me.'

'*Have* I? How frightening. Rather nice, though.'

She was half cross, half amused to realize how what had
begun as a prim little exchange had taken on the character of
flirtation.

'You're quite beautiful, you know,' he added, in the same loud
voice. It was a tone which would have been more appropriate
for assessing the value of a horse, or telling men to fix bayonets.
Tibba felt affronted by his insolence, and yet glowed at the same
time. It was not the sort of thing one could imagine, in a million
years, proceeding from the shy, courteous lips of Captain de
Courcy.

'How very rude to comment,' she said, furious to be blushing
with pleasure.

'I only said *quite*,' said Peverill. 'Your hair's a boring colour
and your legs are a bit on the fat side. But you'll do.'

Quickening her pace, she tried to hurry on to escape this
boorishness, which had suddenly ceased to have anything amusing about it. She longed to make the rest of the journey in
silence and solitude and not to have this brash companion at her
side. If she felt entirely confident of getting the word out without
a stammer she would have referred to his beastly *spots*, some of
which absolutely glistened with life in a way which (she now
thought) was quite revolting.

A chance to humiliate him did not arise, however, because
coming round the corner at the brow of the hill, she bumped into
Meg. It was reassuring to be greeted with her 'Hallo, old thing,
let me take that bag.'

'Good morning, Mrs Gore,' said Peverill, removing his boater
with a stately bow. It now occurred to Tibba that he might have
offered to carry her bag. He seemed unembarrassed by Meg's

grabbing of it. 'Fox and I met down at the station,' he said. 'I went down to meet my dad off the London train.'

'But he's waiting at the house,' said Meg. 'He's been there ages. It was because I had to offer Sir Anthony a glass of sherry that I was late coming out to meet you,' said Meg. She seemed to be rather pointedly speaking to Tibba. 'Added to which, the Humber's gone fut.'

'The Garden Gnome' was standing in the hall, when they all came through the front door. He was expensively dressed not in astrakhan, but in a soft, camel-haired coat and very glossy black shoes. Half his orange head was bald and the other was covered with thick, closely cut white hair. He seemed coated in un-English sunshine as though just back from the Bahamas. He had a very small moustache which was like neither Harold Nicolson's nor Captain de Courcy's. It was more like George Orwell's: the difference being that Sir Anthony had none of Orwell's wistfulness of expression. He looked excessively self-confident and plutocratic. He was several inches shorter than Tibba and bore no noticeable resemblance to his son.

By no stretch of the language could it seem appropriate to regard him as shrivelled. In the absence of a beard, pixie hat or plaster shovel, it seemed equally hard to picture him adorning the gardens of the humbler suburbs.

'Chasing the girls as usual,' said Sir Anthony Peverill, with a manly clasp of his son's shoulder and a laugh which revealed several gold teeth. Tibba felt her feet sort of freezing and sticking to the lino in her uncle's hall. She knew that until Sir Anthony and his son had disappeared it would be impossible for any sound to proceed from her lips. It was hard enough even to look up at his vulgar grinning.

'I drove up in the MG,' said Sir Anthony. 'It was time it had a spin and I thought you'd enjoy having a drive this afternoon.'

Meg shot Peverill a sharp glance as if to indicate that he ought to know perfectly well that it was against the school rules for boys to drive, even when accompanied by their parents. If Monty had returned from taking morning school, he would have made that clear. It was somehow awkward for her to do so, in front of Tibba, as she feebly reasoned with herself.

'I'm not sure there'll be time after the match,' she said.

'Oh, there'll be plenty of time,' said Sir Anthony, at which his son grinned. 'Besides,' he added over his shoulder, as he walked away through the door with his arm linked in that of his heir, 'I shall go back by train so that Piers can play about with the car tomorrow morning if he likes.'

Meg and Tibba watched them go.

They heard Peverill yelling that he wanted Lobster Thermidor, a pretty vain desire, they both thought, in that remote part of Wiltshire. Tibba was sure that her aunt would immediately venture on some comment, some exclamation of disgust, some explanation of the Peverills. But she merely sighed and said, 'I expect you want to go up to your room. Travelling on the railway makes you feel so dirty, I always think.'

When she came downstairs again, having bunged her night things under her pillow and hung up her only decent dress on a coat-hanger on the back of the door, Monty was back from his teaching morning.

'I *say!*' was his mode of greeting.

Tibba was swept up into her uncle's arms and given a kiss which lingered more than she would have chosen. He grinned at her absurdly, his face enlivened with a high flush. 'This is good,' he said. 'D'you want to come through for lunch with the boys?'

'No, Monty, Tibba and I are going to eat some ham in the kitchen,' said Meg. 'But there's time for us all to have a glass of sherry beforehand.'

'House Matches this afternoon,' said Monty, as he fiddled with decanters. 'Will Gore's beat Talbot's: that's the question that's on everyone's mind.' The sherry dribbled down the edge of the glass and on to his fingers as he handed it to Tibba. Once again, in this action, there was more contact than was necessary. His knuckles almost rubbed against hers as he placed the glass between her fingers. He could so easily have put it down on the little wine table.

'It's a good day for it anyway,' said Meg abrasively as she gazed out into the large garden. Damp seemed to hang over everything. It was that deadest time of year when nothing was in flower and the half-shorn trees looked soggy against the grey sky. Beyond the garden gate was the Close, and the main school buildings, lumpish and ugly.

'I think we've got a good enough team but old Reggie Talbot told me his blokes have been training like billy-o this last week or so.'

'Our boys have trained too,' said Meg.

'I know Peverill's Captain of Big Side,' said Monty. 'But he's sloppy. All the other boys in the school have been out on runs each day this week to get fit for the House Matches; not ours. If you ask me, he's fundamentally soft.'

Tibba was interested that Peverill's name had cropped up again. She hoped it would now be possible to discuss his coarse behaviour during her walk from the station. She even contemplated getting him into trouble by 'sneaking' on him about the surreptitious cigarette behind the station awning.

Monty grinned while he spoke of the boy, but Meg did not. Monty was plainly obsessed by Peverill's awfulness.

'Don't let's get on to that subject,' Meg said wearily. And they did not have to, because at that moment a little boy of thirteen poked his head round the drawing-room door and told his housemaster that the boys were all ready for lunch. In the hall, he held open the green baize door which divided Monty's part of the house from the part where the boys lived. Momentarily, they heard the roar of talk in the dining-hall echoing down the corridor. Then the ritual 'Quiet Please!' followed by complete silence. Still the Cheshire cat, Monty walked through the door and it closed.

'Peverill seems to be quite a ...' Tibba paused. *Character* did not seem to be a word which would come to her lips. She quickly contemplated *personage* and *nuisance*. She decided to begin *nui-*

sance, but she only got past the first syllable, so she changed it to 'new face around the place'.

'Don't for heaven's sake talk about Peverill. It's Peverill this and Peverill that every blessed moment of the day.'

'Is he really Head of House?'

Meg sighed despondently, refusing to devote so much as a word more to the subject.

'He was smoking down by the station,' said Tibba.

'Don't tell Monty,' was Meg's surprising reply. 'He's always thinking he can catch Peverill out, but it never works. Of course he smokes, and he drinks vodka in his study and there are all kinds of things he does. But you can *never* pin him down. Now I really insist on talking about something else.'

As they ate their salad at the kitchen table, Tibba told Meg about Giles. She wished that her aunt, who really was not very clever, would not insist on asking about her father's work. Meg understood nothing of it.

Tibba knew that even she, with all the advantage of having lived with Giles for seventeen years, and of having been taught by Miss Russenberger, could not understand either the interest or the fascination, let alone the contents of the *Tretis of Loue Heuenliche*. It was infinitely remote and strange. Their lives were lived on a level of politeness which would have made any such rebarbative subject impossible to discuss: but she always assumed that he had no interest in the religious side of it. He surely knew – his frequently contemptuous remarks on the subject could not leave the matter in any doubt – that Christianity was the most boring and cruel and *contemptible* mode of thought. The idea of these old women being walled up and told what to do by a superstitious parson was (Tibba allowed herself the modernism) obscene. It was extraordinary that their manual should have occupied so much of her father's attention, over so many years. But she knew enough to know that his interest in it was nothing to do with its *contents*. It was the language, as he had always said. Meg was always asking about its 'philosophy'. Giles said it contained no 'philosophy'. But she would not be snubbed.

Tibba did not know what this meant. But she had quickly picked up the idea that most people never used the word 'philosophy' correctly, and it was therefore banished forever from her vocabulary.

'He did explain it all to me years ago,' Meg said, 'the manual for nuns. It's extraordinary that he is still determined to go on with it, really, in the circumstances.'

'It is nearly ready for publication,' said Tibba. 'He could not possibly stop now.'

'But doesn't it involve a lot of ... well, reading, and checking and that sort of thing?'

'Miss Agar does all that,' said Tibba. As she said it, her face crinkled into a smile, the first since her arrival. Somehow you couldn't think about Miss Agar without it seeming funny.

VI

There seemed to be nothing odd about making love on the floor of Trinity College Library. A rug of sorts beneath them added a furry softness to their gentle slow rhythms. Manuscripts were scattered on the periphery of the rug, some in bundles, some carefully wrapped about with ribbon, some bound, some loose. Giles could feel his bare toes rubbing against vellum as she lay on top of him and kissed his eyes.

There was more a feeling of *having had* this experience than of living through it at that moment. It seemed, indeed, not a thing of the moment, but a whole voluptuous past. Afterwards, they sat upright, naked as Adam and Eve, and as happily innocent. And they spoke in low murmurs as she stroked his hands and his cheeks.

He had assumed, while he held her in his arms, that it had been Carol who was his companion, but as he watched the hands reaching up to his cheeks, he realized that it all belonged to a much earlier phase. Those small, perfectly white hands were Mary's. So was the trembling contralto of her words. 'It was *all right*, all right, all right.'

The words referred, or seemed to refer, to nothing specific, of the moment; but their power to reassure was absolute. His heart felt a glowing, warm, sense of release as she spoke, stroking his forehead. He knew instinctively that she was talking of all those lost years of their estrangement, those bitter years of anger, while she had her love affairs and he buried himself in his work.

'But we will never get them back,' he said to her, meaning the years. She needed no explanation of what he meant. Indeed, it was hard afterwards to know whether, exactly, they had used words for their communication, or whether their thoughts had passed silently into each other's brain through gesture and touch and sight. For, although he could not remember what she said in reply to his painful realization that *we will never get them back*, her embrace seemed to be an answer which brought the sense that he had been viewing it all the wrong way about.

'These are the only years that we can have; joy is the only experience that lasts': these were the vague thoughts which her movement towards him conveyed, her burying of his face against her bosom, her gentle rocking of him in an entirely childish glow of affection. It was a kiss which had within it all the ecstatic pleasure of high passion while remaining, essentially, indistinguishable from the first kisses he could remember from nursery days.

'We said we hated each other then,' he reminded Mary. 'But we didn't.'

'We *couldn't*,' she laughed. There was nothing flippant or shrill in her laughter as there had been in the old days. It was a rich, full laughter which filled him with happiness rather than simply amusing him.

'Your hair is so beautiful,' he said. 'A woman's hair is the most beautiful thing about her. Never cut your hair, my darling.'

She smiled confidingly as though he was only beginning to discover a delicious secret. Was it his birthday? Was some 'treat' in store? Thoughts as childish as this occurred. Because it was obvious that she was holding back from telling him of some glorious surprise, something that would confirm this indescribably beautiful sense that the past was redeemed.

'What is it, Mary, what is it?' he asked. He felt so very happy that he was afraid that his heart might stop beating. It was, after those many years of unsatisfactoriness and misery, all right, all right. Something like a curse had hovered over them, some black cloud. Perhaps it had been there even before he met Mary, but it had descended upon them and destroyed his happiness and, since its descent, things had never been right. Even if the outward circumstances of his life had been happy they would not have been right, because he now felt that this curse, this nebulous torment, was an inner thing. But now, as Mary caressed and touched him, the unhappiness evaporated and the knowledge dawned that this was the only solid and true thing in his existence, this love of his for her. It made him sense that the curse, the cloud, the torment, had been illusions.

The fruitfulness of his love was tangible. Mary, as she sat beside him now, was so young: little more, it seemed, than twenty. And yet he knew that she was the mother of his seventeen-year-old Tibba and that she was to be the mother of the next, the child in the womb. *That* was the secret, the good thing which was to come. *That* explained her smile. Beyond her white angular naked shoulder he looked through the library windows to the Italianate courtyard baking in the sun. A variety of geraniums stood about in pots, gloriously pink and white against the terracotta. Cypress trees stood in the corner of the cloister, and beyond, against the most brilliant of blue skies, Giles could see the hills.

She leant towards him and just before she embraced him she said the words, 'Marry me.'

In the very split second before he woke, he realized that he was about to embrace Miss Agar.

In his state of half-sleep, half-waking, he knew that he must not open his eyes. He kept them closed quite deliberately, savouring the memory of the blue skies, and of the colour of Mary's hair and of her playfully happy eyes. Something told him that he must not open his eyes, that to do so would be disillusioning. But he had forgotten what this disillusionment would entail.

He was in a strange place; that he knew. His bedding was different. At home, he liked thick stiff linen sheets of a high quality, tucked about him tightly with three blankets in the summer and five in the winter. A strange collection of articles were attempting to keep him warm here. The bedside rug he had thrown over the collection of unzipped sleeping-bags and flimsy blankets last night had worked itself round to his side so that it felt rather as if he were sharing a bed with a sheep.

The Beloved, this strangely fluid conglomeration of Mary, Carol and Miss Agar, had gone now. He was conscious, as the thoughts passed through his brain, that he was thinking, not dreaming. Quietly and semi-consciously, he reviewed his past, his character, the part these women had played in the drama of his existence. Why had the dream made him so happy? It was not unconnected with a revival of erotic pleasure. But it was very far from being just a piece of sexual fantasy. It had been a dream in which the bitterness of his own nature was capable of being expunged. It was not merely that he was being urged by Mary to make a new start, to turn over a new leaf. It was nothing so moralistic. The conviction had come to him in the course of the dream that all the bitterness was unnecessary. Such a strange, delicious dream. There had been a library, hadn't there? And a cloister, and a sky. But already its details receded. Had he really been making love to Carol, or had he just thought of it now, this waking instant? Had it not been Mary all along? He could not remember. He still felt overpoweringly moved, as if he had seen a really good film. Only the film had been all about himself: not an entirely disagreeable prospect.

Where was he? His bare toes, sticking out of the end of the bed, knocked a pile of papers down on to the floor, and his big toe seemed to be tracing the binding of some folder or other. He remembered then. He was lying on the divan in that little room in whatever street it was. Somewhere off the Chesterton Road. Miss Agar had tried to explain to him where it was but her topographical powers of description were limited.

He blinked. A mistake. It was to be, again, yet another of those bitter wakings when he had to get used to being blind all over again. The happiness of his dream life was a curse. For something over a third of his existence he could still enjoy the delights of the eye. And then the deeply disillusioning mornings came again. Or at least, he supposed it was morning. He checked the watch that Meg had so kindly given him, a special gadget dreamed up by someone at the RNIB, but the thing appeared to be bust. It said three o'clock. It could not be only three o'clock in the morning. But, even as he had the thought, a distant chime outside the room seemed to confirm this, some church or college clock tolling the hour.

At some stage in my life, he thought, *I made up my mind to be bitter*. He wondered when it was. He remembered, as long ago as his undergraduate days, when some don, perhaps the chaplain, had said to him that the only response to existence was *le oui éternel*, an Everlasting Yes. Which French sage had written it? Pascal? Or some modern such as Gabriel Marcel, whom Giles had never read? He remembered the titter which went round the room when he, aged nineteen, had said that he was so far from giving an unconditional *oui éternel* to existence as to echo Eliza Doolittle's *Not bloody likely*.

They must have been in a play. Those were the days when he was in the Marlowe Society.

Perhaps he had been acting ever since. It was easier to be cynical, cold, sceptical, pessimistic; easier, because almost everything in the world justified a pessimistic interpretation; easier, because if you said cynical things people supposed you cleverer than if you said positive, obvious things. Was it ever as crude and as blatantly self-conscious as that? Being back in Cambridge, Giles was able to survey his undergraduate self, and the thought that perhaps it was. Undergraduate life is too short and too rapid to be able to deal in subtle tones. Giles, as a youth of twenty, had overplayed his part of the hardened cynic who professed to find almost everything intolerably boring, almost everybody intolerably ugly or stupid. While his contemporaries fell in love or attached themselves to religion or politics, he stood self-consciously aloof, knowing that his teachers admired his linguistic ability and that a very small circle of friends enjoyed his contemptuous attitude towards life. With what predictably withering epigrams he had managed to dismiss those fools who thought the world was worth saving by a change in its political systems! With what equally brief violence of phrase he had dealt with the ideas of the God-squad!

Such attitudinizing could not make him popular, but he did

not seek popularity. His work was outstanding, he would indubitably get a fellowship.

And then, inexorably, the cynical pose had been hardened into an actual habit of mind; events began to take him at his word. The King's Fellowship had eluded him. (Fancy meeting old Lightfoot after so many years.) Well, something else would turn up! Yes, at the first moment of disaster, he had secretly started to spin himself the optimistic lies. But it was too late. He had told Life that it was the vale of tears. Such it would become. It was no good suddenly turning round and saying that the fairy story would have a happy ending. How often he had said himself that there were no more corrupting words to put into the heads of infants than the phrase *they all lived happily ever after.*

It would have been nice, in his well-appointed college rooms, hung with nice paintings and filled with choice furniture, to give these bitter thoughts expression. But now he learnt that they were true. 'I shan't expect to be elected,' he had said to a contemporary dazzled by his cool nonchalance. 'It is well known that committees of dons always make the wrong decision.' And they had.

Lightfoot's fruity voice the day before had recalled all the agony of that phase of life. Up to that point, Giles had secretly believed that he was too clever to be unfortunate. There was no possibility that the unfolding of existence would involve at each stage anything but the effortless fulfilment of his ambitions and desires. The failure at King's had been the first chilly indication that Life was to be as bleakly cruel as he claimed it was.

There are human beings, in fact the majority of human beings, who survive the passage from birth to the grave without being Fellows of King's College, Cambridge. For the most part, the fact that they lack this distinction does not affect their happiness. But that fact was unconsoling to Giles. It was somehow made apparent to him that there was no point in considering an academic career. And this fact fell upon him like a curse.

By the time that he met Mary he was already half eaten-up with bitterness. He was established in London as a librarian and he had little difficulty in building up a professional reputation for himself. Even by his mid-twenties, he had a prodigious knowledge of the whereabouts of manuscripts. It had been built upon over the years, and now, in his blindness, it was the one great contribution he could still make in the library. If visiting scholars came in search of material, Giles would almost certainly be able to direct them to the exact manuscript they required. He held catalogue numbers in his head in the way some people could remember train times or great poems. And his knowledge was miscellaneous, not merely restricted to his own 'period'. (When people asked him his 'period' he always liked to shatter them with the pedantic reply, 'Somewhere between 1213 and 1215.') He could send historians round twenty-five libraries of great houses, giving them the exact place to find letters of Lord Melbourne or wills from the reign of Edward II. He could provide students of literature with the whereabouts of seventeenth-century holograph poems, or the typescripts of modern novels. He was a mine of information, and he had begun to be this even when Mary walked into his life.

Their falling in love (he was twenty-nine at the time, she rather younger) had not diminished his professional ambition, for she was deeply ambitious on his behalf. But she had never quite seen how corrupting his ambition was. There was nothing so blatant about it as a desire for position, money or success. He wanted to establish his cleverness, to know so much, to be so useful to the learned world, for one reason only, and that was to prove the Fellows of King's wrong, and to show the world that he had deserved to become a don.

A Tretis of Loue Heuenliche had been an important – as it turned out, the most important – part of this scheme, for in its discovery, and his further collation of it with other medieval evidences, he was surreptitiously managing to disprove many of the scholarly assumptions put about by his former teachers in the field. He appeared to be acting in terms of scholarly selfishness. In fact, in an egomaniac way, he had been merely fouling his own nest, and showing the dons that they had all been wrong.

This aspect of things had never occurred to him before. But as he lay there in the darkness, still glowing from the peculiar experience of the dream, still deeply close to Mary, as though she were more alive than ever and curled up beside him like this old acrylic rug (dead sheep or whatever it was), he also reflected that he had never allowed, even in his moments of 'forgiving' Mary, for the possibility that he might also be in need of forgiveness.

She had committed adulteries while he got on with his work in the library or the study evening after evening. He had eaten the cold pasta in Hermit Street while she slithered out of her clothes in the flats and hotel-rooms of actors in Notting Hill. There had therefore been no question in his mind, when their time of reconciliation came, that *he* was in a position to forgive *her*. In the dream, however, it had felt as though she was forgiving him; it was as though he had been longing for forgiveness all his life and was too stubborn to see that it had been doled out to him years before he had even become aware of the longing. And as he lay, almost snoozing again now, in the chilly bedroom (could it really be only three? there was no way of telling), he knew what he was forgiven *for*: it was hatred.

It had begun as an affected hatred of existence. But it had quickly become a real hatred of people, in particular the dons who had failed to make him one of their number. The habit spread. How easy it was to regard the majority of the human race with contempt. Viewed in the right (or the wrong) light most people had something fairly deeply despicable about them. So, even in their early years of married life, when their love had been happy, Giles had liked to spit out his contempt for colleagues who had been foolish during the working day, or for Mary's friends in the evenings. She egged him on, actually enjoyed his expressions of satirical world-weariness at first. But it did not take long for her to realize that the habit of mind had taken him over so completely that there was no one, logically, who could be excepted from it. *There is none who doeth good, no not one.* It had never occurred to him, even in his most forgiving moods, that the reason Mary had that first love-affair was that he made her feel so very inferior (morally, intellectually, in every way except socially) that life with him turned into a constant reproach. In a perverse way, it was as though he wanted her to do it in order to show that he was the more virtuous partner. He wanted to build up an unsurpassed knowledge of manuscripts in order to spike the dons' guns. That was doing a good thing for an evil purpose. But by the time of Mary's first infidelity he had moved into the more dangerous waters of longing for an evil thing for an entirely evil purpose. He longed for everyone to see how patiently he, how woefully she, was behaving. The wounded bitterness, the anger, was something that he had wanted to express almost since he met her, to stamp upon all the good impulses, all the natural sweetness of their love.

And now, in a phantom, all those years later, she had returned to him, as young as the first day they met, but as knowing as she had been in her days of maturity, and bubbling with a certain, confident joy. For that irrational desire of his to stamp on their joy and expunge it from his existence was not something that had ever been feasible or possible. His stray moments of self-abandonment, of happiness with her, of pride in the offspring that happiness produced, were infinitely more solid and real than the blackness which had tried to blot them out. And there was a simple proof of this (even if *proof* is a word from the language of logic, and there was nothing logical about this rambling reflection of Giles's; even so, it had all the feeling of a logical progression). The proof was in the dream; it was in the firm sense that he could not blot out the happiness of his love for Mary, memory wouldn't allow it. Nor, as he searched about in memory, could he find a single *reason* for his sudden cooling towards her, his desire to find fault perpetually, his delight when she at last erred and could be rejected and despised. All this extraordinary corruption of spirit which had occurred in the middle years of his marriage now seemed unreal and fantastic, as though like a sulky child he had been allowed his foolish play while everyone knew the realities at its peripheries to be stronger and deeper than any of the sulks. They were real and powerful too; he could not control them; they were ready to take over again as soon as he gave himself up to them.

The more he thought about these things, the less dozy he became. His mind had begun to race with it all. He had thought, up to this point, that his life was a series of blows stoically borne: and of course, there was a perfectly good case to be made out for that way of interpreting the last twenty years of his personal history. He had never before admitted to himself that he had *wanted* things to go wrong from the first. He had not told himself that he wanted to lose his first wife, go blind, lose his second wife. On one level he wanted none of these things to happen. How could anyone have *wanted* such things? But, having swiftly abandoned the idea that the world was going to heap upon him, as a very young man, reward upon reward, he changed course to the conviction that the world would heap upon him calamity after calamity; the concomitant of which was that he was worthier of the world's attention, admiration and pity.

This was a pretty fantastic line of reasoning, but it *was* the middle of the night and his head buzzed with insomniac absence of precision.

Sex, he suddenly thought, was the only area of life where he even came close to self-abandonment.

Not that self-forgetting had ever been a conscious ambition of his; merely that, without it, he would have gone round the twist in those earlier days of his widowhood. And as he thought of the progression of girlfriends, the endlessly repeated quest for erotic ecstasy which followed the consumption of noodles or the seeing of films, he remembered slowly and sadly how very dead Mary was. And Carol had come to replace her. And the sex and the companionship, the domestic solidity and the gasping excitement of their lovemaking, had been and gone too, disappeared forever like a thing that never was. And death and loneliness and bitterness had triumphed as never before in his dark, blind world.

Into this complicated and (to Giles) endlessly fascinating self-history had to be fitted the two quite new features of life: one was the mature companionship of Tibba, her almost constant presence in his life (so that now, without her, he felt bereft as a child at a boarding school). The other was Miss Agar.

Tibba, the mature Tibba who cooked his supper and read to him afterwards in the faltering tones he loved so much, was an emergent presence. She had always been there in the shadows. His love for her had grown, so deeply and so slowly that there seemed no part of memory which was untouched by her. It was impossible, imaginatively, to accept the fact that there had been a period of his life before she existed. Miss Agar, on the other hand, was something altogether new; she brought the remarkable novelty: a certainty that he was loved, and wholeheartedly approved of. He rather doubted now (it made the final frittering away of the last tatters of the dream seem doubly painful) whether he could have conceived of the remembered Mary as wholly *forgiving* him if he had not known Miss Agar. The *real* Mary had contributed as much to the chilly unhappiness of those middle years of marriage as he had himself. As someone once wrote of Dean Inge: *He casteth forth his ice like morsels: who is able to abide his frost?* Mary's coldness had been a match for his own. This sense of a Beloved who stubbornly could not notice his coldness, who treated him as if it had all been unreal – or redeemed, or purged away – this was a novelty, in waking as in dreaming hours.

By Giles's ordinary standards, the previous thirty-six hours had not been enjoyable. The tea at Girton had been sticky in more senses than one; the supper in Chesterton Road full of beans in only one sense, and that far from palatable. Brenda, the Accredited Supervisor, had chosen to cook a cassoulet, he now realized (with a deep sense of its pathos, and its ignominy), because she believed him incapable of slicing up meat.

How had he managed to survive for forty-seven years in the world without having social life of the kind provided by that supper party? Hard chairs, a cramped little dining 'area' in what was obviously a living-room, hardly any room to stretch legs or elbows round the table; cold, rough, red supermarket wine in tumblers tasting (his at any rate) faintly of onion and washing-up liquid; the cassoulet, cooked not quite long enough so that every bean had to be vigilantly chewed with the knowledge (and here he was, the wakeful proof of it) that it would 'keep him up in the night'; the lettuce with an over-vinaigrous dressing (why didn't people realize that a good dressing is made with nearly all *oil*, good simple olive oil, and that all its other ingredients, whether lemon juice or mustard seeds or vinegar or salt or pepper were to be used sparingly?); the extraordinarily unsuccessful 'mousse'; and the black coffee filtered so that it was cold by the time it reached one's cup . . .

Thousands, perhaps hundreds of thousands of his fellow-citizens ate such meals every week of their lives. In Cambridge, more people than not were probably forced to suffer these indignities night after night, in the name of conviviality. But in London, too, they must have been 'dying thus around us day by day'; in some extraordinary way he had escaped them, and in consequence he slept at night. Now he realized that, whatever the risks of disturbing the household, a visit to the lavatory was essential.

He gingerly made his way to the door and remembered, in feeling his way along the hall, not to knock the little glazed picture which swung precariously to his right. A bitter wind from the direction of the front door attacked his pyjama-clad shins. When he reached the door of the bathroom he paused. He was more or less certain that it was the bathroom. If, however, it transpired that it was the broom cupboard, there was the danger of a cascade of mops, tins or brushes arousing the household. If it were the door of someone else's bedroom, the possibilities of embarrassment were even more farcically acute. He realized, suddenly gripped by doubt no less than by a fairly immediate need of that consolation which only a lavatory can provide, that the cheap red wine had gone to his head; that he was not merely sleepy but still distinctly tight.

He opened the door a crack, and the smell of cheap soaps reassured him that he was in the bathroom.

Once perched on the seat, the noise and smells were volcanic. He felt awkwardly certain that he must be waking the whole tiny household. But peace and silence followed, as he continued to sit there, quietly recovering from the violent shock to his system. At least some of the vinegary lettuce and cheap wine and beans must have gushed out into the pan, and the experience must have been purgative.

Shivering slightly, he remembered the supper. He had been so chilly and silent throughout the meal, and the young people really so nice. Brenda had tried to draw him out on the subject of 'Breton lais', but he had not felt inclined to say much on the subject. Miss Agar, holding his hand under the table, suggested that he bored the party with accounts of *The Tretis of Loue Heuenliche*, but he had only muttered a few words. She had given a glowing (and, he felt, rather inaccurate) version of their tea-party in Girton and been amused by some of its social niceties which had been lost on him. They all seemed to find it very funny that her old supervisor had silver sugar-tongs. Since he so resolutely declined to 'take up' any conversational lead, and made it so clear that he was embarrassed to be present at the supper, it was not surprising that they had all fallen to gossip which could not possibly concern him: who might or might not get minor academic jobs currently vacant, and finally, church, church, church. One of them sang in a choir, another was contemplating taking Orders: to his gradual amazement, Giles discovered that everyone about him round the table did not merely practise *some* liturgical observance; they were avid and frequent churchgoers, sermontasters ... *believers*.

This, again, was a category of person from whom, hitherto, Giles had spared himself; like the plonk-drinking bean-eating diners-in-discomfort. Meg, his sister, believed something or another; he knew that. She always had. He put it in the same category as her voting Liberal and knitting things for hospitals. It 'went' with being a housemaster's wife at Pangham in a way that conspicuous unbelief, such as his own, would not have done. He could no more have prepared boys for confirmation than he could have refereed a football match. They were both areas of experience not merely alien, but alien in the same way.

But now, here he had been, bombarding his system with hopelessly indigestible food, stiff, cold and uncomfortable on an upright chair wedged between a tiny corner bookshelf as he fingered it nervously for hour upon hour, and what felt like a lamp made out of a wicker-covered Italian wine-bottle, and surrounded by six people whose natural subjects of conversation, when unrestrained by the politeness which had characterized the beginning of the evening, were such questions as The Alternative Service Book, the Ten Propositions, or the General Synod, three things of which Giles had never heard. It seemed that all the people round the table (except himself) believed fervently in the importance of belonging to the Church of England, and considered it of conversational interest not only which church one attended, but also which of its clergy one liked, whether something called Series III was or was not better than Missa Normativa, and why priests no longer wore their stoles crosswise.

Giles was baffled. Presumably, since these people went to church so often, and thought the Decline of Evensong or the Ordination of Women appropriate subjects for dinner conversation, they also believed the whole bag of tricks, or enough of the tricks to make their membership of the Church something more than a whimsical mockery. They actually believed, these bean-swilling, kind, good people, that the wrath of God the Father on account of *their* iniquity could only be appeased by the obscenely cruel public death of a Galilean peasant, to outward appearances human, though (in the considered judgement of the girl who had poured so much vinegar on the lettuce) one and the same Person as the Creator of the universe and the Future Judge of Humanity.

For Our Lord in His courtesy chose to hide His nobility under the humble cloak of our human nature, like the prince who hid his fine raiment under the beggar's robe. And behold, He has done yet more. For He has clothed us with that same princely raiment with which He was clothed. Like as the priest prayeth daily in the holy offering of the chalice that we put on that clothing,

of virgin spotlessness, those wedding clothes of the Lamb, even as he has
condescended to wear our vesture of filthiness in the flesh: ejus divinitatis esse
consortes, qui humanitatis nostrae fieri dignatus est particeps.

This opinion of the author of the *Tretis* was shared, evidently, by the north-country female voice to Giles's right at dinner; a voice which had been so hostile to the Ten Propositions that she did not even pause to explain what they were. They sounded like a bland, not to say racy, alternative to the Ten Commandments. The Church of England was *capable de tout.*

But it was not the Ten Propositions which stunned Giles so much as the recognition that he was sitting at a table where every person (except himself) was speaking as though the eighteenth-century Enlightenment, and the Darwinian revolution in scientific thought, had never been. They were, presumably, unaware that there had been Hitler, Stalin, the gas chambers, the Bomb, to think about since the previous unsuccessful revision of the Book of Common Prayer in 1928. Were they also unaware that the Logical Positivists, in philosophy, had established not so much that God did not exist as that all religious use of language was, quite literally, meaningless? Perhaps it was mere aestheticism which made these people able to tolerate worshipping a divinity whom they claimed as all-powerful: responsible, therefore, for all the woes or calamities of the modern universe: a God capable of stopping world starvation, disease and war, but who chose not to do so. And this was their God of Love. It was the same God, according to the creeds which they felt so anxious to safeguard from erosion, who minded so much about the prehistoric error of a Mesopotamian Ape-Man that He insisted on punishing everyone else who has ever been born, holding them guilty of sin until they had been washed with baptism . . .

These arguments for atheism had flowed effortlessly from Giles's tongue in the old days, and, never having spent any time in the company of religious people since his undergraduate youth, he had rather forgotten that religion existed. He was shocked by Miss Agar's friends because they seemed to think religion was true; this offended him much more than their inability to make salad-dressing, or their considering church gossip an adequate substitute for conversation.

And yet he was irritated by them for a different reason. What they said was uninteresting. But as they spoke, he envied them. His envy seemed half-mingled now with his recollections of the dreams he had been having. In both cases, at the dinner-table and in the dreams, he had felt alienated, cut off, solitary. In the dream, it seemed possible to bring this alienation to an end: to reach out, simply, to Mary's smiling face and *accept* it. Accept *what*? Not forgiveness, thank you. Not in waking life.

But if he did not want forgiveness, what was the reason for his uneasiness among Miss Agar's friends?

He envied them, he thought, their *niceness*. Perhaps he had never been, by their simple standards, *nice*. But there had been a time when he had assumed that he was likeable; when he had thought of his cynicism and pessimism as a pose. At some stage, the niceness, real or assumed, which he imagined to be there, had simply worn away. He was no longer, quite, nice.

It was a chilling, terrible thing to realize; worse than the recollection that one is no longer young. Could 'niceness' ever be recovered? Never mind for a moment lost innocence or the Garden of Eden or Original Virtue: could he ever again be simply *nice*?

And the other thing he envied them was the ancientness of their beliefs. There was something very distasteful to him about arguing a thing from the position of modernity. But, as he sat there quietly on the loo, it occurred to him that all his distaste for Christianity (very little of it actually expressed at the table) was based on the thought that it was *old hat*, a method of thought surpassed by more recent intellectual fads. It was odd for some-one in his position to be taking this line. It now seemed very much less certain (chillingly less certain) to him that a thing might not be true simply because it had been disputed, for the first time in nearly two millenia, by a number of neurotic Victorian clergymen.

Miss Agar, he suddenly realized, was closer to the *Tretis of Loue Heuenliche* than he had ever been. In recognizing the fact, the work seemed less hysterical than it had ever done before. He could not understand, still less enter into, the cult of virginity. But he had a deep surge of regret for his own lost innocence (a much more general matter than sex) which coincided with a sense that Miss Agar's innocence was still clinging to her like her acrylic woollies. The last twenty years of disillusioning experience had made of Giles a creature which he would not have thought, in his wildest nightmares, could possibly have existed when he was a youth of twenty-five. If he could creep back behind the years, to those times when, however lofty and cynical his words, he still felt nice *inside*, would he not do so?

The maidens to whom the *Tretis* was addressed knew nothing of the intellectual depravity of which man (twentieth-century man at any rate) would be capable. Their innocence was more absolute, even, than Miss Agar's.

It had never occurred to Giles that there was something perfectly sensible about wishing to hold on to innocence. He had always gone in for the idea that since we only pass this way once, *experience* counts for everything. Again, the modernity of this attitude, now it occurred to him, filled him with remorse. From his own point of view, he had been greedy for all the 'experience' he could get, sensual, intellectual, visual. Yet this had not been his attitude on Tibba's behalf. His own immediate desire, as his schooldays came to an end, had been to lose his virginity as fast as possible. (And the fact that he had to wait twelve years after leaving school, until he met Mary, was what increased the brittle cynicism of those years, he now believed.) But he would consider such an ambition on Tibba's behalf not merely distasteful, but almost inconceivably foolish. He had not noticed it before. He had not been away from her before. But he only considered 'sensible' in Tibba courses of action which would never involve her being out of his presence for more than an hour or two at a time. Who else read aloud so well? Who else knew how he liked his olives and his noodles and his moderate intake of good wine? Other ambitions she might have for herself (one day she would go to University for instance) he regarded as merely tiresome.

If anyone had suggested to him that Tibba was fitted to the life of an anchoress, Giles would have resisted the assertion with force and bitterness. And yet it was hard to imagine, in twentieth-century terms, a teenage girl having a more sheltered life than his daughter. Had he been subconsciously *sparing* her all these years? Did he, even before this dream, this dinner, this strange stream of rather alien thoughts, did he want to delay her headlong plunge into the unpleasant world of experience? Did he want her to stay nice?

Blinking, he remembered the dream again. Less and less of its detail remained, but the extraordinary feeling of well-being was still with him; unwontedly. And he could still recollect the smiling pale face of the young Mary, paper-white, though freckled very very slightly about the nose; her hazel eyes dancing with something which augured joy. Five or six hours lay ahead before anyone else would stir.

Pondering these mysteries, he fumbled for the handle of the device on which he had been perched. A swirling of waters bore away the ill-effects of his hostess's failure to cook the beans 'through'.

Gingerly, pausing with every step, he found his way out into the passage, and along the short distance to his room. Or what he took to be his room. When he came through the doorway, which he had deliberately left open, he was surprised to hear Miss Agar whisper, 'Brenda wondered if you were all right.'

'Perfectly,' he said, disappointed that Brenda was included in the wonderment.

'I mean, I've made you some Alka-Seltzer.'

This was welcome tidings indeed. She took him by the arm and guided him to the bed. It had been tidied up a bit and she had tucked in, where possible, blankets and sheets. The bottom sheet was refreshingly smooth and cool.

'There you are,' she said, putting the fizzing glass into his hand. 'Drink it up.'

'Hold my other hand while I do so.'

She was beside the bed, not on it. It was embarrassing that not only she, but Brenda, seemed so exactly *au fait* with the state of his digestive organs.

'Stay with me,' he said quietly. 'Stay the rest of the night with me.'

She patted his hand but did not move. 'Do you feel like any breakfast?' she asked.

'What time is it?'

'About quarter past eight.'

'It seemed earlier.'

She squeezed his hand more tightly, sympathetically.

'Brenda's out at the Eight,' she said. 'I thought you'd probably want to lie in.'

'The Eight?'

'She's gone down to St Giles's.'

He sighed. *That* again. 'Have you never doubted?' he asked, a little sharply.

'You mean . . . ?'

'Yes. Actually come to the conclusion that religion was all based on a lie.'

'We've *all* doubted.' Her voice had a slightly matter-of-fact tone, as if we had all from time to time caught cold or eaten bad food; not a thing to complain about endlessly, nor perhaps even a thing to discuss.

'But what . . . what made you *stop* doubting?'

'It isn't easy to say.'

He felt her squeezing his fingers nervously. He squeezed hers back, an insistent more than a loving gesture, at that moment.

'You doubt everything one week,' she faltered, 'and then another week, it isn't so much that you want to believe, as that you find you have *always* believed, really. The passages of doubt . . . Oh, I can't explain it.'

'You must explain it.'

'Why must I?' She was suddenly sharp herself. 'I haven't asked you to explain yourself. I don't want you to. It isn't a matter of explanations. I find that I believe because in some funny way it fits the pattern of my experience.'

'Your what?'

'My experience.'

'You haven't had any experience.'

'I don't mean *that*. Honestly, Giles ...' Her voice had a sort of childish reproof in it.

'I didn't mean *that*, either. Or not just that. But you haven't had experience.'

'I'm twenty-six,' she asserted. 'I may not have had a very exciting life by some standards, but there have been ups and downs, days of sunshine, days when the sky went black ...'

He sighed. Why had he ever allowed her to start on this?

'It *"fits"*, that's all,' she said.

Was she still talking of Faith? He had forgotten. He drained his Alka-Seltzer glass and sighed.

'Giles.'

'Yes.'

'It isn't that I don't know that you have had a very *hard* life, and you have had to suffer more than I can understand ...'

'Well?'

'You can't go on and on just letting it get you down. I know you're depressed –'

'Depressed!'

'There you go.'

'What do you mean?'

'That tone of voice. You weren't really very cheerful or friendly yesterday, were you?'

The words shot through him little stabs of embarrassment. He had assumed in some thoughtless way that his rather silent behaviour would go unnoticed.

'I think Brenda wondered if we'd offended you or something, you were so quiet at supper.'

'I'm sorry. It wasn't that I didn't enjoy myself.'

'Oh, Giles.'

He felt her moving closer to him, and holding his pyjama-clad, thin little body in her ample arms. He had felt, until this weekend in Cambridge, so much in control. Now, everything was changed.

'You know that I love you,' she whispered. This seemed to be a reply to his fumbling towards her breasts. Already, to his disappointment, she was dressed. The easily explorable nylon nightdress had been replaced with a thick, much-buttoned cardigan, and a string of beads, and a skirt which went down over her knees.

'Kiss me,' he replied.

It was as full a kiss as they had enjoyed since her proposal of marriage ten days before.

'Do you want just coffee and toast,' she said, disengaging herself, 'or shall I boil you an egg? Brenda gets free-range ones from some nuns.'

VII

Peverill stood in Monty's drawing-room clutching a bottle labelled 'Gun Dog'. It was a kind of sherry. His father had gone back by train the previous night, having bought him dinner at the Foley Arms. But there were a sprinkling of parents dotted about the room, whom Meg, Monty and the house tutors and their wives were seeking to keep amused.

Stuffy Smith's voice, louder than most people's, was saying to a man with glasses, 'No, I think you need three Bs for Bristol; at least three Bs.'

And Mrs Stuffy Smith, referring perhaps, Tibba thought, to some public functionary, rather than a person at the school, was saying, 'I think she's doing an absolutely splendid job. The only way to get inflation down is to be tough.'

Tibba wondered if Peverill was meant to have just taken the sherry bottle, and to be filling up people's glasses (and his own) as if he were the host ('hosting', people now said, to her father's annoyance). Meg was talking to a red-haired lady from Barnes about Voluntary Service Overseas. Monty was discoursing on what he called 'the arcane mysteries of Oxbridge' to another parent. Tibba was in distinct danger of being left on her own to talk to Peverill, had it not been for the Old Panghamian Bishop who had advanced on her before she had a chance to escape.

'And you are?' he inquired.

She stared at the prelate helplessly. He was not particularly prelatical in appearance. He wore a light grey suit and an ordinary celluloid collar like any other parson. The only difference was that the shirt thing was a rather ugly pinkish purple and he wore round his neck what Tibba thought might be a hearing aid, but which she recognized at last as a cross on a chain.

However much the bishop beamed at her, she did not feel able to get out the first syllable of her reply.

'Mr and Mrs Gore's . . .' the bishop prompted.

Niece was all that she had to say, but she hadn't time before the bishop had done her work for her with 'daughter? Jolly dee.'

She was so speechless that she could see the poor man beginning to wonder whether she was completely dumb, and, if mute, perhaps stone deaf as well. A condescending deliberation entered his tones, as he said, unnecessarily distinctly, 'And do you go to school in Pangham?'

She shook her head.

'Nearby?'

'London,' she said. Her interlocutor looked relieved that she was at least capable of speech.

'But just home for the week-end?'

Peverill had come round with the Gun Dog before she needed to attempt a reply to this.

'Ah, Piers,' said the bishop, who had already taken a shine to the boy. 'You read that first lesson wonderfully.'

'Thank you very much, sir.'

Tibba was not sure that you were meant to call bishops *sir*. But Peverill's charm had clearly worked on the suffragan of Devizes.

'Splendid stuff, the Book of Joshua,' added the bishop.

Tibba, to whom Matins had been excruciating, thought that Peverill had read the lesson disgracefully badly and that, if it came to that, the bishop's sermon had been about the most tedious twenty minutes of the year. But she could not, of course, say so.

'Let me fill up your glass, sir.'

'Ah, good man, Piers. Wine that maketh glad the heart of man, you know.' It was an unnatural, booming laugh that he let out.

'How about you, Fox?'

Tibba had been successfully avoiding Peverill ever since his remark, the previous day, about her legs. Of course, she couldn't care less about the stupid boy's vulgar comments. The fact that she was now wearing her corduroy trousers was, she had insisted on telling herself, simply because it was a cold day. She knew, from Meg's glances before they had set out for chapel, that she was expected to put on her 'one nice dress'. But, for reasons no longer clear to her, she had decided to swathe her legs in brown corduroy and wear a Shetland jumper. One got fed up, she had told herself, with wearing a skirt every day to school. Trousers were her usual (anyway her frequent) wear on Saturdays and Sundays.

She allowed Peverill to pour some more Gun Dog into her glass. She could not help admiring his special aplomb, the way in which he charmed this futile little bishop.

'You'll be going up to University soon, I expect,' the bishop asked her.

'No fear,' said Peverill. 'I've got the next five years planned out. My dad's going to fix me up with a business course in America when I leave this place. Then a year or two in the City.'

'Indeed?' Since Tibba seemed unwilling to give any account of her own plans, it was only natural that the bishop should express interest in Peverill's arrangements.

'I'd like to go into Parliament,' the boy continued. 'But it's a good thing to have a firm footing in the business world first.'

'I couldn't agree more,' said the bishop. 'If only more young people like you felt public-spirited enough to contemplate a political career. I'm awfully excited by this new party myself. It's time we broke the mould.'

'I shall vote for them,' said Meg gaily, as she led up a parent to be introduced. 'Bishop, this is Mrs Greatorex. I believe she knew you when you were at Chelmsford.'

Peverill had made no effort to affirm or deny his interest in the new party. Tibba did not know that there was one; nor had she heard of the mould which was in such apparent need of destruction.

'It's a pity your father had to go yesterday, Peverill,' said Meg. 'He'll have to send someone for the car.'

'He wants me to drive it back to London tonight,' Peverill said. 'Didn't he mention it? He said he'd square it with your husband.'

Meg gazed desperately across the room to where Monty was guffawing with mirth and stuffing into his mouth a cheeselet, proffered by the nervous father of one of the new boys. It seemed hardly the moment to start an argument about the MG. She was profoundly angered by the sight of it parked in her drive, and she very much hoped that Monty had not agreed to let Peverill drive it. The notion that Sir Anthony had 'squared' her husband seemed profoundly insolent.

'We pulverized Talbot's yesterday, anyway,' said Peverill. It was the third or fourth time that morning that he had mentioned their victory in the House Matches. He could not know how, over their Ovaltine the previous evening, Monty had told Meg and Tibba that he had almost been hoping his own House would lose, just to 'pull that bloody boy down a peg or two'. The dwindling daylight on Saturday afternoon had been spent on the touchline, Meg in a headscarf and Barbour, cheering whenever Gore's did well; Monty himself running up and down to keep level with the game and shouting out esoteric advice which was Double-Dutch to Tibba. 'Feet, feet, feet. Now pass! Well done, H-Squared. Pass, boy! Now, bunch and take, bunch and take!' Thus it had gone on until the same little boy who had announced luncheon, now blue with cold, had carried an enamel bowl of sliced oranges on to the field for the players' refreshment.

Tibba had, in spite of herself, found the game rather exciting. She had no notion of what the rules might be. But it was impossible not to admire the barbaric forcefulness with which Peverill (something the worse for his big lunch) had spurred his side on to victory, scoring two of the tries himself. Afterwards, when the boys all came off the field, drenched with mud and sweat, and clapping each other on the back for their part in the game, it had seemed almost like a moment in *Coriolanus*, which she had done the previous year. She recalled the vigour with which Miss Russenberger declaimed the lines:

> See him pluck Aufidius down by the hair,
> As children from a bear, the Volsces shunning him:
> Methinks I see him stamp thus, and call thus:
> 'Come on you cowards! you were got in fear
> Though you were born in Rome . . .'

Peverill's demeanour on the pitch had not been at all unlike that. There was something, perhaps, a little churlish about Meg's refusal to congratulate him. Tibba heard herself saying, 'You were the hero of the match.'

'But of course.' He laughed as he said it, and closed his eyes without much irony concealing the conceit.

'I wish these people would go,' said Meg *sotto voce*.

As one looked around the room, there were still a dispiriting number hanging on, even though most parents had taken the hint and departed when their sherry glass was not refilled. Stuffy Smith was still stuck with the man with glasses, explaining something called Conditional Offers, and showed no signs of stopping. The common ground of Chelmsford, likewise, looked as though it could occupy the bishop and Mrs Greatorex all day unless someone moved in to stop them.

'I hate to break anything up,' Meg suddenly said in a rather forceful voice, 'but the bishop has got to be over at School Field in five minutes.'

'Gosh, is that the time!' said he of apostolic consecration. 'How wonderful to have such an efficient social secretary.'

Meg – for the bishop was quite a small man – stood behind him and pointed down at his head as a signal for the Stuffy Smiths to hurry up and take him away.

While she did so, Peverill said to Tibba, 'I'm afraid I ought to be going to have lunch too.'

She smiled at him. Just for a moment, there was a very faint trace of courtesy in his voice.

'I'll come round afterwards and see you, Fox.'

'I'm not really called Fox, you know,' she said seriously.

'About two-thirty – or is Ruddy G. going to take you out for a ten-mile walk? Then we could say goodbye properly.'

She smiled again. A hike was all too probable, unless it continued to pour down in such buckets.

He did not make any further ceremony about his departure from the room, beyond putting the empty Gun Dog bottle on the polished table by the telephone. She wondered why on earth she should want to 'say goodbye properly': and what he meant by the phrase. But such an ambition had formed itself in her brain by the time Monty had shooed the last of his guests out of the front door and they were settled down over the roast beef and Yorkshire pudding.

While they munched the rather tough beef, Meg and Monty chattered like monkeys. Tibba simply wasn't used to their level of good humour, and she was not interested in their subjects of conversation. She found her mind drifting off into little private conversations of her own while her aunt's voice and her uncle's grin enveloped the atmosphere of the luncheon.

'Quite a nice bish.'

'A jolly good egg,' Monty grinned.

'There aren't as many OP bishops as there were. I don't know why it should be.'

'Only plebs become parsons these days.'

'Let's go away!' said Captain de Courcy.

'But where? I sit – a plate of Yorkshire pudding before me. This morning, I sat – and there were eggs. I try to write – but the words won't come. I try to speak – and they don't come either. But if we were alone . . .'

'We could go to Rodmell, and eat tongue and drink lemonade.'

'And afterwards we could smoke cigars and read Sir Thomas Browne.'

'I think a lot of the trouble is that they are selling off all the old rectories,' said Meg, rudely interrupting. 'In the old days if a nice girl married a parson, she at least knew she'd get a decent house even if they couldn't afford to heat it properly . . .'

'I love you so much that I can't bear it.'

'I love you too,' said the Captain – at last: the words had never been said between them before, so explicitly. 'Haven't you guessed, you old donkey?'

'Even in the early days?'

'From the moment you came to see me.'

'What was it that made you know?'

'But of course if you can't furnish them,' Monty said, 'there's something rather depressing about living in one of these dirty great places. I mean everyone in the old days inherited a bit of furniture. Some of these chaps now haven't got a stick.'

'Why do we feel love, why do we have to? Sometimes it hurts so much that I think I am going to die. And it's all so pointless. Because we shall never be able to get away, never able to . . .'

'Unless we decided to get . . .' How gallantly shy and awkward he was about it, sucking slightly on his moustache.

'Tibbs,' said Meg, 'finish up the roast potatoes. I can't bear them cold.'

'D'you remember how your old dad liked cold roast potatoes?' Monty asked.

'And cold rice pudding. The CRP he called it. He used to have it for breakfast!'

They both chuckled about this. Tibba had never known her grandfather. Giles had never mentioned the CRP, but she had heard about it a thousand times on Meg's lips.

It wasn't a rice pudding. It was a rather nice apple sponge with cream. Monty gave them all huge helpings, which was a good thing. Then he fell to talking about Peverill.

'The bish couldn't get rid of him. Did you see the way he was sucking up, pouring out my sherry . . .'

'He is the *limit*,' said Meg. 'And his father has gone back to London without that sports car.'

'I've told him he mustn't drive it,' said Monty.

'And I wonder how much good *telling* him will be.'

'I don't think he'd risk driving it. The Bodger is very firm on that sort of thing. The strange thing about Peverill is that he knows when to toe the line.'

Tibba remembered this comment later in the afternoon when, out on their walk, they were passed by Peverill in the sports car, roaring along the lane which led down to the station. He waved cheerily to them, the lord of the manor greeting village churls who were only too happy to leap into the hedgerow to avoid the privilege of being run down.

This audacious outrage was not to be an occasion of original eloquence on Monty's part. It was, he averred, the last straw. Meg confirmed that this was it.

The last hours of Tibba's stay with her uncle and aunt were entirely dominated by their attempts to have Peverill dismissed from the school on the spot.

'It's extraordinary,' said Monty, coming back from a telephone-call in which he had successfully disturbed the headmaster's Sunday afternoon repose.

'What did the Bodger say?' was Meg's anxious request.

'He said you can't get rid of a boy like Peverill *just like that*.'

'But it's a major offence, driving a car. The Bodger is always going on about it.'

'I know he is. But you see' – Monty's grin became almost ape-like in its pathos – 'he's right in a way. There'd be a hell of a hullaballoo if we just gave old Pevvers the boot. There'll have to be some sort of arrangement with Sir Anthony . . .'

'Arrangement? But you said . . .'

Tibba couldn't listen to it. It was too involved, too local. At the same time, in an odd way, she couldn't sympathize. Why should they dislike Peverill so very much? It was amusing, rather, to have him about: she hated to admit that she had enjoyed anything without Captain de Courcy; but she had enjoyed this visit to Pangham more than any previous ones.

'Look,' said Monty, coming up to her in the hall, 'we're neglecting you.'

'I'm driving her to the station in a moment,' said Meg.

'In what?' asked Monty.

'In a moment.'

'No, I mean in what vehicle? A wheelbarrow?'

'I'd forgotten about the Humber.'

'I can easily walk,' said Tibba.

'We'll wander down with you,' said Monty. It was extraordinary. His hand had slid round to the base of her spine, even as he spoke, with Meg standing there smiling. It made Tibba feel extraordinarily uncomfortable in their presence. She wanted to run out of the house like Cathy Earnshaw and let the rain sweep across her hot flushed cheeks. She said, 'There's really no need.'

'Seems *awful*,' said Monty. He was patting now; patting the bottom. For some reason then she felt she would do anything to escape. The bag was packed, the coat was hanging there on the hatstand in the hall.

'I don't mind waiting at the station,' she said abruptly, 'and you have this Pe –'

'Well I hope when we next see you it will all have worked out,' said Meg, looking down at the floor. 'There's been so much about Peverill this week-end that we've hardly talked about the family . . .'

And she suddenly began to pour out information about Helen, her daughter, the much-loved grandson, Daniel; if Tibba had let her, she would have gone on about her sons, the boys Giles always dismissed as 'those rough cousins of yours'.

Although it was still raining, and her shoes were still soaked from their walk, Tibba was happy when she had been kissed for the last time and allowed out.

It was not that she did not love Meg; it was impossible not to. She loved Monty, too, as she thought of it, 'technically'. But the embarrassment of having her bottom touched by him drove all other thoughts out of her head, and she scampered, rather than walked, down to the station.

Nobody seemed to be waiting to inspect her ticket. The place wore such a deserted air that it was hard to believe that the London train would ever draw up at the platform. She wandered out into the yard again to look at the timetable. 16.22. What was that?

'You didn't turn up, Fox,' said Peverill. She jumped at the words, but she didn't feel altogether surprised to see him.

'I couldn't,' she said.

'Ten-mile hike?'

'Something like that.'

'I saw you.'

'Look, you're in fearful trouble,' she said with sudden earnestness.

'Oh dear, what's up?'

'Don't you know you aren't supposed to drive?'

'I told you. Dad squared it with Ruddy G.'

'Uncle Monty doesn't seem to think so. He's in a fearful bate; he's been ringing up the headmaster and everything.'

As they spoke, it had not occurred to Tibba to do anything but stroll along at Peverill's side. They had now reached the offending object, red and glistening by the kerb.

With unwonted courtesy, Peverill held open the door. She sniggered. It was impossible not to find his outrageous cheek disarming.

'I'll miss my train,' she said.

'That's the idea,' he said. 'I'll drive you back to London.'

Tibba thought how angry Meg would be at the very suggestion. She thought of what a waste it was not to use her return ticket on the train. She thought of the next morning when Chantal and Rosemary would be discussing their week-ends and their boyfriends.

She tried to make her 'Okay' sound casual, as she threw her bag over the back of her seat and slunk down into the car. It felt extraordinarily low compared with other cars she had been in; almost as if she was sitting down on the road.

Peverill's heels clomped in a military way on the tarmac as he walked round to his side of the car. When he had slithered into the driving-seat he leant over her so that their faces almost touched. She froze. Not *that*. Not so soon.

'Please don't,' she said.

'I'm only putting your belt right,' he smiled. 'Don't worry Fox, I'm not going to eat you.' As he spoke she smelt his breath which was sweet, like honey.

It was true that all he did was to stretch the seat belt across her chest and click it into place. But she did not know what he might not have tried to do if she had not been firm. The car started up with a deep roar and they shot off towards the motorway.

'Did you notice that?' he bellowed at last.

'What?'

'A sort of noise.'

Tibba had not noticed anything except that they were going very fast. As shades of evening fell, fences, houses and street lamps seemed to whizz past at a greater and greater pace.

'I don't think we're firing on all cylinders,' said Peverill.

'I'm all right, thank you,' Tibba shouted back. Conversation was really rather difficult against the roar of the engine.

When the motorway was reached, it was dark and the rain was coming down harder than ever. She wondered at the way in which Peverill could drive the car at such speed, with the added distraction of flashing lights on the hissing surface of the road. She watched the little speed-clock by the steering-wheel register eighty, ninety and finally a hundred miles an hour. The speed was thrilling. She felt her legs turning to jelly with it. Few experiences in life had ever been so wonderfully liberating. It had all the thrill of some fairground device – the big dipper or the helter-skelter – with the added, dreamy sense of escape. As they sped on through the dark, Tibba forgot that they were just driving back to London. It felt as though they were flying through time on a winged horse.

'Scared?' Peverill yelled, as the clock started to show 110.

'No!'

He liked the way her eyes were ablaze with excitement. As she sat back in her seat, chewing the end of a small piece of hair, only her eyes were really visible, and the elegance of her firm profile against the flashing lights of the window.

They passed signs for Wantage, and then, in next to no time, Newbury. Peverill stayed in the fast lane all the time, unless he happened to come up behind some slow-coach driving at a mere eighty or ninety. In which case, he dodged past them on the wrong side, laughing if angry motorists honked their horns or flashed their lamps as he sped by. Tibba hoped that he was not drunk.

It was beyond Newbury that the whirring, or roaring, got worse and Tibba thought she smelt burning.

'Is everything all right?' she yelled.

'As I say, I'm not sure we're firing on all cylinders.'

It smelt as if they were firing all too many. At least Peverill seemed to be slowing down. They were only doing sixty now, and he had stopped swerving about from lane to lane.

'Shit,' he said, unnecessarily.

Tibba had never heard the word. She had seen it written and remarked its ugliness. She knew that it meant excrement, but that it had a metaphorical application to persons. Now, she gathered, it could be used as a common expletive. It seemed no less ugly said than written.

The car had begun to shake and hiss. It was smoke, and not fog which clouded the windscreen as they juddered and shook on to the hard shoulder. Tibba wondered if they were about to blow up.

Giles made a conscious effort to be biddable, friendly, *nice* that Sunday. He had listened to music on the wireless while Miss Agar went to mass with her friars. Afterwards, they had luncheon at something she called (presumably its accepted appellation) the University Centre. He could not understand why the word centre (presumably imported from America) had come to describe such a wide range of distinct places: shops, offices, restaurants, and now, in this case, a club of sorts. There was nothing, particularly, central about it. They clambered down

Little St Mary's Lane towards the river, arm in arm, in order to get to it. Inside, it echoed like a cave. But they were able to recline in armchairs and drink. Their host was, to judge from his tones, a Yorkshireman. Giles had not heard his name before, even though they worked in a similar field of philology.

It had been much the most comfortable and civilized of the social encounters Cambridge had offered. The food was served in a 'cafeteria', which Giles found himself unable to cope with, so he was put at a table while they chose for him. It was what you would have expected from a cafeteria. Miss Agar brought him chicken and chips followed by jelly; a slightly childish repast, it seemed, but they were both quite palatable. Their host had had a range of decent topics of conversation. Miss Agar had fallen rather quiet while he and Giles talked about Italian opera-houses.

When they parted from the Yorkshireman, Giles, having affected good humour since breakfast, found that his spirits had, in fact, lifted. He contemptuously pretended that it was the prospect of leaving his old university once more which lightened his spirits. But as they took a final turn along the river, Miss Agar squeezed him with joy.

'It's been such a lovely week-end,' she said. 'The most wonderful week-end of my life.'

'It makes me afraid, you know, that you allow your happiness to depend on me,' he said.

'Don't be afraid. You think I'm just a silly inexperienced child.'

'Now, Louise, I never said –'

'You did.' There was nothing ill-tempered about her contradiction of him. 'You said I hadn't had any experience.'

'That was somewhat different.'

His prim little conversational adjustments amused and charmed her so much that she always wanted to hug him the more when he gave them utterance.

'I know you think I'm a baby,' she continued gaily, 'and I probably am. You should have seen the look on your face when I brought you jelly for lunch.'

They both laughed before the *tactlessness* of her comment could sink in. And when it *did* sink in, they laughed again, and Giles kissed her, because he had never imagined that it would be possible to find anything funny about being blind.

'I don't see what's so marvellous about the so-called grown-up world, anyway,' she said.

'Now, you're being self-conscious,' he said. 'Stop it or it will develop into affectation.'

'But you needn't worry about me, Giles. That's what I mean. I'm stronger than you think.'

'How do you know what I think?'

'I don't. But I know enough of what you think. You think that I'm just childishly in love with you, and it pleases you to think so, because it makes you feel superior to me. You aren't in love with me ...'

'Louise –'

'No, you aren't. You like being adored, but you aren't in love. But I *am* in love with you. It isn't just a silly little fantasy, you know. I really do love you – for what you are. And you can't stop me doing so by warning me that it might make me unhappy.'

'I didn't say that either.'

'You did.'

She paused, and kissed him fully on the lips.

'I wanted to make love to you last night,' he said.

She merely laughed and walked rather briskly on, tugging at his hand.

After that, they wandered back to Brenda's house, made appropriate farewells, and bundled their luggage into the taxi, railway-bound.

'The truth is,' said Giles, as the train started, 'that I never really *liked* Cambridge.'

'I loved it. I still do.'

'The young build up expectations which can't possibly be satisfied.'

'You'd never be satisfied,' she said crossly. He heard a rustling and knew that she was reading a newspaper.

The smell of Liverpool Street did him good. Home was not twenty minutes away. Tibba would be there. A toasted bun. A chapter of Scott.

He wondered what to do about Miss Agar. It would give Tibba no pleasure if the research assistant were invited home. On the other hand, it would have been discourteous not to suggest that she came in for the single cup. Moreover, he found in himself a desire to perpetuate their coagmentation for as long as was socially feasible.

'You'll come in for tea?' he said.

Since they seemed to be sharing a taxi, the question came inevitably.

'I must ring mother,' said Miss Agar.

'Apart from anything else,' said Giles, ignoring the allusion to Northwood Hills, 'we have said nothing all day about the *Tretis*.'

His draft introduction to the work would, since the visit to Trinity on Saturday morning, require a minute emendation on page xlvii where he discussed evidence of early Kentish formations in the language of the Trinity scribe; evidence scotched by Miss Agar's eagle-eye, which felt certain that he spelt the word kiss *kisse* and not, as Giles had supposed, *kesse*. *Thow noldest nimme thaet cluppunge and kisse of thi leofman, nat of fleschli pruckunge but a gastliche kisse from the sweote wordes of the muthe of Gode* – a muddled sentence, made inelegant by its double negatives, but which she, in her translation, rendered, *The embrace and kiss of thy lover will be of no carnal kind, but in the form of a spiritual kiss, formed from the sweet words of God's mouth.*

'We'll have finished soon,' she said.

'In three weeks,' he said. 'It could not take us longer now.'

They said no more as the taxi wound its way the short distance north-west. Miss Agar sighed. Three weeks was such a very short time, and she felt by no means certain, yet, of Giles's affection for her. Cambridge had been, from that point of view, a chilling experience. She *had* childishly assumed, that first day of her declaration in Hermit Street, when Giles had kissed her with a vigour so far from *gastliche* or spiritual, that he loved her as she loved him. It had all seemed too good to be true, but she had still thought it *was* true. How quickly, since love had been confessed, she had come to sense the complexities in his nature. Almost nothing had been *said* between them, concerning his feelings, concerning his past; still less had been made of plans for the future. Unspoken, hanging before them, was the delivery of the typescript to the Early English Text Society. After that, there would be no further excuse for them to meet. Explanations would have to be made to Tibba.

It now occurred to her that his initial desire to keep their 'courtship' secret had been a little disingenuous. She felt, on the strength of two days with him, that she could size him up a little more dispassionately. He had been biding his time. She saw that now, as they drew up outside the dark little house.

'Ring,' he said, when the taxi had been paid. 'Tibba will let us in.'

'The house looks rather deserted,' said Miss Agar. She so much hoped that this was not going to be a trick. It would spoil the week-end, if Giles tried to lure her into taking her clothes off and being silly, when they had had, on the whole, such a nice time.

'I must ring mother,' she repeated.

'You must ring the door-bell first,' said Giles. 'Tibba will have made some tea by now.'

'I wish you'd l-l-let me catch the train.'

'Don't go on about it, Fox, for heaven's sake.'

'I'm cold.'

'It's better than being burnt alive.'

'What's the time?'

'Only seven-twenty.'

'But it was six when you telephoned.'

'He said they might be a bit of time.'

Other cars, more fortunate, rushed, swished, thundered past them as they sat, cold and vulnerable, in the conked-out MG. It was hard not to feel that Peverill was to blame, though he could not have wanted the car to go wrong.

'That's really the last thing I feel like,' she said, as he slid his hand over her thigh in the darkness. The sentence had a wordly sound to it, as though there *were* times when it might be the first thing she felt like.

'You're rather beautiful you know, Fox.'

'So you said.'

Leaning over to kiss her was not all that easy. She did not struggle when he put his lips to hers. She simply sat there icily, not responding in any way. He found it more disconcerting than being slapped down, and he soon stopped his fumbling about in the dark.

'Like a sweet?' he asked. It seemed rather a come-down, after his romantic endeavours, to be proffering a little roll of peppermints. 'I've run out of cigarettes rather annoyingly.'

'I don't smoke anyway,' she said. 'I consider it a disgusting habit.'

'You aren't in a bate, are you, Fox?'

There was no answer to this. She sucked hard on her peppermint, gazing out at the rain, and the dark, and the unrelenting ugliness of the motorway.

'Are you sure there isn't a note; nothing to indicate where she is? Look again. Look on the chimney-piece.'

'There's nothing, Giles.'

A note would certainly have been conspicuous in the Hermit Street house. It had a bare, uncosy feel to it. Miss Agar had never seen rooms with so little furniture, almost none of it upholstered. She had grown accustomed to the study where she worked with Giles: a carpeted room containing nothing except a large mahogany table, fitted bookshelves and four upright dining-chairs. The kitchen, where she had been entertained for tea, was, likewise, not a place where one would expect much padded upholstery. The little parlour, however, where Giles had expected Tibba to be waiting, was a sanctum which Miss Agar had never penetrated. She was astonished by it. There was no carpet. A circle of spindly, but uncomfortable, little chairs surrounded a tiny grate. It seemed like a room in a museum, not a place to be comfy in; a room where you could imagine someone having written *Rasselas* or the *Letters of Junius*.

'Look upstairs!' Giles urged. 'Look in the bedrooms.'

So she did: and once more, beyond three of the doors she turned, she was confronted with a complete nullibiety of domestic reassurances, an atmosphere where her own gestures towards decorative enlivenment (a poster of Winnie the Pooh stuck on here and there with Blu-Tack) would seem not merely childish but alien. She gulped. Climbing the stairs, she had expected a revelation, even if only a minor one: a sight of Giles's dressing-table, some trace of idiosyncratic untidiness, a pair of slippers lying at an angle by some bed. No such trace survived. In each room she entered, there was the same absence of recognizable personality: here was only the spindly beauty of iron bedsteads, or Jane Austenish grates in which there might be room for, at most, three pieces of coal. It was impossible to tell which of the rooms, if any, were inhabited at all; still less was it possible to know which of them was 'Giles's room'.

The truth, unknown to Miss Agar, was that Giles did not have a room. The three rooms which contained beds were kept as alike as possible so that he could sleep in any of them at whim. The large wardrobe in the annex to the bathroom was the closest he came to having a dressing-room. He had few clothes, and did not go in for a wide choice of cuff-links, neck-ties or shoes. Since reading had ceased to be a part of his existence, there was no reason for him to accumulate clutter; there being no reason, Giles did not do so. The enforced anonymity of these beautiful, unreformed rooms, looking much as intended by the architect who designed them in 1824, told Miss Agar nothing. She had never seen rooms so bare, so stark, so unfeeling. To throw open the door of Tibba's bedroom was, therefore, to receive an exaggerated impression of the girl's personality. For this was the first, and the only, room in the house where there seemed a trace of human habitation: habitation, at least, since the days of William IV.

The bed was thrown together rather than made, and covered with a patchwork quilt that belonged to different traditions of simplicity to those of the Regency. There seemed something Hardyesque about it, a quilt in which Tess of the d'Urbervilles might have committed uncleanness; or Jude the Obscure's children slept their final sleep.

The walls! They were the first touch of colour in the house! An egg-yellow, with pretty, splashy curtains. The contrast was so absolute between this and other parts of the house that it felt like bustling in upon forbidden territory; like opening a private journal or reading someone else's letters. Giles's personality was nowhere in evidence in his room (whichever that was); but Tibba's personality was traced, or so it seemed to Miss Agar, in almost every detail of the room's decoration. On poster hangers, a large photograph of Virginia Woolf was suspended from the delicate red picture-rail: it was a side view of a young, lean-necked, spotlessly beautiful woman. The shelves contained a complete set of much-thumbed grey paperbacks, the works of Mrs Woolf, some Shakespeare, the poems of Stevie Smith, Alistair Cooke's – rather incongruously – *America*.

'No sign of her?' Giles called up.

There seemed so many signs of her that it seemed wrong to shout back, 'No!'

'This is extraordinary.'

'I'll wait with you – if you would like that,' she said. Once home again, with his coat off, he seemed sharper, and larger. The house, she realized, was in scale.

'So that perhaps if I could ring my mother ...' she said awkwardly.

Giles sat tensely while communication was made with North-wood Hills. His perfectly manicured nails drummed the crisp creases of his trouser knees. His lips were taut, and, in their anxiety, thin.

'Anything might have happened, anything,' he said.

Miss Agar had been slow to appreciate what was always clear to Giles, the infinitude of life's depressing possibilities. Each of the potential calamities listed in Giles's cold, precise tones, came as surprises to her. She had begun to share only in a vague sense of unease. Her mind had not worked its way, with Giles's swift precision, to his sense that 'her train might have crashed; she might have been kidnapped; she might have been raped.' Between each phrase he paused. Miss Agar did not know whether she was to agree that these things were all too likely, or whether the silence was intended to be broken by her own protestations of certainty that Tibba was safe. 'She might have foolishly attempted to walk from some bus stop instead of taking a taxi. I have told her repeatedly that I do not like her to walk the streets of London.'

'There may be some other explanation,' said Miss Agar.

'There may,' said Giles. 'She could have been run over by a drunken motorcyclist and left for dead in the gutter; or she could have been seized with a violent attack of appendicitis and, at this moment, be lying, gasping, in some darkened side-street, unable to call for medical assistance . . .'

Both these suggestions were so specific in their fears that Miss Agar believed them. They made her acutely sad. She did not immediately consider that they could not both be true. They had such a deadly circumstantial quality to them that some sinking feeling in her stomach allowed her to enter into, rather than console, Giles's misery.

'It is only to be expected, perhaps,' said Giles.

'What is?' This could not mean what it appeared to mean.

'I have lost everything else,' said Giles calmly. 'Why should I be allowed the companionship of the one person left to me in the world?'

After these hours together, Miss Agar felt that the exclusiveness of his remarks was unnecessarily cruel. He had a right to be anxious about Tibba; but not, surely, any need to persecute her on account of the girl's absence.

'The only person whose companionship means anything to me at all,' he repeated to the chilly silence.

'We don't know . . .' Miss Agar was so shocked that she could not finish her sentence. She wanted to protest at his cruelty. Was he now rejecting her love? 'We don't know that she has left your sister's,' was eventually said.

'We don't.' Giles conceded the point without enthusiasm. 'But had she remained in Pangham any longer than expected, we should certainly have been informed.'

'But you have been back only half an hour. We do not know that your sister has not been trying to ring you up all week-end.'

'That is less than probable.'

'But your sister might know *something*.'

'That, again, shows how little you know my sister.'

He was prevailed upon, nevertheless, to lift the instrument and speak into it when Meg answered. Miss Agar heard merely, 'It is now nearly eight o'clock ... And by your timing ... Precisely. Which means she has been lost for at least three hours ... And you definitely saw her step on to the train? You *didn't* ... No, merely a strange detail to have withheld, in the circumstances ... I fail to see what difference it makes whether you were deliberate in your failure to mention it ... But of course. Police, hospitals, everything. With Carol, the police were kind enough to come to my door. When Mary died, I was summoned to the hospital ... I don't see the logic of that; being seventeen does not, as far as I have heard, render a girl immune from mortality ... It is events, not I, which are depressing ... Of course; and if you hear, similarly ... I am glad ... Send mine to him ... Goodbye.'

How odd that the crisis, such it had become, was making Giles harden into a caricature of himself. Miss Agar, for all her longings, had never had a sister. If she had one, she felt sure she would not have spoken to her as Giles had addressed, in those minutes, the instrument. There seemed no familiarity in his tone towards the sibling.

'She's left Pangham then?' Miss Agar asked.

'Evidently. My conviction is that she is dead, but that is because of my experiences.'

Miss Agar realized that she knew none of Giles's life in detail. She had always been too polite to ask about it. She had gathered

from Tibba that her mother was dead; it was that information
that had inspired her with the confidence to make her proposal
of matrimony. She knew nothing of the Carol episode, still less,
of course, of the evenings of music, noodles and fornication
which had preceded it. She had come on the scene not merely
late, but a-tiptoe, hoping to pick up all she needed to know of
Giles's history by inference.

'Tell me your experiences, tell me why you are so bitter,' she
said.

'There is really nothing to tell.'

'Who was Carol?'

'You do not know?'

And he told her a long version of the story. It was not a
continuous narrative. For, as it proceeded, she gained in confidence, and began to ask questions: 'So you've only been blind
five years?' ... 'But wait, when did Mary die?' he was affronted
by none of the inquiries. He expressed no surprise about her
previous lack of curiosity, no assertion that it might seem odd
to propose marriage to a man you know nothing about. She
dreaded some such reproach. Whether delivered in playful or
acid tone, it would still make her seem, and feel, foolish. But no
such reproach was proffered or intended. He wanted, for once,
only to tell; she merely to learn. This seemed suddenly a higher
need than the importance of discovering Tibba. Giles was, in any
case, insistent that there was nothing, in relation to Tibba, that
could be done. As his tale unfolded, Miss Agar came to recognize
what he had meant by saying that, 'With Carol, the police were
kind enough to come to my door.' It must have been extraordinary to lose his second wife so suddenly, and by the arbitrary
operation of a motor-car. The news that he had *had* a second wife
surprised her in the extent to which she was not upset by it. She
surely should have *known*. And yet the figure of Carol had never
been mentioned, never cropped up. There were no pictures of her
in the house: what use would that have been to Giles? Nothing
of hers, if it remained, seemed distinctively hers. She was gone;
and he did little to bring her to life. He described her as 'one of

the kindest women I have ever known; I wish you had been able to know each other.'

How was one to take this? For, if they had known each other, it would not have occurred to Miss Agar to claim Giles as a husband. It seemed a chilling, off-putting wish when first considered. And yet, equally, there was a hint of intimacy in it.

'She was also extremely beautiful,' Giles said. 'I know that, even though I did not see her.'

'How?'

'Sit nearer. Because it is in the same way that I know you are beautiful.'

She glowed with an intensity of emotion which was so strong that she did not know whether it was painful or pleasurable. There seemed no answer to it. To be thought beautiful was something she had abandoned any hope of. Yet to be thought beautiful by a blind man was not merely – at best – a dubious compliment; it had with it a pathetic sense that she was deceiving him.

'You mustn't think that,' she said honestly. 'I'm not. I'm afraid if you could see me you wouldn't . . .'

'I can't see you. I will never be able to see you. Isn't that obvious?'

'Yes, but *if*.'

'There are no ifs. How can you mock me by saying things like *If I could see you . . .?*'

'I am not mocking you, Giles, but it's just that I don't want you to be deceived. You see,' she giggled, 'I'm not really a great beauty.'

'I don't want to hear your own vain or silly opinions, any more than I want your cruel speculations about whether, if I had my sight, I would form this or that opinion. I was merely expressing a fact, which is that I find you beautiful. The ability to perceive beauty seems a purely visual thing when you have eyes. But when you lose your sight, you still go on perceiving beauty; not merely moral beauty, or the beauties of sound and sense. Please do not contradict me because you could not possibly know what

I was talking about. Any more than I could possibly know what you are talking about when you say you believe in God.'

The story of his life, which these remarks almost concluded, was interrupted by the telephone ringing. The slight colour remaining in his cheeks vanished as he went to the instrument.

'Yes? . . . Yes it is . . You *have*? Thank you.'

It was replaced. The brevity of the conversation told Miss Agar nothing: neither who was ringing, nor from where. But the relief which spread over his face beneath the shadow of the dark glasses was obvious. The creases round his mouth relaxed. He smiled helplessly.

'It was Tibba,' he explained.

'But where *was* she?'

'She had been having supper with some friends,' said Giles.

Momentarily, all his former anxiety on his daughter's behalf seemed contemptible. He pursed his lips and sat upright. He heard the clock tick. He thought only of Tibba. His confession to Miss Agar had been brutal because it was true. His sense, knowledge, that Miss Agar was of an overwhelming comeliness – those pudgy hands! – could scarcely blot out the bleakness of the truth that Tibba was all in all to him. Such a devotion was what would be called 'unrealistic'. It would be thought that she 'had her own life'; a hypothesis probably true. But he had been unable to disguise the anguish that her removal would cause him; an anxiety which, perhaps, no substitute could assuage. For she was the last survivor of those old happy times. And it was with Tibba, Tibba alone, that he could redeem his wasted years.

The reflexion led him into a silence which made him half forget Miss Agar's presence in the room. Yet it must have been a sympathetic silence, not to say telepathic, for she broke it with, 'Does Tibba know nothing about us?'

What was there to know? That Miss Agar had declared affection; that, physically, this was reciprocated? Her expectations were firmer, less realistic than his. How could Tibba know anything of this?

'Tibba knows nothing,' he averred.

'It seems dishonest; it will make it so much harder for her when we do tell her.'

The knowledge that the girl was on her way inspired this sudden desire to get things straight; but it also made any extended discussion of the matter inappropriate.

'It must be faced,' Giles said, 'that Tibba will not be pleased if she is told. Do you not think that we should wait until there is something to tell?'

'But Giles – there *is*.'

'I am not sure.'

Miss Agar stared at him, panic-stricken. 'What aren't you sure of, Giles? If you mean you aren't sure of your affections, I understand that. I can wait. I will wait, until love has grown.'

'You speak of love as if it were a potato. These horticultural metaphors mean singularly little to me.'

'Please, Giles, don't be cruel after our lovely week-end.'

Had it, after all, been so lovely? Doubts and a quite irrational anger swirled back. He recognized the sensations; unaccountably, it was just like the moments before he had deliberately manufactured altercations with Mary.

'But if things became different, if you were to change your mind . . .'

'You know I never would.'

'I know nothing of the sort. Consider. You knew nothing of my history until tonight. You did not even know how often I had been married. Are we, on such flimsy foundations, to risk –'

'Why do you say flimsy? I have told you how I feel.'

He sighed but he could not answer. The door opened and Tibba entered. Miss Agar looked up at her. She looked quite superbly pretty and young, her cheeks flushed with the cold night air, her loose hair flecked with light rain which looked like dew on a hedgerow. She went to kiss her father, but barely acknowledged Miss Agar's presence in the room.

'We tried to ring you up,' she said. 'But there was no reply. You must have only got back this instant.'

'Louise and I have been waiting rather longer. But you are back, and that is everything.'

At 'Louise', Tibba started. Since when had this endearment been affected? But she had surprise weapons in her own armoury, for she said, 'Mrs Crapper drove me home.'

There seemed no delicate way of responding to this intelligence. Just before making brusque inquiry as to this Crapper's identity, Giles realized that Tibba was not alone.

'M-M-Mrs Crapper, this is my father.'

'Giles, I can't *believe* it!' It was a voice which seemed the worse for cigarettes, but it was not immediately familiar to him. He knew no one of the name of Crapper. 'But how *are* you?'

A figure had borne down upon him. There was a jangling of costume jewellery, an atmosphere of skin lotions and a strong scent of something expensive from a French *parfumier*. The cigarette-weary tones, faintly colonial in emphasis, had taken on the condescending note used by the vulgar to address the afflicted. Even more surprising, he found himself being kissed. Moist, tobacco-odoured lips were being pressed to his own, with what smudges of lipstick he did not care to speculate.

'I didn't know ...' Tibba was clearly surprised by this development. Miss Agar (translated, as the first stage in Tibba's initiation, into Louise) awkwardly held her peace.

'Peggy Chandris,' persisted the voice, 'I'm Piers's mother.'

'And who,' Giles asked, 'is Piers?'

'Anthony – that's my number one – was *idiotic* enough to let P. have the MG to drive up the motorway, if you please! Needless to say, knowing Piers, the big end had to go in some god-awful place like Swindon.'

'It was Reading,' said Tibba. 'The AA drove us to the station at Reading.'

'Just like Piers to have picked up *yet another* beautiful young lady! I got the shock of my *life* when they turned up on my doorstep – hadn't even put my face on. Still, that's what mums are for so I gave them a couple of steaks out of the deep-freeze and here she is to tell the tale.' In spite of this assertion, Mrs

Crapper appeared to have cast herself, and not Tibba, in the role of the tale-bearer. 'Bloody silly thing to do to *let* Piers of all people drive the car; honestly, one pays the *earth* to send them to places like Pangham and then they just let them do as they please. Why in *hell* didn't his housemaster stop him? Of course, when Piers said Tibba here was called Fox I never even *thought*, even though now I look at you together I can see she's the spitting *image*, but fancy, Giles, this is simply glorious after *all these years*. I think it calls for a *very* considerable celebration.'

As her rasping voice grated on, the name of Peggy Chandris slotted itself falsely into place in Giles's brain. She had been one of the three or four girls with whom Mary had shared a flat some twenty years before. Never liked by Mary, and only met by Giles in a gaggle of other girls, never often, his brain had blotted her out, as it eliminated so many early memories of the days when he was, humiliatingly, deeply in love. Now, quite wrongly, he thought she must have belonged to a much later phase of history, to the era of noodles and fornication. Had she been the blonde who shared a flat with a girl called Tamsin in Holland Park Avenue? He rather thought so. It troubled him that he could not remember, however hard he racked his brains, whether Peggy herself had been one of his mistresses or not. All those girls had been fleeting presences in his life: what some would have called 'one-night stands'. He was never so undiscriminating as to suppose that, after a bottle of Valpolicella and a glass of grappa, all girls are alike. But it was disconcerting how they blended together in his memory. It was, as men measure, only eight years, probably less, since his one evening – at most two – in that flat. He was not sure, now he thought about it, that it *was* in Holland Park. Wasn't Tasmin the girl with a 'place' in Hereford Square?

Why not come back to my place for a coffee?

Yes, that was Tamsin. The high vulgarism of placing the indefinite article before the word *coffee* stayed, ludicrously, firm in the mind. So did a memory of Tamsin's breasts as she pulled that thick woolly blue jumper over her head. Peggy had only been there at an earlier stage of the evening. Or was Peggy, after all, Tamsin's friend? Did she belong to a different occasion? Surely, this slightly slobbering, smelly, gin-sodden woman would be remembered if she had been anything more than a passing acquaintance? But it was all before Carol; it was before his blindness; it was probably, too, before fifteen or twenty similar experiences. It was, simply, impossible to keep them all in his head.

'I am very tired,' said Giles.

'Nonsense! I think we should *all* put on our little bonnets, and come back to our place where I've left Piers to switch on the washing-up machine.'

'I ought to be getting back,' said Louise Agar.

'Must you? But come to our place first – I can drive you home. Where do you live?'

Mrs Crapper was not a type of person with whom Miss Agar had ever had to deal. She was, if you weren't used to that sort of thing, rather alarming. It suddenly seemed painfully obvious to Miss Agar that she had been making a mistake. Somewhere, unmentioned even in the long catalogue of his emotional biography, Mrs Crapper had been lurking. Giles, for all his expressions of diffidence, had been used to an atmosphere of alcohol and ear-rings which, if he still had his sight, Miss Agar could not have matched.

'It's very far north.'

'Nonsense! Course I can drive you – Canonbury, St John's Wood, Primrose Hill, whatcher call north?'

'It's N-Northwood Hills,' said Tibba.

'Northwood Bloody Where? Christ,' said Mrs Crapper.

'I can easily get the train,' said Miss Agar, who did not want in the least to be conveyed in the Crapper family vehicle.

'We must all have early nights,' said Giles. 'Tibba has to start school early in the morning. Miss Agar and I are engaged in a most important piece of work which will resume, I hope, tomorrow.'

This was to be his farewell. Miss Agar left while Mrs Crapper, who had lit up a Gitane cigarette, was still announcing an implausibly convivial programme. Mention was even being made of a nightclub.

'I'll expect you at nine forty-five,' was Giles's only valediction; nothing about having enjoyed the visit to Cambridge; but perhaps it would have been hard to say much in the presence of Tibba and this new woman.

As she sat on the Metropolitan Line train, Miss Agar felt more bewildered and unhappy than she had ever done in her life. The depression sank on her in deep clouds, she couldn't stop it. She wished that she was not in love, and so deeply in love. She wondered why God could have allowed her to fall so painfully in love; whether it was to be used in His eternal Providence, or whether it was the temptation of the Devil, an aberration, a falling away from the Divine Purpose. Perhaps she should, after all, have pursued a religious vocation. Perhaps she should have been happier with her lot and been prepared to do more for mother, particularly now she had her hip.

There were so many obstacles to overcome in loving Giles. There was his stubborn atheism; there was Tibba, there was his past; they were all enemies to Miss Agar's love, she could see that now. If only she had *thought* a bit. She hoped Giles didn't realize what a surprise it had been when he poured it all out, the story of his first marriage, and then of his *second*! He could have knocked her down (or so she believed) with a feather when he mentioned the second.

Was it really conceivable that she could have been so incurious? '*We felt you should be . . . well, quite honestly, Louise, just a tiny little bit more mature.*'

She felt such a *chump*. How could she have believed that Giles, with his sophisticated friends like Mrs Crapper, could possibly think it worth wasting his time on the likes of her? She started, as the train glided out of Preston Road station, onwards and northwards, to count the hours and the days she had spent with Giles. There had been, perhaps, two or three hours a week for a year.

That made a hundred hours. More, lately. Since her declaration of passion for him (what an *idiot* he must have thought her!) they had spent, perhaps, forty waking hours together. Only now, in the last two of them, did she really know anything about him beyond what could have been learnt in that initial advertisement: that he was a blind scholar.

Mrs Crapper suggested a whole past, about which he was visibly shifty and awkward. Another past, to add to his second wife, and his first wife, and all his professional disappointments. Miss Agar was crushed by it. She could have dealt with present rivals; she could even, she felt, have felt equal to risking the inevitable clash with Tibba. But you could not fight against someone's past. It provided an invincible rivalry: all those years and years before she came on the scene.

Her mother had stayed up, in dressing-gown and curlers, for her return. It felt like the middle of the night, though actually they heard the last of *Your Hundred Best Tunes* together as they drank their Horlicks.

VIII

The recriminations were delayed until the evening of the following day. They both had enough sense of decorum for that. It was, moreover, a purely practical question. When (as he optimistically put it) they had '*finally* got rid of Mrs Crapper', it was much too late for explanations. The evening is no time for quarrelling if you value your sleep. The morrow was taken up with school on the one hand, and with the *Tretis* of virgin wisdom on the other.

Tibba, equally, had felt no particular inclination to betray anger in the presence of Miss Agar. It was bad enough that it was now Christian names all round. But she really saw no reason why The Agar should be treated with the intimacy which a flash of rage would have implied. And The Agar stayed and stayed. It was dark by the time she left, for, in the previous thirty-six hours, the clocks (like everything else in their quiet existence) had changed.

The intervening day gave them time to make their own separate adjustments to the revolution thus effected.

Anger was what Tibba felt, or imagined she felt, from the moment of waking. But it was anger tinged with a quite wretched feeling of disillusionment. She had learnt for the first time the shocking fickleness of her own heart. 'Happy those early days,' Miss Russenburger tossed off later that morning with her usual telepathic appropriateness, 'when I shined in my angell infancie.'

There had been the usual theatrical display of shock when no one knew who had written the lines.

'Vaughan,' Miss Russenberger had said. 'The only Welshman

of genius. Dylan Thomas had what we can call *exuberance*; but I don't think we would describe him as a genius.'

This was only an aside. They had almost finished the play. Debbie had falteringly asserted that

> We are not the first
> Who, with best meaning, have incurred the worst.

And Miss Russenberger, having pulled out the *vox humana* stops for the famous 'Come, let's away to prison' speech, had talked of the two sorts of *childishness* in the King: his petulant 'spoilt child' self at the beginning of act one scene one and the pleasing, quiet child-*like*-ness when he emerged from his madness. She had gone on at once to ask why Tibba was not writing this down.

Tibba had forgotten her pen, but it was more than that. All day, she had the dreadful sense that her evening was going to be the exact opposite of Lear's idyll in the prison cell.

> When thou dost ask me blessing, I'll kneel down,
> And ask of thee forgiveness

was scarcely to be their attitude when the supper things were cleared away. Something awful had happened. A great change had taken place. Their quiet companionship, the father's and the daughter's, had been rudely intruded upon.

There was no point in blaming Peverill. She could quite easily have taken the train. There had been no need to accept the ride in his silly sports car. But that single piece of thoughtlessness, that act of treachery, had started the whole thing, revealed a gaping blackness beneath life's tranquil surface. It seemed like a punishment that Giles should have *known* Peverill's mother. He had pretended not to, but why else should she have called him *darling*? Tibba could not imagine why someone once called Peggy Chandris, now Mrs Crapper, should have been Peverill's mother. There must have been any number of marriages in the history. But she did not feel it, as she would have done in the days of her angell infancie (that is to say, before Friday), as a simple betrayal of her mother. It was much more like the exposure of a lie which they had both been living all along. Like father, like daughter, as she saw now. Oh, she could say that she still loved Captain de Courcy; and there was no doubt that she did. But she could never love him in the same way. Not after she had *let* Peverill kiss her like that in the car; let him, even rather enjoyed it, and made absolutely no effort to resist. He had even touched her chest, and it had been extraordinarily thrilling. Goodness knows what more might have happened if the A A man had not come up in his van. Afterwards, in the comfort of the train, she had lolled in Peverill's arms, and she had assented to his suggestion of adjourning to his mother's house *because*, and not in spite of, his declaration, 'She's bound to be out but we can make bacon and eggs or something.' She *would have done* what Peverill wished. That was what shocked her now. The fact that no such possibility afforded itself – merely the raucous supper with Mrs Crapper, who wasn't out after all – made no difference, morally, at all. How *could* she have been so fickle? For now, when Captain de Courcy said, as he perhaps would on the following Saturday, 'I hope you had an enjoyable time with your aunt,' the scepticism he managed to inject into the word *aunt* would be fully justified. He would be bound to sense that Peverill had been fingering her jumper; and that, even if she were still, technically, a virgin, she had been *kissed* – in *that* way – and really, after that, it was simply a matter of time before the rest followed. In days of absolute infancy, when she had called those long embraces 'film kisses', it had never once occurred to her what was involved. She had been completely astonished when, during the second kiss on the train, Peverill's tongue slipped into her mouth. She felt violated, disgusted, and yet profoundly thrilled. The door slammed shut on her Past. And if, if (but now, she saw, they never would be) Captain de Courcy's lips were pressed against her own, she would not be pure. She had failed, quite simply, in loyalty. And to fail even once in loyalty is to know that one can never trust oneself again, that the whole of life must be potentially tainted and corrupted.

So, instantaneously, it had been. For Mrs Crapper, doubtless, the very concept of loyalty did not exist; else how could she be Mrs Crapper *and* Peverill's mother *and* someone in her father's past called Peggy Chandris? Tibba had hoped, and because she had so deeply hoped she had also believed, that the whole Carol episode was irrevocably over. And what she meant by the Carol episode was not just the horrific vulgarity of Carol herself – that ghastly armchair she had bought and put in the parlour! – but a whole attitude to Tibba's mother. In the restitution of Giles's quiet routines – musical or literary evenings, and early bed, seeing no one but Tibba herself – she had felt him to be living loyally and closely to her mother. But now, *incredibly*, Miss Agar had become *Louise*. They needed to say no more about how they had spent the learned week-end in Cambridge. She herself had been sitting in a train allowing Peverill to put his tongue in her mouth while her own father, with the plainest girl on earth, was canoodling in some college bedroom. 'The wren goes to't,' as Miss Russenberger had said so violently earlier in the term, 'and the small gilded fly does lecher in my sight.'

That was Tibba's position. Giles, during his separate day, had formed very analagous feelings in relation to his daughter's week-end. The Crapper woman had more or less boasted as much: that her boy, this Piers, a pupil of that ass Monty, had been misbehaving with the girl.

Giles was grieved and shocked by this in a brooding sullen fashion as he wrestled all day with his introduction to the *Tretis*. The philological part of his introduction had been written years ago, before he lost his sight. He needed merely to add ten pages or so on the historical significance of the piece.

Christianity inherited its reverence for virginity from the Platonists, he rehearsed.

Christ himself belonged to a language group which did not even have a special word for what the Greeks called parthenos. *And of the evangelists themselves, only Matthew and Luke make the very improbable claim that Christ was born of a woman who 'knew not a man'.*

Pausing, he emended the word improbable to *unsemitic*. After a paragraph or two on the mystical writings of the neoplatonists, the origin of the monastic movement and the self-castration of Origen of Alexandria, he began to speak of the cult of virginity in Western Europe in the twelfth century. But the words came out less Gibbonian and incredulous than he had envisaged or planned.

It is necessary to recall that this tradition of thought grew and flourished before the cult of courtly love, certainly before any attitude to love which we might term, however loosely, romantic. Chaucer himself, writing what is generally considered the most moving love story of medieval times one hundred and sixty years after the Tretis, *still concludes* Troilus and Criseide *with the very specific injunction to 'yonge fresshe folkes' to abandon 'worldly vanitee'.*

> *And loveth him, the which that right for love*
> *Upon a cros, our soules for to bye,*
>   *First starf and roos, and sit in hevene a-bove ...*

Love itself is a concept the poets borrowed from the theologians, and not the other way about.

He frowned, because, although he had not meant to write anything so discursive, he realized that what he had conceived was true, and the truth of it was not something he had ever recognized so clearly before. He drafted a few more paragraphs of a less general kind, comparing the *Tretis of Loue Heuenliche* with *Halo Meithhad, Ancrene Wisse* and other works of a similar date and character.

To us, the eremitical austerities of these pious manuals seems less absurd when we consider the historical conditions in which these young women, many of them probably little more than teenage girls, were expected to find husbands. Regrettably, the world was not a safe place for young women in the Age of Chivalry.

It was pointless to be rehearsing these very questionable sentences. The general editor of the Early English Text Society would not think them in the least appropriate for the purpose of introducing the *Tretis* to scholars, all of whom would know more than they needed about the 'Age of Chivalry'. All the introduction had to do was to give some facts; where facts were not available, some speculations, about date, provenance and language. The historians could make what they would of the book's contents.

He blamed Mrs Crapper for the intrusion of these irrelevances into his mind at such a crucial stage of the edition's history. Peggy Chandris. The more he thought about her, the less he could remember. Her calling him *Giles, darling* was intolerable, and he made haste to point this out to Louise when she arrived.

'There's really no need to apologize, Giles,' the girl said.

'I was not apologizing, I was explaining.'

'It's a part of the past, I could see that.'

'I don't even remember her. She sounded disreputable. Did she look it?'

'That's not a very kind way of thinking.'

'I wasn't trying to be kind, I was trying to be accurate,' he sighed and handed her his draft introduction, 'though you would detect no particular passion for accuracy there. Put a pencil through all passages which do not directly relate to the matter in hand.'

'Please, Giles, just before we get to work, I must say ... about last night ...'

'What?'

'I've been a fool, I can see that.'

'I do not know what makes you say that.'

'Nobody mature would have behaved as I've behaved.'

'Mature?'

'You said yourself that I hadn't had any experience; of *that* and other things.'

'I never thought that was to your discredit.'

'It's undignified, all the same.'

'Being what you call immature is undignified?'

'My whole position, I see it now. It is terrible. I don't know how I could have been so awful, bursting out with it like that.'

'Bursting out with what?'

'Saying I loved you, saying I wanted to marry you.'

'Wasn't it true?'

'It was just putting a pistol to your head, wasn't it? I didn't bother to find anything out about you. I didn't even know how often you'd been married.'

'And that makes a difference?'

'I feel such a bloody fool.'

Sniffing followed the employment of this grotesquely uncharacteristic epithet.

'Are you weeping?'

'I'll be all right.'

'That isn't an answer to my question.'

He rose and blundered his way towards her. When their bodies collided, he tried to put his arms around her but she struggled free.

'Louise, don't. I've told you, I don't even remember the woman.'

'It's nothing to do with ... the woman.'

'Then what is it do with?'

'The whole thing.'

'That's scarcely very specific.'

'Oh, I would have written it, but the only way I could have done so would be to get Tibba to read it to you and that wouldn't do.'

'Indeed not.'

'I don't want to marry you, Giles. It is simply that.'

A very icy pause descended.

'I see.'

'Oh, I'm putting this all so terribly badly.'

'That part of the message seems very clear. A week ago you wanted to marry me. Now that you know me a little better, you don't. I admit that my behaviour at Cambridge was cold and unfriendly. It simply happens that, had I known we were going there for so long, I would have liked to see some of my own friends.'

'You never said.'

'You never asked.'

'Giles, it has got nothing to do with our visit to Cambridge. I knew you were unhappy. I didn't mind that. But I was so *immature* that I thought that my loving you would just make you happy, like magic.'

'And you have now changed your mind?'

'You are not making this very easy for me, are you? You see, I do love you. I have never been in love before, not properly, not like this.'

'What does properly mean?'

'I've never told anyone that I loved them before.'

'But it was in telling me that you consider yourself at fault.'

'Don't try to tie me up in knots.'

'I am interested in all these other men that you loved, but whom you did not tell. Why not, I wonder.'

'Well, one was a friar.'

'Indeed. So pleasant was his *in principio*.'

'Don't mock me, Giles, just because I haven't had your experience. It was pathetic.'

'Why do you say that so suddenly?'

'I've been awake all night thinking about it, that's why. I only loved him because it was impossible. He left Cambridge anyway in my second year. They posted him up to the far north: to get away from me, I think.'

'The *femme fatale* of the friary.'

She ignored this ribaldry. 'I must have been such a bore to them. I was round there all the time: tea on Sundays, every mass poor Brother James celebrated I went to; all the discussion groups he led. I even went to his Church History lectures.'

'I think you do wrong to say that people are *bored* by being loved. The opposite is true.'

'I was just being a silly little baby.'

'Why should you think that your feelings for this fortunate ecclesiastic, however fantastically grounded, should affect your position in relation to me?'

'They don't, oh, they don't. I can't tell you how I love you . . .'

'Please don't cry. I can't bear it. You will make me weep, which is not something I like doing.'

'But I can't marry you, Giles, I can't. Don't you see, you are so much more mature ...'

'I am rather old if that is what you mean.'

'And there's another thing.'

'Another friar?'

'You said I'm beautiful,' she blurted out. 'I'm not. I'm fat and I'm boring. I can't bear it when you say I'm beautiful.'

'By all means say so if it makes you feel happier.'

'Oh, *Giles*. Sometimes you say such cruel things.'

He manufactured a laugh.

'It merely seems, in the circumstances, a rather irrelevant consideration. I find you beautiful to hold, and beautiful to kiss and beautiful to be with. Your lips are beautiful and your hair is beautiful. Your appearance means nothing to me, but that does not deprive me of the right to say that I find you beautiful.'

'But I'm not.'

There was a long silence, punctuated once more by her sniffs.

'Perhaps we should resume our work,' said Giles.

'But only if you are quite clear that it's all over between us. I can't marry you. I won't. It was quite wrong of me to suggest it.'

'Since it was your idea in the first place, you are entitled to withdraw the suggestion, I suppose.'

His observation provoked no response. 'I should consider it a pity,' he added. 'But still ...'

'Last night ...'

'What about last night?'

'What you said about Tibba.'

'I forget what I said about Tibba.' He did not want to be reminded of his stray daughter, and the horrible world she appeared to have been sucked into.

'You said that she was the only person whose companionship meant anything to you at all.'

'I didn't mean it.'

'You did. You wouldn't have said it if you hadn't meant it. You also said Tibba wouldn't be pleased if she knew about us.'

'That must be faced.'

'Well, it needn't be faced. We aren't getting married, and that's that.'

'Tibba has very evidently decided to lead her own life. She can scarcely object if I decide to lead mine.'

'That's not what you said last night.'

'Do we have to revert to last night?'

'Last night,' said Miss Agar, 'was the first time you and I have ever spoken to each other *properly*.'

'I don't know how I would distinguish speaking properly from merely speaking. We haven't been wholly silent with one another.'

'Giles, why should you upset Tibba? You are all she has in the world . . .'

'That is plainly untrue. There is, we learn, someone called Piers, and a woman I have never met called Crapper who puffed cigarette smoke at me and called me darling. Tibba, moreover, has friends: girls at her school, you know. She is quite a popular child. Not that she is really a child any more.'

'You know what I mean.'

'That, precisely, is what I don't know. But if you can pardon the vulgarism, I get the message. For whatever reason, you have decided that you do not want to take on the responsiblity of being my wife. I don't blame you. I'm really rather a tiresome person to live with.'

He had begun to finger his typescript.

'Oh, Giles, we can't leave it there.'

'There is namoore to seye.'

'But do you understand?'

'Let's get on, shall we?'

They hadn't managed to do much. She made no useful suggestions about what he had written, though she said she would take it home to type. She reminded him to delete the reference to the Kentish *e* in the word *kesse*. The whole burden of his argument, constructed over nearly two decades, had depended on a belief that there were Kentish *es* in the Trinity manuscript, written by an evidently non-Kentish scribe, and therefore copied from a Kentish original. The elimination of this vital prop from his argument would, ten years before, have plunged him into something very like despair. But today, he was in a melancholic haze. No longer seeing the words on the page, *kesse* or *kusse*, was part of the reason why he murmured, 'Make such alterations as are necessary.' She replied that she would, recognizing that, while she was about it, she would have to retype many pages of the *Tretis* itself incorporating necessary emendations. Somehow, the gravity of this scholarly earthquake passed them by. They were both engulfed in the painfulness of having to mention kissing in so drily philological a context. Giles's gloom made him concentrate wholly on Louise. She, in her turn, at that crucial moment in both their lives, was overcome by a sudden impatience to get the typescript finished, done, in the post. These problems, she thought airily, could be dealt with by their general editor at the Early English Text Society. She thought only, with agony, of whether there would be a reason for seeing Giles again on a regular basis. By tea-time, she was gone.

Tibba, who knew that recrimination would be in the air, was torn between putting off the embarrassing moment of confronting her father, and making the moment worse by delay; for, the longer she was out, the more certainly he would suppose that she was 'up to no good'. Thus, she throbbed and juddered and chuntered on an omnibus, gazing blankly over the afroid wool hair, the cigarette smoke, the headscarves, the cloth-caps of the other passengers, into the black and brightness of the City as they left it behind them crawling up Goswell Road. And the dome of St Paul's, hemmed in by little towers and blocks of plateglass, was gradually lost to sight as they turned the corner, and she pushed the bell to stop the bus.

'Tibba?' her father asked when, the short walk accomplished, she turned her latch-key.

'Father.'

'You have a moment?'

He was in the parlour, sitting on the piano stool. She kissed his cheek, and as she did so he began to play some of a Schubert Impromptu (the one in G) very slowly and softly. She stood with her hand on his shoulder for about five minutes without saying anything. Perhaps the conversation they had both been dreading all day was not going to take place. It seemed, while the notes drifted in and out of ear and soul, as though, perhaps, the Change had not befallen them after all. But a little sigh, as he played, reminded her that everything *was* different. She had her guilty secret about Peverill. And, for his part, Miss Agar had become Louise.

They continued to say nothing, but, when he made a very minor mistake in his playing of the impromptu, and paused, she leant over his shoulder and played the phrase correctly. As she did so, she could not help noticing how beautiful her hands were against the ivory keys.

Tension built up gradually, the silence became more and more pregnant. She said that she must do a little school work before she prepared the supper, and she disappered to her bedroom for an hour. As she descended the staircase, she could hear her father breathing: sharp little intakes of breath, heavy, almost asthmatic exhalations. They were designed, she concluded, to hasten the preparation of the *tagliatelle*.

They ate it as usual, simply, *al burro*, to the accompaniment of a slice or so of very peppery salami and one or two olives. The wine in the decanter was a vintage Rioja. They drank a glass each. Some lettuce, dressed properly, was consumed *à la française*, with a knife and fork and a piece of Brie. Then some coffee was drunk.

After Tibba had washed up, she returned to the little parlour to find her father sitting on one of the upright chairs by the fire.

'Are you cold?' she asked. 'I could light a paraffin heater.'

'I dislike the smell.'

'That doesn't answer the question of whether you are cold. I think I am going to put on a cardigan.'

Once more, she lingered in her bedroom, delaying the commencement of the battle. She saw in her looking-glass that she looked quite ashen. She felt a sudden gush, not merely of distaste for the coming conversation, but of actual *fear*. It was a childish sense that she was going to get into trouble. It would be worse if they didn't manage to talk about it all tonight. But how to start?

Her footsteps seemed noisy as they clattered down the little wooden stair.

'I think perhaps,' Giles said at once as she returned, 'that you owe me some explanation. You can, of course, befriend whom you like. But it was very worrying. We had no idea where you were.'

'We?' she countered. It was necessary, from the beginning, to remind him that he had *his* explanations to give, too.

'Meg and I,' he said dishonestly. 'We spoke on the telephone. When you failed to appear, I assumed that you might have been staying another night with Monty and Meg. When it became clear that you weren't, I naturally thought there had been a calamity.'

'A boy called Peverill offered me a lift. He's in Monty's House.'

'So I gather.' Giles was surprised at the directness of her confession. It left him a little startled.

'He is quite a nice boy,' said Tibba brazenly. But before he could slip in some withering aside, she continued rapidly, 'Rather brash, b-b-but what would you expect with a mother like that?'

So far, they both awkwardly were aware, Tibba was winning.

'I think that she must have been mistaken in believing herself to be an acquaintance of mine,' said Giles.

'Is that why she called you darling?'

'Please, Tibba, there is no need to be vulgar.'

'I should have thought it vulgar to be asking me about Piers. I am eighteen in February you know.'

'That seems a *non sequitur* if you will forgive me for saying so.'

'I don't mind you being a friend of Peverill's mother. It's rather a funny coincidence really.'

'Its comic qualities elude me.'

'You should hear the things Meg and Monty say about Peverill.'

'They approve of him, I suppose,' said Giles, who had gathered that the regrettable young man enjoyed a position of eminence in Monty's House.

'Absolutely n-n-not. They c-c-can't stand him. The v-v-very m-mention of P-P-Pi, of him makes them furious.'

Giles smiled. He had not realized that Peverill was a source of irritation to the Pangham establishment. It somehow endeared the boy to him, but only momentarily.

'I suppose you will continue now to see him at intervals?' Giles asked, morosely.

'We haven't said anything about that,' said Tibba.

She did not lie. He knew that. Her attempts to be untruthful were so rare and so conspicuously unsuccessful that he knew her to be a person of sincerity. He sighed. It appeared that he had been over-dramatizing the situation.

'Mrs C-Crapper seemed pretty keen on seeing more of us though,' said Tibba. 'Now that she thinks you are such old friends.'

'I probably did meet her once or twice years ago,' said Giles. 'One can't remember everyone.'

'What about *your* week-end?' Tibba pursued, feeling that she had emerged victorious from the first round of the contest.

'It was tiring.' Giles sighed as if to suggest that he was still slightly out of breath from having sat next to Miss Agar while she read a manuscript.

'And are you any nearer completion now?' asked Tibba.

'Completion?'

'Of your edition.'

'A few weeks.' He drummed his fingers as he said it. 'No more, certainly. Miss Agar has some retyping to do. But I should be able to hand it all over to my general editor before Christmas.'

'Are we to call her Louise now?' asked Tibba with a sort of commonsense sprightliness; as though it was not a particularly important matter, and one that had only just occurred to her. Giles reflected how very cruel one is when young.

'It seems unnatural after so long an association not to call her by her first name,' Giles said. 'I think you are a little unkind about the poor girl.'

'No worse than you are,' said Tibba. 'Or than you *were*. It was you who said her voice reminded you of *A Diary of a Nobody*.'

'Did I say that?'

'You know you did.' Tibba laughed, trying to extract a few last drops out of the happy era when Miss Agar was nothing more than a joke. 'Anyhow, as you say, there's no need to be unkind.'

'She's very –' Giles's voice stopped suddenly. His sentence was broken by a convenient sneeze.

'Very what?'

'She's very anxious that you should like her.'

The words fell like lead upon Tibba. She had begun to hope that her speculations were false, and that her father had lapsed merely into a confusing and uncharacteristic modernism in his styling of The Agar *Louise*. Not so. For of what possible importance could it be that Tibba should like The Agar or not, unless plans were afoot to make her a regular part of the Hermit Street existence?

'I see,' said Tibba.

'So, try to be kind to her, won't you.'

The victory of the early stages of the conversation was being fast routed by these cruel sallies. She felt tears welling up inside her, tears of rage, of helplessness, simply of childish fear. Her grief for her mother came back to her. She knew that the only person who could help her out of her difficulties was this dearest, loveliest of mothers, lost to her forever. No one could stave off the catastrophe except Mother. It was thus, illogically, that her sorrow shaped itself, rather than the chronologically more exact reflection that all this was happening because Giles was a widower.

'If you don't mind,' she said, 'there is rather a lot of work I've still got to do on *King Lear*.'

'Oh, but surely you can do it in the morning,' said Giles. 'We had reached such an enchanting moment in *St Ronan's Well*. Josiah Cargill is so like oneself. And I like Touchwood so much. Please read a chapter.'

'I really am rather tired, and rather busy,' she said, trying to keep the tears out of her voice. What a departure from tradition! She had never refused to read to him before.

'Well, if you will gad about in motor-cars,' he said, for her demeanour angered him.

'I wasn't gadding any more than you were.' It was the volume of this riposte, and its note of tragic fury, which shocked Giles, for there was nothing in the words themselves that could be seen as a threat to tranquillity.

'All right, calm down,' he said.

He only heard the door slam and her feet banging up the stairs. The silence which followed was deadly. It was cold and horrible. He felt the chill and misery enter his soul more completely than at any time in the previous three days. It would not have been so painful if he had been able to issue Tibba with an ultimatum: *Miss Agar and I are to be married*. Now, however, he had to acclimatize himself to Miss Agar's own change of mood, or inclination. Yet, that hopes were still alive in those directions was confirmed by his willingness to upset Tibba over the question. He could have said something to hint that he was enjoying no more – and the ludicrous phrase suddenly leapt to mind, in spite of all sorrow – than

> An attachment, *à la* Plato
> For a bashful young potato
> Or a not too French French bean.

Louise was certainly a bashful young potato, poor creature. If only he could have her without complication, and on his own terms, whatever those terms might be. He had never felt less certain of his own emotions: in relation to Miss Agar, or to Tibba, or to his own past self.

Tibba, upstairs, lay on her bed and sobbed. She gave herself up, as never before, to the melancholy sense of her own failure to be loyal. Her father, too, as well as Captain de Courcy, had been betrayed by that kiss – the second kiss – on the train. The first had not mattered because she had not enjoyed it so much. But the second, which had seemed at first so revolting, was, in restrospect, one of the most rapturously enjoyable things of her life. And yet, it shocked her that the parting of the ways must be so sudden. If Father had been 'swept off his feet' by some vulgar lady like Mrs Crapper, Tibba felt that she could (almost) have borne, or at least *understood* the insult to her dead mother. But The Agar! Apart from anything else, Tibba knew that the ordinary diurnal experience of shared existence with Miss Agar would be intolerable. If Father were to marry her, it would mean that she had to leave home at once – go to University or take up a career or travel or throw herself on the mercy of some kind friend like Chantal. She *couldn't* endure the prospect of breakfast with that *silly*, round, ugly and yet so self-satisfied face. She *couldn't*. It was all right for her father. He was blind.

How wrong she had been to think, when Carol died, that Trouble was over. In fact, it had only been a brief respite of a couple of years. And this was far worse: Carol had many qualities Miss Agar lacked. She had been, in her repulsive way, genuinely well-meaning, kind, demonstrative. She hadn't been absolutely vile in appearance. It would almost have been possible – if she hadn't been Tibba's stepmother – to find her self-confident vulgarity rather a joke. But Miss Agar had nothing to her credit, really. That silly round face. 'I'm sorry,' said Tibba, 'but I can't help repeating myself. And all this odious Christianity. Oh God, I wish she was dead!'

But the icy remembrance of how effective her last curse had been – polishing poor old Carol off in less than twenty-four hours – made her suddenly silent with guilt and rage and impotent misery. It was in imagination, Peverill, not Captain de Courcy, whom she clutched as she held to the pillow for reassurance and sobbed till her throat was sore.

She did not even hear the telephone ringing downstairs.

Giles resented it, and thought to let it ring. But its persistent, and annoying regular, trilling made him lift the receiver.

'Giles?-Peg.' It came over all as one word.

'Meg? What do you want?'

'Listen, darling, this is a biggy.'

'I'm sorry. Who is that speaking?'

'It's Peg Crapper.'

'Oh, hullo.'

'It's rather important, it's about my Piers.'

'Whom I have not had the privilege of meeting.'

'Look here, Giles, darling, you've got to help. They're being simply bloody about this *stupid* business of the motor-car; I mean, frankly, I don't see how anyone can be so petty in this day and age.'

'I'm afraid I don't know what you are talking about.'

'Well let me tell you.'

Giles sighed. He could hear her lighting another cigarette, and could almost smell the atmosphere of drink, fags and expensive, sickly scent, coming down the wire.

'You'll have gathered, since I was kind enough to drive her home, that your daughter Tibba had supper at my place last night. No, seriously, she's a sweet kid and I *adored* having her. No problems. But Piers only came to London in the car last night because he'd taken it into his head that he had to drive her home.'

'Why couldn't she have come on the train?'

'Now, as you probably know, Piers's housemaster is none other than your brother – have I got this right? – who's called Gore.'

'He's my brother-in-law.'

'Brother-in-law. Sorry. No problems. My very simple point is that if *his* car hadn't been broken down, Tina wouldn't have had to hitch a lift from my P.'

'Tibba.'

'Tibba, then. You see my point.'

'Not really. Tibba had a railway ticket. There was no question of her being driven back to London by my brother-in-law.'

That would presumably clear the matter up, bring this tedious conversation to an end. There was a pause.

'Oh,' said Mrs Crapper. 'So let's get this right. Your Tibba was coming back in the train, right?'

'That's what I've just told you.'

'You see, my *darling* husband, who gets everything, but everything, wrong, seemed to think there was some arrangement with a car. When he heard about Tina's family connection with this housemaster he thought it was worth a try. And while I've got you on the line, I do think, even if he is your brother-in-law, that this housemaster has behaved *pretty* shabbily.'

'I'm very sorry.'

'I mean Piers has been a *very* good pupil. He's been Captain of Rugger, he's been Head of House . . . He puts one foot wrong, and they have to take this terribly harsh attitude. Not that I think Pangham is all that it's cracked up to be. Very far from it. I've been telling Anthony for months it would be better if P. came home and lived with me and got up his O's at Davis's or Westminster Tutors.'

'Well, goodbye,' said Giles.

'But, Giles, darling, you'll do me just the tiniest favour, won't you . . . *for old time's sake?*'

'I'm sorry.'

'I mean, get this bro of yours to change his mind, for God's sake. It looks so bad from your point of view apart from anything else. I mean, your own *daughter*.'

'What are you saying?'

'They're trying to give Piers the sack. I mean, would you believe such a thing in this day and age. For driving a *motor-car*, for God's sake. I mean, it's medieval.'

Giles wondered in what sense the adjective was being used.

'Positively medieval, isn't it,' she repeated, 'to sack a boy for driving a *car*. I mean, he's passed his test, what more do they want?'

'I'm sorry. I don't see what I can do. I don't even have a very clear sense of what happened yesterday evening.'

He regretted saying this. She proceeded to tell him. It was a pretty incoherent, rambling account. She still clung to the theory that Meg had promised to drive Tina home in the Humber and that, when this failed, Peverill, out of the goodness of his heart, had driven Tina home instead. She seemed unmoved by his corrections to her many errors of grammar or nomenclature. But as she spoke, his mind raced ahead. He had never met the regrettable Peverill. But he was evidently a young man of considerable charms. With more than a share of deviousness, it occurred to Giles that Wiltshire was further away than Knightsbridge, and that Pangham was a boarding school.

'I mean, let's face it, we pay the fees,' she said.

'I think you have a case,' he heard himself saying. She was telling the story of the second time Piers took English O-level, and why she blamed the English master (a Mister Shotover) for his failure.

Giles reflected that if Piers were sent to the crammers in London, he would have far more opportunity to see Tibba; that there would be more tears, slamming of doors, refusal to read *St Ronan's Well*. This sort of tantrum, he saw it clearly now, was just first love wreaking its boring chaos in her life.

'I'm not in any kind of authority at the school myself,' he said. 'But I'll certainly ring Mr Gore up if you like.'

'Giles, you're an angel. And we *must meet soon*.'

He doubted whether this meeting was of obligation, but nor was he entirely hostile to the notion.

At Pangham, there was an air of triumph which was almost bloodthirsty. Meg and Monty had almost never looked at each other with their eyes ablaze with such exultant feelings of victory. The excitement equalled the day when their eldest son won an exhibition to Sidney Sussex or the thrill of Daniel, their first grandchild, being born. But there was, added to the simple glowing pleasure of triumph, the vindictive sense, deeply satisfying, that they had scored a point and crushed a foe. The Bodger had spoken. There could be no turning back. Peverill was to go. Meg and Monty had been turned into parodies of crowing excitement, like a Prime Minister and spouse on election night, not without a touch of the Macbeths.

Meg had opened a bottle of *Asti Spumante* to celebrate, and, as if to crown a perfect day, Anna Ford was reading the news, her delicate throat pulsating, her eyes moist with that mixture of intelligence and sultry passion Monty enjoyed; especially after a glass or two.

Who on *earth*, it might reasonably be asked, would ring at such an hour? Meg answered it in the hall, and was puzzled when Giles asked if he could speak to Monty. It must have been the first time he had wanted to speak to Monty since 1952. Couldn't *she* help? Monty was slightly busy at the moment. (In a funny sort of way, while being irritated by Monty's uncomplicated heterosexuality, Meg liked the way he drooled over pretty girls.)

'You'd better go,' she said, putting her head round the door.

'Who?' he whispered.

'Giles!' she whispered back, with many a melodramatic shrug and shake to indicate that she didn't have the foggiest what her brother could want. While Monty was out of the room, Anna stopped reading and it conveniently switched to Alistair Burnett. Meg thought *he* was rather a dish; she liked his hair. But she suspected that women never *drooled* over members of the opposite sex in the way that men did. She preferred Alistair Burnett anyway to the ghastly little trade unionist who came on next whingeing and whining as usual for more money.

'Where's it going to come from?' she shouted back at the set.

She was so happy that she could have danced, or swung from the electrolier that hung over the middle of the room. Peverill gone! The terrible boy had been a thorn in Monty's side ever since he arrived. She thought of all the *endless* trouble it had been, of how much she hated the parents: greasy little Sir Anthony with his cigar-ash dropping on to the carpet and that wretched mother – Meg momentarily forgot Mrs Crapper's name – who was really little better than a tart.

'Well, well, well,' said Monty, with a hint of puzzlement in his grin. 'It seems old Giles has palled up with Pevvers.'

'You're *joking*!' Meg roared.

'He was asking me if the decision was irrevocable.'

'Giles asked that? You can't be serious.'

The last assertion, though probably true in general terms, was contradicted. 'I can. That's what he said. Had we really made up our minds? Wouldn't it be better for Pevvers to take his O-levels here rather than be moved to one of these swindling crammers?'

'But what on earth . . .?'

'Peverill's mother has been on to Giles. He said that she was an old friend whom he had not seen for a number of years.'

'Mrs Whatsit? I forget her name.'

'She's Lady Peverill, presumably. Lady!' He snorted.

'We have Harold to thank for Sir Anthony's knighthood,' said Meg, 'but mum isn't married to him any more. Don't you remember, she got married again in Peverill's second term. He had to be excused end-of-term exams to go to the wedding.'

'I remember now.' But he didn't.

'Crapper, that's it. She's called Mrs Crapper.'

They both laughed.

'Fancy Giles knowing her.'

'He mixed with some strange people years ago,' Meg conceded. 'But she's never been mentioned before. I can't believe they're very close.'

'He said it would, in the circumstances, be embarrassing for us all if we gave Pevvers the boot.'

'But we have given Pevvers the boot,' said Meg firmly. 'There's no going back on it now.'

Monty's conversation with the knight had seemed, at the time, brief, businesslike, and to the point. He had told Sir Anthony that he was very sorry to have seen, after repeated warnings, that Peverill had been driving the M G. Sir Anthony had said it was *his* impression that the boy was allowed to do so. Monty had denied this. Sir Anthony seemed to think that Monty had given special permission. Monty was once more firm in his negation. Then, Sir Anthony had hoped that the whole incident could blow over amicably. His son had, he believed, recently driven the car back to London. He was at present staying with his mother in Knightsbridge. Monty had said that, in that case, Peverill should stay with his mother until further notice. He was sorry to say that the school authorities took the very gravest view of this matter. Peverill was not to return.

Now he looked back on it, though, he wished that a letter *had* been written, and that they had got things more cut-and-dried. The Bodger said he would handle the matter. But you could not always trust the Bodger to do things properly. Monty wished that he had more to go on. He had certainly seen the boy drive the car. He had even had the insolence, the previous afternoon, to wave to his housemaster. He and his father freely admitted he had driven to London. But of course, as he saw now with chilly fear, the brazen way in which he admitted it all, and claimed that he did not know he was doing wrong, might, in some ears, seem rather a strong defence.

'We haven't actually written a letter,' said Monty. 'Not to Sir Anthony.'

'Why not? And do you have to write a letter?'

'You needn't worry,' he grinned. 'The Bodger has spoken.'

It was, nevertheless, a slightly disconcerting twist to the otherwise wholly joyous series of circumstances. It was so hard to see what Giles's motives might be for taking the wretched boy's side.

'Did Tibs get back safely, by the way?' Meg asked.

'I dunno. I didn't ask. Somehow, in the general confusion, I didn't think.'

'Presumably she did. The train's often late on Sunday. He was in such a flap last night you'd have thought that she'd run off to Australia. Had I actually seen her get on the train etcetera.'

'No, I'm sure Tibba got back OK,' said Monty. 'By the way, we never said anything about driving her back to London, did we?'

'In the Humber? It's gone fut.'

'That's what I told him.'

'But she had a ticket.'

'I know. Apparently Mrs Peverill –'

'Crapper.'

'Crapper, then, thought we were going to drive her back in the Humber, and that the reason Sir Anthony left the car was so that Tibs could have a lift –'

'Tibba a lift with Peverill?'

'That's what it sounded like.'

'But they've never met Tibba.'

'Sir Anthony did, briefly, on Saturday. And Peverill met her on the Sunday morning.'

'Yes, but not before. Anyway, we saw Peverill driving the car when we were walking along with Tibba, don't you remember?'

'Of course I do. We went and rang up the Bodger straight away.'

'*Typical* to drag her into it,' said Meg; though what it typified she was not sure. 'They surely aren't suggesting now that Peverill drove Tibba back to London?'

'Giles didn't say.'

'I wish I'd talked to him more. Apart from anything else, we ought to work out our Christmas arrangements. I suppose they'll be coming down on Christmas Eve as usual?'

Monty sighed.

'I know,' she replied. 'Last year was awful. And the year before. He tried to be a complete wet blanket . . .'

'Succeeded,' said Monty. 'What was it he called the carols from King's?'

'Christian caterwauling,' said Meg hastily, feeling the phrase to be rather blasphemous. 'He's still bitter about that place, you know, after all these years. It's rather pathetic in a way. But I think it would be too hard on Tibbs not to have them. You know

Giles takes no notice of Christmas at all. If they stayed in London, it would just be like any other bleak old day; and poor Tibbs wouldn't even get a slice of turkey.'

They planned their Christmas party for a while. Two of their four children would be coming, with spouses, and baby Daniel. It would, they agreed, be company for Tibba. Meg was of the opinion that it was never too early to start Christmas shopping. Catalogues from Barkers and Bourne and Hollingsworth started to arrive by post in September.

'Giles is an impossible person to give presents to,' she sighed.

'What did we give Tibba last year?'

'Alistair Cooke's *America*: an *inspired* choice,' said Meg.

IX

The parcel had been dispatched to Oxford; and the task of twenty years was now complete. It was Miss Agar who had accomplished the final prosaic details. When the typescript had been checked so often that she was no longer able, clearly, to read it, she had found out a shop selling office supplies, which had copied the thing on a Xerox machine. *A Tretis of Loue Heuenliche, edited by Giles Fox; with the assistance of Louise Agar.*

This formula, wholly surprising to her, had been composed by Giles. She had felt overwhelmed when she saw it, duplicated and reduplicated, slithering out of the machine in the shop off High Holborn. When she answered Giles's advertisement, she had not hoped for glory such as this. But her initial feelings of pleasure in the compliment were accompanied by a chilly sense that Giles's courtesy had a note of finality to it. When she had posted the thing, wrapped in its layers of corrugated cardboard and surrounded with stout brown paper, she returned to Hermit Street with the change and placed it on Giles's table.

'That's that then, really, isn't it?' she said.

'Until we hear from the Early English Text Society. You remembered to send it Recorded Delivery?'

'Of course.'

'I hope we shall keep in touch,' he said. He did not add, 'In spite of our last conversation.' That unspoken conditional was understood by them both.

'That would be nice,' said Miss Agar.

'I have said already that without your help this edition would never have been completed.'

'It's been really lovely for me,' she said brightly, as though she had been a child asked to help bake a cake and lick the basin afterwards. 'I've done nothing.'

'Your mother will wonder what has happened to you,' he said with abrupt sharpness. 'You must go.'

'Goodbye, Giles.'

She leant forward and kissed his forehead. How different this was from their earlier kiss, after her embarrassing outburst. Now they seemed stranger to each other than on the first occasion of their meeting.

'Goodbye,' he said. He made no attempt this time to grab her or to embrace her with passion.

'And as I say . . .' Her voice trailed off. She had not been saying anything.

'Goodbye.'

'The money's just there on the table.'

'Thank you.'

He listened to her go. Silence and gloom swirled back as he sat there, upright on his neat little chair, alone in his sightlessness. After a few moments, he felt his spirits plummeting to the depths. He was unhappier than ever. It seemed now as though there was nothing at all left in the world to live for. *A Tretis of Loue Heuenliche* had always been in the background of his life. Even on days when he did not really do anything about it, he would devote the odd thought to it, or feel guilty that he was not doing so. This peculiar work had been his oldest companion. He felt that he knew every nuance and inflection of the author's language. In that author's sense, Giles loved the *Tretis* more, perhaps, than any other book.

For what is love? It is a drawing back of our souls to the home and household of our belonging. It is that which tugs at the heart of a traveller in foreign lands and makes him turn for his own country. It is that which makes a man ride to war to defend his own, even as now Christian men make war upon the infidel in defence of Holy Church. It is that which makes a woman suffer all to defend the children of her bosom. This tender attraction we call love, this attachment, this knowledge of our belonging. For, know this in your hearts, we choose not the thing we love. For love pulls at us with invisible chains into its free thraldom. For as Love himself saith: Non vos me elegistis, sed ego elegi vos etc. And, as Saint Austin bears witness, fecisti nos ad te etc. Thou hast made us for Thyself, and our heart is disquieted within us until it rests in Thee.

It was only lately that he had begun to admit to himself the possession of a heart; but something within him was drawn towards the old book, something more than anything it contained or represented. A part of himself had been discarded as soon as Miss Agar posted the finished parcel. And he felt, not merely that a chapter of existence had concluded, but that his whole professional life was now, effectively, finished with no eyes. He could never work on anything again. He would be condemned, for the years that remained, to draw on the stores of memory (which would fail) of things which he knew already. 'Ask Fox: he *might* just know.' People, in the infinitely tiny world of learning, would, conceivably, continue to say this; half-justifying his place at the library as a manner of consultant on the whereabouts of manuscripts. But nobody would ever again think of his name as a suitable man to start something new. Everyone knew he was finished.

It might have been so very much less depressing had he been able to marry Miss Agar. But his past, and, the inheritance of his past, the chilly blasts of his uncharitable nature, had frightened her away. Poor innocent thing, poor Louise. Her declaration of love now seemed, in retrospect, one of those embarrassments too acute ever to be smoothed over by the resuming of apparently 'normal' social relations. Moreover, although he had of course not *said* to his daughter that there had been intimacy between himself and his research assistant, it had been all too painfully sensed.

The unspoken recognition, between father and daughter, of 'Louise', and all this threat implied, had ushered in a new era. For Tibba's sobs and sulks had confirmed that they both knew that their intimacy was not exclusive. One day, if not a 'Louise', some other person could come into Hermit Street and change everything. And this impulse, if impulse were needed, had precipitated Tibba's change of allegiance. She was now – Giles did not ask how often they saw one another – a person with a boyfriend. Sometimes, without any objection from him, she made a cold supper and left him to eat it alone. She had even absurdly suggested that he listen more to the wireless. Such nocturnal entertainments and outings were not, admittedly, of quotidian frequency. But they had made their point.

The day when Tibba went altogether was the time for which they were both preparing. They might call it marriage, or university, or a job, or an opportunity to travel. Any name might be supplied for the excuse; but the separation would come. He sensed that she had come to long for it. She was no longer a happy, domestic little presence, quietly going to work in the kitchen and preparing their meals as though ministering to dolls. There was no air of repose as she read to him now, or played the piano. There was always the sense that she was generously fitting him into her timetable of events, a programme which now contained secrets which he was too self-protective to inquire after.

She was of course as kind and as polite as one could expect. In April, only five months off, she would be eighteen. He winced to recall what he had been like himself at that unattractive age: assertive, cruel, snobbish. Perhaps women found it easier, he really didn't know, to be simply *nice*. He thought guiltily of his parents, and of Meg, saying to him (the Christmas he was eighteen), 'How could you be so vile to Mum?'

What had it been that provoked this outburst? He had not bought his mother a Christmas present, perhaps, or perhaps he had complained about the food or said something disrespectful about the King. All that had pained him at the time was that Meg went on calling their mother *Mum*. His contemporaries at King's (the ones whose lives he had wished to emulate) all seemed too clever or too well-born to have mums. They would surely have divorced women whom they called by their Christian names, or stately figures called Mother. Not *mums*. When he thought about it, he could hardly believe his own cruelty. For his mother had been totally baffled by his refusal to call her *anything* after this. Indeed, communications had completely broken down because of this tiny point of snobbish awkwardness. Must he prepare himself for some severance as absolute from Tibba?

The thought of this, his first undergraduate Christmas, and of how badly he had behaved, prompted thoughts of the coming festivities. Meg had written that morning to invite him and Tibba to spend Christmas at Pangham 'as usual'. The 'as usual' had been rendered with cruel weariness by Tibba as she read the thing aloud over their brown toast and Marmite, their apples and black coffee, the breakfast they still took together at twenty to eight. She had left the house soon after that. There had been no discussion of the Christmas arrangements. But, after over two hours of quiet sitting in his chair, he felt ready to discuss it. And he did so when she had returned from school and made a pot of Earl Grey.

'Won't they be rather hurt if we don't go?' she asked.

'Probably.'

'And what would we do if we didn't go?'

'Do?'

'Yes.' Her voice faded and died. His monosyllable suggested contempt for any form of activity, particularly for activity undertaken with the specific aim of promoting jollity or diversion.

'I feel no need whatsoever,' he added finally, as if to make the point abundantly plain, 'to do anything at all.'

'We could always stay here,' said Tibba. 'They'll probably be having Christopher and Jenny or Philip or —'

'Those rough cousins of yours,' he said reproachfully, as though she should be capable of reforming their characters.

'And they'll have the baby,' Tibba reasoned.

'So you think perhaps they won't be hurt by our not coming at all?'

'I don't know.'

She was silent. She wondered what on earth her father was plotting. It did not cross her mind that his unwillingness to go to Pangham had the simple purity of a negative wish.

'Did . . .' she faltered, for the name still did not come naturally to her '. . . did Louise come this morning?'

'Yes,' he said, 'it was a momentous day.'

She could imagine so easily *how* momentous. She wondered whether they had yet fixed the date. She thought less bitterly of it now. It seemed, from her new position of wisdom and experience, all rather pathetic. She imagined them worrying about the difficulty of 'telling Tibba'. That, in all probability, was what they had been discussing that morning.

'We finally finished with the typescript,' said Giles. 'It was posted off to the Early English Text Society before lunch.'

'By Louise?' said Tibba, just for practice, just to get used to saying the silly word.

'Yes. Louise went to the Post Office.' He sighed. Tibba could not be expected to realize what an important day it was for him, how extraordinary it felt to be rid of the typescript, to have finished a whole chapter, an aeon of existence. Women had come and gone. Fortunes had fluctuated, with health and money. But for the last twenty years and more, The *Tretis of Loue Heuenliche* had been a constant feature of his life. His daughter's insensitivity in the matter was wounding.

Giles had no idea himself what it was that Louise had bundled up and delivered to the Post Office: a diligent retyping of the entire work, incorporating many of her own notions which, in the solitude of Northwood Hills, had suddenly seemed to make sense.

Tibba, for her part, chose to ignore the import of the visit to the Post Office, the dispatch of virgin wisdom to Oxford. It seemed to her that her father was being merely shifty. She was consumed wholly with the thought, not of the *Tretis*, but of the complacent, dumpy form carrying the parcel: a future stepmother, it was certain now.

Moreover, Tibba's thoughts had been dominated so much, in the previous three weeks, since her visit to Pangham, with her own emotional state that she had found little time to devote to thinking of the main business of her father's professional life.

Since then, there had been two visits to Captain de Courcy. She had come to despise herself, utterly, for the 'crush' she had once felt. Once felt? She still continued to feel, in spite of all that had evolved since her adventure on the motorway, her crush. But it had all changed now. She blushed to think of the Captain, but she had now managed to make of him a joke. The moustache, the club ties and the blazer seemed comic, and she did her best to conquer the infatuation which still possessed her by pricking its bubble with private cruelty. He was, perhaps, after all, rather a fraud. She felt capable of pitying him. The low-brow books, glimpsed under his arm on the day, now months before, when she had met him by 'Returned Fiction' in the public library, confirmed the impression that he was not all that she had hoped for, longed for, dreamed.

That, of course, had been in the period, aeons since, at least three weeks before, when Virginia Woolf had been all in all to her. She had come to tire of the mannerisms of that genius, and to look about for another. She had read a hostile reference to Mrs Woolf (no more than a waspish aside) in the writings of some other novelist. It had been enough. Her heart was ready for a change. She now saw that even an arch-satirist could herself be satirized. One could laugh at *The Waves*. Thus, little by little, Tibba's innocence had evaporated. She had come to enjoy the daily sense that she was less and less childish. And presumably all this had to do with the incident of Peverill.

It was Peverill, of course unwittingly, who had changed her attitude to the Captain. It was the experience with Peverill which had made her relax when sitting in the Captain's modest establishment in Canonbury. It was all quite different now. She worried less about her own feelings, and thought more, flirtatiously, of the adventurous possibilities which a session in Canonbury could provide. If he now went down on one knee and slipped a manly hand around what he doubtless thought of as her 'pretty little waist', she would be equal to the situation. She might even, were she feeling agreeable, allow him to 'have his evil way'. Yes, Sir Jasper. He was the villain of a Victorian melodrama. *Maria*

Marten and not *The Pargiters* was the work of art she had been inhabiting all along, without knowing it.

Her correspondence with Peverill was touching in its one-sidedness, or rather in its double one-sidedness. One-sidedly affectionate on his part; one-sided in its intelligence on hers. His epistles were pathetically brief and ill-spelt, but their abject passion moved and excited her. She had received about nine since his departure again from London. Their mixture of childish, schoolboyish innocence with unbridled filth made her read them again and again, half fascinated, half enraptured.

Dearest darling Fox (said this morning's effusion). *It was super to get your postcard. I think of you all the time and it will be great when term ends and we can meet again. You were great at kissing Fox but I really want to have it off with you as soon as possible. Their are House Matches again this afternoon; I expect we'll win we usually do. With passionat kisses and love from Piers.*

The suggested encounter would, presumably, take place. It was simply a matter of waiting for it, and the waiting consumed Tibba's thoughts so that even Miss Russenberger and *King Lear* had come, recently, to be neglected. She found that the only company she wanted was that of girls of her own age, Chantal, Rosemary and the others. It was cruel, perhaps, to leave her father so much on his own. Yet, without explanation, she felt bound to go out in the evening where she could sit in Chantie's bedroom, drinking instant coffee and playing records and discussing, endlessly, the importance of Peverill in her life.

She had never felt so close to Chantie, or, in a different way, to Rosemary, since the incident on the motorway with Peverill. Chantal *assumed* that the long-expected event *had* happened with Peverill at some stage of the momentous Week-End. It seemed unsporting to disabuse her. Even if he had not managed to seduce her fully, Tibba knew that it had been his intention to do so; and now she possessed written – scrawled – evidence to prove it. To suggest to Chantal that circumstances had actually made It impossible would have been an irrelevance. And it had not involved all that many fibs. When, a little bluntly, Chantal had asked, 'Did you actually do it in bed or was it on a sofa or what?' Tibba had murmured, 'On a bed,' quite quietly, so it wasn't much of a lie. Perhaps it wasn't a lie at all. Chantal had only asked the question so that she could repeat her most recent experiences with a boy who was just emerging from a homosexual phase. She called it 'gay'.

Tibba had never been 'close' to anyone in the way she had grown close to these girls. Their rambling, companionable evenings were things she could no longer imagine doing without. For the first time, her feeling of alienation from her contemporaries had been perforated. Without too much embarrassment, she was able to get Rosemary and Chantal to elucidate the modern world for her as they casually chatted. She came to learn the details one ought to know about it. She learned about the Social Democrats, and the Gays and the Pill and eye make-up. She had invested in some blue stuff from Boots which she smeared on her eyelids. It made her feel more normal, even though she had yet to learn skill in its application. She had started to wear lipstick, and to think that some of her Post Office money ought to be invested in a pair of knickerbockers.

Thus, while Giles sat solitarily playing the piano or listening to the BBC, had his daughter occupied her evenings of late. She assumed that, in the circumstances, it was a kindness to be out some of the time. She did not ask. But presumably The Agar came much of the time and hatched thoughts of some repulsively religious nuptial ceremony. Only the other day, when Tibba had made some remark of average profanity about the ghastliness of Christians, her father had made an unprecedented correction.

'Christians may be ghastly. But the more trivial the world becomes, the less one dreads being ghastly,' he had said. Anything, in short, could happen. Unbelief apparently had its limits.

She could not reconcile herself any the more to The Agar's place in her father's heart. But something, of recent weeks, had made her more tolerant. She knew that her own life would one day take place outside the walls of Hermit Street. She had come to see that it must do so if she were to breathe, and not be suffocated by her father's egoism. And if she were to go, then it followed that someone else must come to take her place. She accepted it coldly, sadly, as indisputable facts must be accepted.

This Christmas business threw the whole thing into relief. She did not know what her father had in mind, but it presumably involved an idea of seeing The Agar on Christmas Day. This scarcely suggested a Yule of Rabelaisian exuberance. But, equally, the thought could not be avoided, that if they were in London, she might see Peverill. He was not sufficiently fluent in the difficult art of forming letters on a page to have been able to go into any detail about what his arrangements for the holiday might be. Whether he feasted with Sir Anthony or with Mrs Crapper, Tibba did not know.

Anyhow, the silence must be broken, and she felt it was she who was called upon to break it.

'What is Louise doing for Christmas?' she asked.

'Louise? How on earth should I be expected to know?'

'I thought she might have mentioned it.'

'Good Lord, no.' He felt like launching into another diatribe against the notion that one needed to 'do' anything, either at Christmas or at any other season of the year, but he was astonished to discover that Tibba was still speaking.

'Perhaps she would like to come here.'

'What did you say?'

'I said that perhaps Louise would like to spend Christmas Day here after ...' she stabbed about, a little desperately, for some seemly reason why this desire might exist in the bosom of The Agar '... after all her work with you this year.'

'It is indeed an extraordinary thing,' Giles conceded, glad that the girl had mentioned his life's work at last, 'to have posted that little parcel today. To think of all those years and years I have been working on it. "Actual life comes next!"'

The quotation was lost on her. Even if she were temperamentally equipped to enjoy Browning, which she was not, where would be the time? The advent of Peverill had made 'actual life' important to her too, and she resolved, with some absence of self-knowledge, to live henceforward less in and for books. People now mattered; the personal crisis caused by the eruption of The Agar into Hermit Street needed to be faced with bravado.

'I thought she might like to come here, that's all. Louise, I mean,' she persisted gallantly. For, really, she did not like the idea of spending Christmas Day with The Agar, and only thought of the invitation as an excuse which would enable her to slip out and have exciting encounters with Peverill.

'But she has her mother,' said Giles.

'Perhaps she would like to come too,' said Tibba. Presumably, Giles had met Mrs Agar by now; even discussed the choice of hymns with her.

'I hadn't thought of it.' He was puzzled by the suggestion, but the kindness of it was touching. He wondered what Mrs Agar was like. She was a shadowy figure. He did not spend much time trying to 'reconstruct' people he had never met. He could remember very little of what Louise had said about her mother, except that she was a widow with a hip.

'Not if you don't want to.'

'I hadn't thought you would want to have them,' he said.

'It would be nice.' The lie was grotesque. 'But only if you want to. Then you can say to Monty and Meg we can't go to Pangham because we have made other arrangements.'

Well, that was hard strategy and he saw the force of it.

During dics, Monty felt exceedingly angered by the way that Peverill bawled the evening hymn and by the raucous way in which he said the Lord's Prayer. In fact, when the final imprecation had been pronounced, Monty could not wait to get back behind the green baize door and mix himself a pretty stiff one.

The recurrence of Peverill, after his dismissal had been made so unambiguous, was bad enough. But the shock of the Bodger's announcement that Peverill was to be Head Boy of the school in the Lent Half was something from which Monty did not think he would ever, properly, recover. Meg was surely right when she said that *you simply couldn't do that kind of thing*. At Pangham, perhaps at all public schools, it was thought to be an immutable law that the housemasters were sovereign. When Monty made it clear that Peverill was to be dismissed for the serious offence of driving a motor-car, that, in Meg's opinion, was that. All the other housemasters' wives agreed with her. Apart from anything else, the Bodger's action made Monty look a complete fool. There had been no consultation. The Bodger had simply button-holed Monty one day in the Quarter and said, 'This Peverill business is more complicated than you think.'

It had emerged, after all their perfectly understandable denials, that Tibba *had* been driven back to London by the wretched boy. This news, which had astonished Meg and Monty, had never been properly explained. They had written to Giles about it, but there had been no reply. *Why?* That was what they would like to have known. She had a perfectly good railway ticket. Why on earth should she have accepted a lift from, of all people, Peverill?

'You'll see it puts us all in a pretty embarrassing position,' the Bodger had said.

Monty did not see this, but Meg had. A 'stink', it was believed, could or would be raised by Sir Anthony if it were known that a housemaster had dismissed a boy for doing what he had, misguidedly, thought to be a kindness to a housemaster's niece.

Monty was ashamed at himself for feeling so profoundly jealous of Peverill. For himself, he could think of nothing nicer than whizzing at speed down a motorway with Tibba at his side, her wonderful legs, in their thick white tights, temptingly near the gear handle. It was because he could imagine it all so vividly that he felt unable to probe into the matter. He accepted the Bodger's definition of the incident as a delicate matter.

But clearly the delicacy of it was more complex than the Gores believed at first. Meg said that, if you asked her, there had been some funny business. But nobody did ask her. Monty said that it was not as blatant as it looked. Sir Anthony had, apparently, agreed to give money to the new language laboratory *before* Peverill's drive down the M4. Meg said that, all the same, it was the principle of the thing. Was it true that the Bodger had been seen lately, as Sir Anthony's guest, at a banquet in the Haberdasher's Hall? Well, everyone knew it was true, because it was one of those big livery dinners and the names of the guests were printed in the next morning's *Times*. The invitations for that, it was reasoned, like the cheque for the language lab, had been written weeks before Peverill's misdemeanour.

The Gores felt, therefore, cheated. It was not simply that they were like dogs from whose jaws a delicious marrow-bone had been snatched before they had the chance to slobber over it. There *was* an element of disappointed revenge, certainly; and there was the very decided and actual irritation of still having Peverill about: not merely about, but even bigger for his boots than before, since his elevation. It was all nastier than that. There was an element, somewhere, of jiggery-pokery. They felt like pawns in a game. The Bodger had not played a straight bat, and worse, he had not *consulted* Monty. Meg found herself sadly reflecting that Monty was fifty-six. Only four years before he could retire. In the ordinary course of things, he would have wanted to go on till sixty-five. She had seen them still haunting the school long after he was seventy, a sporty version of Mr Chips. It all seemed chillingly different now. They had been talking the other evening of getting a little cottage in the Scottish Highlands. Monty could do his birdwatching. And they might even get a dog.

The General Editor of the Early English Text Society arrived for lunch at her college in North Oxford with an air of anxiety. It was the busiest time of the academic year. There were entrance papers to mark, and the grind of tutorials and graduate supervisions went on unchecked. Meanwhile, she had the worrying business of this latest typescript, and all available hours in the previous week had been spent checking it against a microfilm of the original manuscript.

She really did not know what to make of it. Some of the mistranscriptions were so glaring that she thought they must have been mere typing errors. But they were so persistent that she was forced to the conclusion that there was something chaotically dogged about the errors.

She did not know Giles Fox. She had merely met him once, years before, over tea after one of the Sir Israel Gollancz memorial lectures at the British Academy. She knew nothing of his private circumstances. *A Tretis of Loue Heuenliche* had been awaited by the Society for years: it had been mentioned to her by her predecessor as a standing joke, the sort of task which would never be finished. But here it had come, at last, in a brown paper parcel addressed iin the biro-writing of what seemed like a child.

The accompanying letter had been extremely curt. She thought of it as she ate her rather gristly ox-tail and heard about a colleague's scholarship candidates.

'This has been an extremely good year,' someone said. 'We've had six applicants for geology.'

While she said something polite in reply, she wondered how on earth she was to deal with the matter.

Dear Sir, the letter had said, though it must have been generally known that Professor Garfield had given up the general editorship years ago. *Here, after many years, is the Tretis of Loue Heuenliche, ready for publication. I hope it will be possible for that publication to proceed without delay. I will be happy to answer any questions you might have about it. Yours truly, Giles Fox.* The signature had been spidery and it was written through, rather than beneath, the words *Yours truly.* She wondered if he was an alcoholic. Only a few hours with the microfilm machine in Bodley had shown her that there was no possibility of the thing being published 'without delay'. It would all have to be redone. And as for the introduction, it was absurd! He seemed to know all the recent work that had been done in the field, for instance, the numerous editions of *Ancrene Riwle* manuscripts. But their indisputable discoveries were dismissed with a sort of acid arrogance which was incomprehensible.

'We need no longer bother ourselves with the fatuities of such so-

called philologists' was a sentence which particularly rankled, dismissing a point she herself had made in the Tolkien *Festschrift*. Bad temper could be explained or expunged; but not so the mistakes. She had never read through the *Tretis* before, though she had known of it since its discovery; and she of course knew its famous *Hymn to Virginity*, reproduced as an excerpt in innumerable preaching-books and commonplace manuals of the period. The work was actually of considerable interest, though she was at a loss to see why Fox insisted so firmly on its being Kentish, when all indications, she could tell at a glance, pointed to a provenance of the West Midlands. There was even a baffling contradiction between the introduction and the text itself. For he claimed that the scribe spelt the word kiss *kesse*, yet when she turned to the relevent passage in the typescript it read (variously) *kusse* and *cusse*, in the former case a mistranscription from the original.

All this, on top of marking, seemed the last straw. After lunch, at which she was quiet over her cheese, she went to the college office and dictated a letter to the secretary: '*Dear Mr Fox, Thank you so much for sending the typescript of the Tretis of Loue Heuenliche. I cannot hold out any hopes that it will be published soon, since, as you probably know we have a great back-log to catch up on.*'

'Exclamation mark,' she said, desperately, hoping that would make it look kinder.

'*At the moment term is still in full swing and we then have the college entrance exam to cope with. So do not expect to hear from me until after Christmas when I hope to have time to devote the time to the Tretis which it deserves.*'

She wanted to add a reassuring little sentence suggesting a conviction that Mr Fox's work would be invaluable to Middle English scholars, a most useful addition to the Society's list of titles. But she could not bring herself to tell a lie.

X

That Christmas Day, they wandered hand in hand, Tibba and Peverill, in those few hours when their families had no claim on them. The Brompton Road was completely deserted and still. It was rather a mild day, with a feeling of damp in the air. The dome of the Oratory, as they passed it, seemed magnificently alien, grand and black against the pale English sky. Knightsbridge was left behind them now as they walked towards Onslow Square and the Fulham Road. Shops were all shut. The pavements were empty. There was not even a cat to be seen. And there was a perfect silence; not a car, not a church bell, not so much as a breeze to spoil it.

Of the six or seven evenings since term ended, and Peverill had returned to London, they had spent four in each other's company. They had seen films, and toyed with meals in restaurants, and been to a party. And the inevitable, the long-awaited event, had taken place. She saw why such rough words were used for the activity (banging and so on), for it had lacked the ethereal dreaminess which she had expected of it. But pleasure had not been absent, even when he had been rather drunk and bruised her with his violence. For she loved him, and felt loved by him in return, and the intensity of this knowledge was so intoxicating that she felt she might go mad with it. She loved him all the more, this quiet Christmas afternoon, when she could merely nuzzle against his coat and enjoy the sound of his clonking footsteps on the damp paving-stones.

She felt so very flattered, so very honoured. For he was, in his own quiet way, a hero. He had risked being expelled from Pangham for the love of her; and if Uncle Monty had had his petulant way, Peverill might be now at some crammers rather than the Head Boy elect. As it was, his name would appear in the Court Pages of *The Times* when the school reassembled for its Lent Half, and she would be able to open the pages of the newspaper and see his name: *P. J. A. Peverill is Head of School.* And this would be he, her lover and her lord.

'I wish we were spending the whole day together, Fox,' he said.

'So do I.'

'You could have come to dinner tonight, you know.'

'It would have been lovely.' But she thought of Mrs Crapper's voice, and her friends, and the way that cigarettes got smoked between courses. Besides, the food prepared by Mrs Crapper was rather richer than Tibba was used to.

'You simply must taste my chestnut stuffing,' she had coughed, when the idea had been proposed of Tibba as a guest at her Christmas table. 'I got it out of the *Sunday Times* and it knocks you *out*.' It was just as well that, then as now, she was able to say, 'We've got our own Christmas arrangements.' The arrangements consisted of tagliatelle, olives and (*St Ronan's Well* being finished) a chapter or two of *The Surgeon's Daughter*.

'I wish Dad hadn't forced me to go back to Pangham next term,' said Peverill plaintively. 'It's a complete dump, you know.'

'But you'll be Head Boy.'

'Besides which Ruddy G. and me don't exactly see eye to eye.'

'Uncle Monty's all right.'

She didn't want to be having these prosaic words. She wanted to drink in the silence and feel his firm arm clasping hers as they walked along.

'But if I'd left Pangham I'd be in London and we'd be able to see each other so much more often.'

'There's time,' she said quietly. 'You don't go back for three weeks.'

'Do you think we could run away together, Fox?'

She looked at him to see if he was serious. He was. It was a wonder how he had changed. He was still galumphing and tactless in many ways, but love had tamed his brashness and his conceit.

'Not really.'

'Couldn't we have a holiday together – go and stay with Dad in Florida?'

'I'm so poor,' she said. The knickerbockers, which did not really become her, had more or less cleared out her Post Office account. On top of which, there had been family Christmas presents.

'Dad'll pay.'

'It's a lovely idea.'

'Well then.'

'No,' she said, 'let's enjoy now. I feel so happy, and I l-love you so much.'

When their kiss came to an end, he said, 'Have you been in love like this before?'

'Not like this.'

It was true. Captain de Courcy had inspired aching and longing, but she wondered now whether it had been *him* she loved. The de Courcy phase seemed like no more than a rehearsal for the real thing. She was simply going through the motions and might as well have been in love with a teddy-bear. Her whole life had been a preparation for this.

'Have you been in love?' she asked. 'Before?'

'I've got around,' he teased. 'But it's different, this.' His face was scarlet as he said the words, so that flesh and acne blended into an even hue. 'You were so fantastic yesterday.'

It was a blatant observation, but it thrilled her. Much of the 'success' of the most recent escapade was owing to some intimate advice of Chantal's. But it would have happened anyway, the pleasure and the excitement, for they had both been carried away on floods of passion which were more beautiful than anything in books could have prepared one for.

'Do you think your mother was ever in love?' she asked.

'I'd never thought about it.' His laughter was embarrassed. 'I suppose.'

'I don't think my father can have been,' she said wistfully. 'I think it must be a very rare thing, what we are both feeling now. Our parents couldn't have felt like this.'

'Why d'you say that, Fox?'

'They just c-couldn't. I mean everything is so b-beautiful, so wonderful now. You couldn't f-forget feeling like this. You just couldn't.'

'You say some funny things.'

Silence resumed, because she could not express properly what she felt. Only, she knew that she was experiencing what all the great poets had written about when they described being in love. It was a shatteringly lovely experience which took over your whole being. You couldn't just have it and then forget it. It was so much more than the sex or the kissing or the writing of letters. Almost every pop song you ever heard was about it; and half the novels and plays you read. People knew it was there, and perhaps they tried to make their own cheap or chaotic emotions *seem* like love, just as she had told herself she was in love with Captain de Courcy. But she now believed it was a terribly rare thing, the absolute surrender of one person to another. It could never be trivialized or forgotten. If her parents had ever been in love *properly* there wouldn't have been all the boyfriends who hung about her mother when she was too young to understand what was going on. And if Mrs Crapper had ever been in love with Sir Anthony, they would never have got divorced. For it was such a special thing, this rare and painful sensation, that you couldn't ever behave as though it hadn't happened. People spoke of falling out of love. But that must simply mean that they had never been in it.

'Oh, Piers,' she said suddenly, stopping outside the barricaded window of a camera shop, 'kiss me again.'

The mother of Louise had been mildly appalled at the prospect of spending Christmas Day with strangers. No doubt the offer was meant kindly. But they had *always* gone to Ethel and Tom for Christmas Dinner since Gran died. Now Tom had his asthma, they couldn't let Ethel down. Knowing that the invitation was meant kindly did not diminish, somehow, the pain it caused; its threat to shatter Mrs Agar's unalterable festal routines was almost insulting.

These were the routines: Midnight Mass – though it had never been the same since Father George went to the West Indies; he had carried the bambino really *beautifully* – was followed by sleep. On waking, there was present-opening and early-morning tea; expressions of surprise at a bed-jacket she had seen Louise (never more than a passable knitter) toiling with for six months; mass again, this time with a sermon; and then on for dinner with Tom and Ethel and the 'brood' on the fringes of Gospel Oak. There was always a Polish neighbour there whom Mrs Agar, hazy over surnames, rationalized into Mr Weetabix.

What on earth did total strangers mean by wanting to disturb this succession of reassuring rituals? If anyone had asked her opinion (a conditional never fulfilled) Mrs Agar would have said that Mr Fox had taken up quite enough of Louise's time as it was, stopping her getting a proper job and settling down as a school-teacher.

A compromise had been reached. They would go to Hermit Street for tea. Louise, who had stressed the loneliness of her blind employer, had won the day. Mrs Agar, grudgingly mindful of the Christian duty to be kind, had denied herself a televised circus performance. As soon as the Queen had spoken to the Commonwealth, Mrs Agar and her daughter had bundled themselves into coats and made their way towards Islington in the back of Tom's Triumph.

Tom shouldn't have had to stir with his cold, but they would never have got a taxi on Christmas Day. Walking the couple of miles from Ingestre Villas was not a possibility for Mrs Agar's hip.

When the Triumph had driven off, the two women stood timidly on the pavement outside Giles's house, Louise, rather red of face after all the wine and turkey and pudding, her mother more leathery of complexion. Mrs Agar had a sensible-looking roundness of posture. She was firm of jaw, bright of eye and rigid of permanent wave. Her wiry little hair-do had a hat ('my church hat') rammed on to it firmly.

'Well, I don't want pneumonia for my Christmas present even if you do,' she sniffed.

Louise rang the bell nervously. She had allowed an awkward time to elapse since her last meeting with Giles. She had so very much regretted her common sense, her withdrawal of the marriage proposal. Since her regular visits to Hermit Street had stopped, life had been very bleak and empty. There had just been her mother, who reasonably suggested that it was about time she started looking about for a proper job. She found herself missing Giles quite unbearably. But she knew that it could never be her who 'made the running' any more. It must come from him. Then, when she had been out at Sainsbury's late opening (because she had forgotten mum's Gingerellas when she had gone that afternoon), there had come the invitation. It was Tibba who had rung.

'What sort of name's that?' her mother had asked.

'Oh, Mum, you weren't rude, were you?'

'Course I wasn't rude, only it's unusual, isn't it? Short for something I suppose, though *what* I'd be blessed if I knew.'

'Are you sure they asked us for the whole of Christmas Day?'

'Well, I'm only saying what she *said*, aren't I?'

So Louise had rung back to check with Giles and to explain about the time-honoured rituals: Tom, Eth, Gospel Oak. His voice seemed very far away when they spoke, and it was hard to tell whether he was bitterly hurt or merely relieved that they could only come for tea. He had asked whether she would like to see him before Christmas, and she had said very much, but neither of them had been bold enough to suggest an actual time or date. It was therefore their first meeting in the flesh for several weeks when he opened the door.

'Mum, this is Mr Fox,' said Louise.

'I'm very pleased to meet you.'

Mrs Agar was struck immediately by how smart Giles was; then by his size. Louise had not told her that he was a titch. He was immaculately dressed, a pansy, she wouldn't be surprised. So much, thought Mrs Agar, for the idea of his being lonely. No one would have put on a suit and silk tie just to give people tea, even if it was Christmas Day. She imagined him going out to a late dinner, and felt mildly conned by his worldliness. When he shook hands, they were as soft as a woman's. You couldn't really see the eyes behind the dark glasses. *Creepy* was a word which came into Mrs Agar's head as he led the way through the little hall (no nice carpets, no nothing) and up a few steps into the lounge. What a shock! Lou had said there wasn't much comfortable furniture, but there wasn't so much as a nice settee. And the other really extraordinary thing was that there was no Christmas decoration of any kind. Perhaps it wasn't worth bothering if you were blind, but you'd have thought the girl might have bought a tree or put up a few garlands or paperchains.

Tea things had been laid out in the little parlour. There was thinly sliced brown bread and butter, and a home-made jam and a seed cake. Mrs Agar thought a little plaintively of the rich fruit cake she had iced and decorated with the little figure of Santa that Lou had liked since she was a kid. They had left it at Tom and Ethel's and it would probably all be gone by New Year's Eve when they were to meet again.

'Tibba is very sorry to miss you,' said Giles. 'She's gone out to see a friend – a fairly long-standing arrangement.'

Mrs Agar wanted to say it seemed sad for him to be all on his own on Christmas Day. But this was too painfully obvious a truth to be enunciated and she suppressed it. Instead, she said, 'What a lovely piano.'

'Yes, it's German.'

'So I see.'

'Do you play?'

'Mum teaches it,' said Louise.

'You never said.'

'She's funny like that,' said Mrs Agar. 'She never says all that much. Never used to tell us a thing about what she'd been up to at school all day. She'd come home and I'd say, "Have a nice day, dear?" and she'd just say, "Yes, Mum."' Mrs Agar laughed. '"Yes, Mum,"' she repeated, laughing. 'But it's a real beauty, isn't it?'

'Perhaps you'd like to play,' said Giles.

She needed no prompting. He heard her heaving herself out of her coat and thumping herself down on his delicate little piano stool. But in a moment the room was full of the most exquisite sound as her fat little fingers ran up and down the keys. It was *Jesu, Joy of Man's Desiring*, and he stood, transfixed by the delicacy with which she brought out all the poignant beauty of its perfect music. When she had finished, it was impossible to speak. All three of them were seized with a silence which was awe-struck rather than embarrassing.

'It's got a lovely tone,' she said at length, because Lou was just gawping as though she didn't have a tongue in her head.

'I'm very feeble myself,' said Giles. 'But since I lost my sight it is my chief source of consolation.'

'Shame,' said Mrs Agar quietly. And then, feeling that moping really wouldn't do, not on Christmas Day, she fixed her features with a determinedly comic expression and played an extra-ordinary little medley of her own concoction. It started with a few familiar bars from the Emperor Concerto and then it became 'Let's All Go Down the Strand – Have a Banana.' That suddenly grew into a Mozartian air, which switched to the Dead March from Saul, played with extraordinary solemnity and blending imperceptibly into

> Merrily we roll along, roll along, roll along
> Merrily we roll along, over the deep blue sea.

She sang this in a high little voice and Louise thought she had never seen Giles laugh properly until that moment.

'You play something, dear,' she said at length. And Giles realized after a moment of silence that she had come forward and touched his hand.

'*Dear*.' No one had called him dear (excepting ladies in shops) since his friendship with a rather distinguished don in his undergraduate days.

'All right,' he said, with studied casualness. And placing himself neatly on the stool, he played; and as he played he sang in a mannered tenor voice Louise had never heard before: she wished her German were better so that she could follow the words.

'Schubert a great favourite of yours, is he?' Mrs Agar replied as soon as the performance was over. He wasn't bad for an amateur.

'Very decidedly,' said Giles. He wondered if the meaning of the love song had communicated itself to the two women. 'Here I stay alone, my dearest one,' was its import, 'until I think that my heart will break, when I remember our last parting. Oh would that you loved me as of yore, oh would that I had you on my breast' – rather too high a note on *Busen* – 'once more.'

'I'm very fond of the Lieder myself,' said Mrs Agar.

Louise brought the hot water to the pot, and they settled to tea; it was more like a China tea with a sort of scenty taste, not what Mrs Agar liked; and of course, not enough to feed a mouse. But conversation made up for these deficiencies. Her good-humoured garrulity did not allow any painful pauses in the flow of talk, and Giles's face relaxed into a position of happiness as she jabbered about the opera. It appeared that she had a long-standing arrangement with a clergyman whom she accompanied to the cheaper seats in Covent Garden two or three times a year. Verdi's *Falstaff* was the one they had seen recently.

'Extraordinary, isn't it, he was *eighty* when he wrote it.'

'Verdi has a little too much, I don't know how to put it ...' Giles said.

'Verve I'd call it. Oh, I *love* it,' she said smiling. 'Of course, I'm old-fashioned, I dare say, but give me a happy ending.'

Louise wondered why she had never been able to *deal with* Giles, get on with him so well as her mother. The older woman had somehow established immediately that she could 'say anything' to Giles without causing offence. Louise had always tiptoed about him as though making her way across a minefield. (She saw, perhaps, that delicacy is not the right manner with the delicate.)

Precisely, and with his thin lips now relaxed and happy, he nibbled his dry little bit of seed cake.

'We should have brought you some mince pies or something,' said Mrs Agar, feeling no need to pretend that she had eaten adequately. You couldn't go on eating bread and butter all afternoon.

'I think they'd scarcely have agreed with me,' said Giles. 'I have a very sensitive digestion.'

'Get off with your bother,' said Mrs Agar. 'Who ever heard of mince pies doing anyone any harm?'

'I can assure you, they do me harm. I do not like anything too rich.'

'Rich.'

What was she doing now? He heard her waddling about and tidying things.

'I'm going to do a bit of washing-up,' said Mrs Agar.

'There's really no need – my daughter will be back soon.'

'All the same,' she persisted.

They heard her rather ostentatiously turning taps and trilling Verdi at the back of the house. At length, the unmistakable odour of tobacco smoke suggested an ulterior motive for her momentary absence from the parlour.

'You mustn't mind Mother,' said Louise.

'Come and sit by me,' said Giles.

'She doesn't mean any harm.'

Louise came and sat on the floor by Giles's chair, so that he could stroke her head as he spoke.

'Why do people want to apologize for their parents? I did, you do; doubtless Tibba will do, if she doesn't already. I liked your mother as soon as she came into the room. You are very fortunate in her.'

'She's had a hard life ...' It was impossible to believe he was sincere and she felt the need to go on with her defence of the old woman ... 'Dad left home, you know. Mum always likes people to think she's a widow, but she isn't really. We never hear from Dad. I think he sends her a bit now and again ...'

'Perhaps she will take me to the opera again. There is no substitute for hearing it in the theatre, even if you can't *see*.'

'Giles, don't be unkind. As I say, Mum's a very *warm* person. She *means* well ...'

'Will you take nothing that I say seriously? I meant it. I genuinely would like to spend an evening with your mother. Perhaps we should all go out together soon: if we can find something with a sufficiently happy ending.'

'Oh, Giles, do you mean it?'

'Of course I mean it. *Christ*, Louise, I've missed you. I'm not asking you to change your mind. I see that you stepped in out of your depth and said something you did not mean: you understand what I am referring to.'

'Yes, but Giles –'

'No buts. I am not going to exert any mental blackmail. I know that you do not love me as you used to do; as indeed, I in my slow and tardy way, have come to love you.'

'Oh, *Giles.*'

'No, my dear girl, let me just have my say. It isn't just a simple case of my having got *used* to you. And it isn't just that you have helped me in my life's work. Without you, that typescript could not possibly have reached the stage it has now.'

'It makes me so proud when you say that.'

'But it isn't just that, Louise. You must see that. Even if you go away from here and we never meet one another again, you must see that I would love you even if we had never done any work together. It isn't our shared *interests* that make me love you. It's *you* that I love.'

'Oh, Giles.'

Her gift of sight made her more nervous than he of the possibility of being spotted; but the ostentatious noise of a pan being run under a tap suggested that her mother was still tactfully occupied. In so far as it was possible to lean over him as he sat, still perched upright on his chair, she put her arms about him and implanted a kiss fully on his mouth. He responded to her embrace, and pulled her down on to his knee.

'Marry me,' he whispered, 'marry me, darling Louise.'

'What was it you said,' she asked quietly, 'when I asked you? "Is it a request or a command?"'

'It's a command,' he said. He felt the tears falling from her eyes on to his cheeks.

She could not reply. It made her shiver, partly with joy, and partly with the sense of old wounds being opened, old confusions beginning again. There was so much that could be said, doubtless, if she could see clearly what ought to be said or done. The noise of her mother's cough, like a goods train doing some routine shunting in a siding, warned her to get off Giles's knee before the old woman returned to the room.

'I've washed up for you. It's a lovely neat kitchen,' she remarked, giving Lou quite a hard stare. What was the girl crying for?

'You really shouldn't have bothered,' said Giles.

'I wish we could play some more music,' said Mrs Agar, 'but we'd really better be off.' She was particularly anxious not to miss 'Christmas Night with the Stars'.

'Well, perhaps you will come again,' said Giles.

'It'd be lovely,' said Mrs Agar. She hoped he wouldn't suggest a date too soon. It didn't do to build up lonely people's hopes. And then there was the fact that you had to have them back. 'Give us a ring on the old blower when the Festive Season's over. You could perhaps come to us next time. And bring your little girl. It's a shame I haven't met her.'

Captain de Courcy ate another of the mince pies and took a swig from the tumbler before him on the coffee table. He wished he had stocked up with more whisky. He was running out; and if he stayed up to watch the late film, he would have to move on to the Ginger Wine. He felt too depressed to read the Desmond Bagley he'd got out of the library. He simply sat. It had been a miserable sort of day. There was one mince pie left in the super-market packet, from which he ate them, scattering crumbs on the carpet. He did not know what time it was. It was presumably about time he put the frozen chicken in the oven; but he was almost reaching the stage where he felt there was no point in bothering. He felt quite pleasantly woozy. The mince pies would do him. If he still felt hungry when the circus was over, he would make himself one of those toasty topper things you get out of a tin. Save trouble. Stick a bit of holly in it if necessary to make it seem more festive.

He laughed aloud at what seemed, privately, rather amusing. Telly had been pursuing its own quiet life in the corner of his room, but he had not been paying much attention to it. He had just been sitting there, getting slightly tighter, ever since he woke up at about half-past eleven that morning.

He had always hated Christmas; but in a bleak way, he preferred it this way. When Mother had been alive, he had had to go down to Bournemouth and share his loneliness with her. It had been awkward, somehow.

The best Christmas he had ever spent was in Germany in 1957. He had stayed on in the Army after doing National Service and got a commission. The married men had all buggered off to their wives and offspring on Christmas Day, and those left in the Mess had been able to get on with some serious drinking. There had been a hilarious game of footer after lunch against the NCOs, and much rumbustious laughter before tea in the showers. Then he'd wandered off into the town and got really plastered.

It was sad he'd ever had to leave the Army, really. He often thought that if he'd played his cards right and got a decent lawyer, that court-martial would never have happened. In the Navy they were more understanding about these things.

It had been a funny old life since. If he'd passed that TEFL thing he'd have made a packet. London was full of wops learning to polish up the Queen's English. But he'd kept body and soul together. Mother had not been exactly over the moon when he came out with the acting idea. Regular work was what she wanted him to have. As it turned out, he wasn't cut out for all those lonely nights in provincial boarding-houses playing in rep, anyway. And his agent had been an absolute shark. He might have actually got some parts if the bloody woman hadn't insisted on his doing that modelling work. It wasn't even *Men in Vogue*. His highest moment of glory had been sitting in a dinner-jacket while some raddled actress fondled an Afghan hound and offered him a mint chocolate. That one had reached the colour supplements of the Sunday newspapers. Then someone had made a remark about his hair-piece. Well, what if it was a wig?

He took it off now and twirled it daringly on his index finger. He was bald as an egg underneath. It itched, wearing the bloody thing all day and every day, but once he had moved into his new lark, he did not feel able to discard it. Somehow, it would have been embarrassing, confronting his clients with the contrast between bald reality and the crinkled, well-coiffured object which art supplied. Twenty quid it had cost him.

This new lark was an enterprising thing to have done, he decided. He had only been at it two years, but it provided a way of life. He more than broke even now, after he had paid the rent and kept his 'cellar' well-stocked, and paid for the advertisements in the *New Standard, Ham and High* and one or two other local papers. LEARN TO SPEAK WITH CONFIDENCE. *Fully qualified tutor (RADA-trained) gives assistance in voice training, speech therapy, elocution, etc.* It was amazing how many people thought that an hour of his company every week would iron out their plebeian tones. His favourite client at the moment was a young clerk in an insurance company. Not much progress had been made with him, Captain de Courcy was glad to say. The little man would take months before he learnt to say *one* instead of *wan*. The Captain wondered if his feelings for this client were in any way reciprocated. Sometimes they sat quite close together as they went through passages of literature preparatory to reading aloud. Then there were women who had just been elected to local councils, and the odd aspirant actor or actress who wanted to brush up on voice production. They didn't usually return for more than a couple of sessions. Perhaps they were hard up. He knew what that was like. Perhaps they saw through him too quickly.

He gulped down more whisky at the thought of this, wondering with a sudden stab of fear what there was to see through. A legitimate licence with the truth had been taken in the matter of his Army rank; and it was not, perhaps, strictly true that he had ever been to the Royal Academy of Dramatic Art. But there was more to it than that. Sometimes he had an odd sinking feeling, in which he was not sure of the difference between the real and the phoney any more. It was a sort of swooping sensation of misery, allied to the knowledge that, if he were to die, sitting like that in his chair, it might be days before anyone found him. Clients would ring the bell, and would go away unanswered. But no friends would ever miss him. Somehow he'd missed out on friends.

He stared blankly up at the swaying chimney-piece and felt that he ought to go easy. He hated puking. The gas fire hissed. The modern ones weren't so friendly as the old sort, encased in their rigid rectangular frames of artificial wood. Above the fire and the beige tiles, a lot of clutter was heaped on the shelf: glasses he hadn't bothered to wash up from the day before, a few bills, the cellophane from a packet of paper handkerchiefs, a jar of Vick, and a tea-caddy containing Mother's ashes. He had never got round to doing anything about them. The bloke at the crem had asked if he wanted to scatter them, and he hadn't, so he had come away with them under his arm, wrapped in a wooden box and brown paper, labelled MRS CASEY. He had hoiked it about ever since, from one flat or bed-sitting room to the next. Against this tutelary vessel leant the only Christmas card he had received that year. It was already curling about the edges from the heat of the gas. It wasn't very Christmassy. It was a reproduction of Henry Lamb's portrait of Lytton Strachey in the Tate Gallery. He was surprised she'd sent it, the poor little schoolgirl who came on Saturday mornings at five quid a time. He never felt she liked him much. She was always rather offhand and withdrawn.

Some people expected you to work magic. He had tried rhythmical speaking, but it was no good. You couldn't really do anything about stammers. He had come to the conclusion they were hereditary. But it was nice of her to have sent the card, and to have written the message inside, in her strong italic hand: *WITH LOVE FROM TIBBA.*

MORE ABOUT PENGUINS,
PELICANS AND PUFFINS

For further information about books available from Penguins please write to Dept, EP, Penguin Books Ltd, Harmondsworth, Middlesex UB7 ODA.

In the U.S.A.: For a complete list of books available from Penguins in the United States write to Dept DG, Penguin Books, 299 Murray Hill Parkway, East Rutherford, New Jersey 07073.

In Canada: For a complete list of books available from Penguins in Canada write to Penguin Books Canada Ltd, 2801 John Street, Markham, Ontario L3R 1B4.

In Australia: For a complete list of books available from Penguins in Australia write to the Marketing Department, Penguin Books Australia Ltd, P.O. Box 257, Ringwood, Victoria 3134.

In New Zealand: For a complete list of books available from Penguins in New Zealand write to the Marketing Department, Penguin Books (N.Z.) Ltd, P.O. Box 4019, Auckland 10.

In India: For a complete list of books available from Penguins in India write to Penguin Overseas Ltd, 706 Eros Apartments, 56 Nehru Place, New Delhi 110019.

AN ICE-CREAM WAR

As millions are slaughtered on the Western Front, a ridiculous and little remarked-on campaign is being waged in East Africa – a war that continued after the Armistice because no one told them to stop.

Primarily a gripping story of the men and women swept up by the passions of love and battle, William Boyd's magnificently entertaining novel also elicits the cruel futility and tragedy of it all.

'A towering achievement' – John Carey, Chairman of the Booker Prize Judges 1982

'Quite outstanding' – *Sunday Times*

'If you can imagine John Buchan or Rider Haggard rewritten by Evelyn Waugh then you have something of the flavour of this book .... Very funny' – Robert Nye in the *Guardian*

A GOOD MAN IN AFRICA

Morgan Leafy isn't overburdened with worldly success. Actually, he is refreshingly free from it. But then, as a representative of Her Britannic Majesty in tropical Kinjanja, it was not very constructive of him to get involved in wholesale bribery and with sensitive local politicians. Nor was it exactly oiling his way up the ladder to hunt down the improbably pointed breasts of his boss's daughter when officially banned from horizontal delights by a nasty dose...

Falling back on his deep-laid reserves of misanthropy and guile, Morgan has to fight off the sea of humiliation, betrayal and *ju-ju* that threatens to wash over him.

'Wickedly funny' – *The Times*

'Splendid rollicking stuff!' – *Spectator*

Winner of a 1981 Whitbread Literary Award

Winner of the 1982 Somerset Maugham Award

David Lodge in Penguins

CHANGING PLACES

The plate-glass, concrete jungle of Euphoria State University, USA, and the damp red-brick University of Rummidge have an annual exchange scheme. Normally the exchange passes without comment.

But when Philip Swallow swaps with Professor Zapp the fates play a hand, and the two academics find themselves enmeshed in a spiralling involvement on opposite sides of the Atlantic. Nobody is immune: students, colleagues, even wives are swapped as the tension increases. Finally, the cat is let out of the bag with a flourish that surprises even the author himself.

'Three star rating for a laugh a line' – Auberon Waugh in the *Evening Standard*

'By far the funniest novel of the year ... the cool, cruel detachment of Evelyn Waugh' – *Daily Mail*

Winner of the Hawthornden Prize and the Yorkshire Post fiction prize

HOW FAR CAN YOU GO?

How far could they go? On one hand there was the traditional Catholic Church, on the other the siren call of the permissive society. And what with the advent of COC (Catholics for an Open Church), the social lubrication of the Pill and the disappearance of Hell, it was difficult for Polly, Dennis, Angela and the others not to rupture their spiritual virginity on the way to the seventies ...

'Hilarious ... a magnificent book' – Graham Greene

'Huge, bitterly funny and superbly presented montage of the false nostrums that assailed Christianity like worms' – *Sunday Times*

Winner of the Whitbread Book of the Year Award

and

GINGER YOU'RE BARMY
THE BRITISH MUSEUM IS FALLING DOWN

Graham Swift in Penguins

SHUTTLECOCK

Prentis, senior clerk in the 'dead crimes' department of police archives, is becoming more and more paranoiac ... Alienated from his wife and children, and obsessed by his father, a wartime hero now the mute inmate of a mental hospital, Prentis feels increasingly unsettled as his enigmatic boss Mr Quinn turns his investigations towards himself – and his father...

'An astonishing study of forms of guilt, laced with a thread of detection, and puckering now and then into outrageous humour' – *Sunday Times*

THE SWEET-SHOP OWNER

A symbol, a token of life, an attitude ... the sweet shop was all that and more. It was the bargain struck between Chapman and his beautiful, ailing, depressive wife. Safely penned up amongst its confectionery and newspapers, Chapman was defused as a threat to her, impotently confined to stocktaking and reorders.

It was a bargain, strangely enough, based on love and courageous acceptance of life's deprivations ... threatened only by Dorry, their clever, angry daughter who will never forgive either of them.

'A marvellous first novel' – *New Statesman*

MONSIGNOR QUIXOTE

Graham Greene

A wonderfully picaresque and profoundly moving tale of innocence at large amidst the shrines and fleshpots of modern Spain, Graham Greene's novel, like Cervantes's seventeenth-century classic, is also a brilliant fable for our times.

'A deliciously funny novel and an affectionate offering to all that is noblest and least changing in the people and life of Spain' – Michael Ratcliffe in *The Times*

HEADBIRTHS

Günter Grass

Should Dörte and Harm Peters – today's quintessential German couple – have a baby?

Formidably gifted, funny and wise, Günter Grass whisks us off on a fact-finding holiday with the Peters, to the sprawling teeming slums of Asia where (true liberals) they contemplate the population explosion, world poverty, nuclear war...yes-to-baby, no-to-baby? And where, in a novel stuffed with fantastic 'headbirths' and outrageous invention, Günter Grass probes the modern German psyche with his own special brand of brilliant and devastating wit.

'Part novel, part film script, part essay, part soliloquy ... Grass is a playful, exuberant, amazing writer' – Paul Bailey in the *Standard*

OH WHAT A PARADISE IT SEEMS

John Cheever

Skating on Beasley's Pond always makes Lemuel Sears feel nostalgic. He is old enough to wonder – after skating, or when he sees a young couple kissing in the cinema – whether sometime soon he will be exiled from the pleasures of love.

Meanwhile, there is Renée. He first noticed Renée, her style, her splendid and endearing figure, in a New York bank. With her, even in polluted, fast-food, nomad America, the illusion of Paradise lingers. Until he returns to find his free skating rink turned into a municipal dump. And until. . . But Renée has always said, 'You don't understand the first thing about women.'

GINGER, YOU'RE BARMY

David Lodge

When it isn't prison, it's hell.

Or that's the heartfelt belief of conscripts Jonathan Browne and Mike 'Ginger' Brady. For this is the British Army in the days of National Service, a grimy deposit of post-war cynicism. It consists of one endless, shambling round of kit layout, square-bashing, shepherd's pie 'made from real shepherds', P.T. and drill relieved by the occasional lecture on firearms or V.D. The reckless, impulsive Mike and the more pragmatic Jonathan adopt radically different attitudes to this two-year confiscation of their freedom. . . and the consequences are dramatic.

VIDA

Marge Piercy

A dozen lovers, two hundred friends, thousands who had heard her speak at rallies...

In the sixties she was a symbol of passionate rebellion, now Vida Asch is forced to live as a fugitive. Years spent fleeing the FBI, travelling in disguise and the experience of bitter sexual and political rivalries threatens to splinter her commitment. In her struggle to survive Vida has learned to trust no-one, but when another outcast, Joel, enters her circle she finds herself reluctantly drawn to him...

THE BANQUET

Carolyn Slaughter

For months Harold watches and admires Blossom before he finds the courage to approach her...

Between them develops a rapport at first exquisite and fragile, then deepening to a consuming passion. Gradually Blossom realizes that this is forever – and that Harold has chosen her for something quite extraordinary. Propelled by an obsession both painful and terrifying, Blossom and Harold are swept towards the affair's horrifying climax.